RUTHLESS IDOLS

GIFTED ACADEMY BOOK TWO

MICHELLE HERCULES

INFINITE SKY PUBLISHING

1

RUFIO

Morpheus's parents live in Everdale, which is an hour away from school. I made the trip in thirty minutes. By the time I pulled in front of their two-story home, Morpheus was almost completely frozen. He had stopped screaming, but his silence was more worrisome.

Morpheus's mother took him into a room as soon as she laid eyes on him and only came out to answer the door for two Idols dressed in elaborate robes. We've been waiting for nearly six hours for an update.

"This is crazy. What the hell are they doing there?" Phoenix asks, sounding as anxious as I feel.

Shoulders hunched forward and leaning my elbows on my knees, I stare at my phone. I've been calling Bryce since four in the morning and nothing. He's never gone off the grid so long before.

"Still no word from your brother?" Phoenix continues.

"No."

I'm about to call him again when the door at the end of the hallway finally opens and the two Idols who had come in earlier exit Morpheus's room. Both Phoenix and I jump to our feet.

The men walk silently toward the exit, but hell if I'm going to let them leave without giving us an update.

With long strides, I cut across the room and block their way. "How is he?"

Both men just stare at me, blankly. It takes me a few seconds to realize they're blind. But are they deaf too?

"Hello? My friend asked you a question." Phoenix applies pressure.

"We did what we could. Now we must wait."

"Wait for what?" I ask, my voice rising.

In that precise moment, my phone begins to ring. I glance down and see it's Bryce calling. *Finally.*

"For Morpheus to take back what the shadows stole," the second man replies.

"What kind of bullshit is that?" Phoenix asks, amplifying his Idol power. It doesn't change their neutral expressions at all.

Fuck. We're not getting anything from these guys.

I whirl around and answer Bryce's call before it goes to voice mail.

"Bryce, where the fuck were you? We've been calling nonstop," I say.

"I can't explain right now. What's going on? Where's Daisy?" He sounds agitated.

I run my hand through my hair as I look at Phoenix. The mysterious Idols are gone. *Great.*

"Shit, man. A lot's happened. You picked the wrong weekend to disappear," I reply finally.

"Just answer the question already. Is Daisy all right?" he snaps, putting me on high alert. Why is he so worried about Daisy? Does he know what happened at the beach?

"I don't know. But listen, Bryce. You have to get back to

school as soon as you can. Shit happened last Saturday, and Daisy isn't safe."

"Why aren't you in school?" he asks.

"Morpheus got really sick, and we had to bring him to his mother."

"What happened to him?"

"We still don't know. But don't worry about Morpheus. Phoenix and I got this. You need to check on Daisy." I put extra emphasis on the latter. I'm fucking worried about both Morpheus and Daisy, but Bryce doesn't need to be. I want him focused on Daisy's safety for reasons still unknown to me.

You're so full of shit, Rufio. You know very well why. I stomp on my pesky thoughts, refusing to believe my motives have anything to do with feelings I abhor.

The call goes silent all of a sudden.

"Bryce? Are you still there?" I ask, getting no response.

"Call dropped?" Phoenix approaches.

"Yeah. Fuck. Today is turning out to be hell."

I call my brother again, only to get his voice mail instead. "Son of a bitch. I think his phone died."

Phoenix rubs his chin and focuses on nothing in particular. "We messed up, Rufio. We were supposed to let Daisy drown."

There's no conviction in Phoenix's tone, but I get angry all the same. "I'm not done with her."

Phoenix peers over his shoulder, brow furrowed. "Cut the bullshit, Rufio. You don't want to kill her or even hurt her anymore."

I open my mouth to offer a retort, but I can't. I just begged Bryce to protect Daisy. I could say I'm protecting her from others because I'm the one who wants to torture her, but what would be the point? It'd be a lie.

"If it makes you feel better, I don't want to hurt her either," Phoenix continues.

I clamp my jaw shut. *What am I supposed to say to that?* In the past few days, Phoenix was the one thirstier for revenge.

"How is that going to make me feel better?" I reply. "She's a Norm who, somehow, has managed to whip both of us."

Phoenix's eyes flash with anger. "I'm not whipped."

Whatever. With a shake of my head, I veer toward the hallway. I'm done waiting for Mrs. Malek to give us an update.

"Where are you going?" Phoenix asks.

"To get answers."

At least *some* answers. Figuring out why Daisy has a hold on Phoenix, Bryce, and me will have to come later.

Halfway down the corridor, the door to Morpheus's room opens and his mother steps out. She looks distraught as she fixes her gaze on me.

"How is he?" I ask.

"I did what I could. The bracelets have been reinforced, but now it's up to Morpheus to regain control of his powers."

"What about the god who was punishing him?"

There's no need to get into details with Mrs. Malek. She's the only adult who knows about what happened on that island of horrors. She's the one who found us, after all.

A spark of fear shines in the woman's eyes for a fleeting moment. "He's gone for now."

"We all disobeyed him. Why was he only punishing Morpheus?" Phoenix asks.

Mrs. Malek averts her gaze. "Morpheus wants to talk to you. I'm going to brew some tea."

With quick steps, she walks around us and disappears through a set of double doors.

"For fuck's sake. What's up with everyone's cloak-and-dagger attitude? Can't they just give us as a straight answer?" Phoenix asks.

I snort. "Please. Since when do fucking parents make it easy for us? If we want answers, we gotta get them ourselves."

I enter Morpheus's childhood room, finding it as warm as a sauna. The curtains are open, revealing a room that hasn't changed much since a young Morpheus occupied it. The shelves on the wall opposite his single bed are still filled with toys and children's books.

Morpheus is sitting up on his bed, propped against a couple of pillows. Several blankets are on top of him, including the bedspread depicting a cartoon superhero. He's also wearing a wool beanie.

"Hey, guys," he croaks.

"Dude, you look like hell," Phoenix points out.

"Thanks for that useless observation, jackass." Morpheus takes a sip of the steamy beverage in his hand.

I notice the shadows are still swirling around his wrists, but I can't tell if they're covering his entire arms like before.

"Your mother told us the god is gone," I say.

Morpheus flinches a little. "Yeah. The Zions were able to kick him out of my head."

"Zions? I thought those dudes were priests or some shit like that." Phoenix rubs the back of his neck.

"Same crap, different name," Morpheus replies.

"Did he tell you why he was punishing you and not us?" I ask.

Morpheus gives me a droll stare. "Do you think that asshole would give us any explanation for his actions? He's a fucking god."

"But you're good now?" Phoenix moves closer to the bed.

Morpheus sets the mug on the nightstand and glances at his wrists. He pulls a sleeve of his sweater up, revealing the shadows are only concentrated around his bracelets.

"The Scions—" Phoenix starts.

"*Zions*," Morpheus corrects him.

"Yeah, yeah." Phoenix waves his hand dismissively. "They

said you had to take back what the shadows stole. What did they mean by that?"

Morpheus shrugs. "I have no clue. My dignity?" He drops his chin, crossing his arms over his chest. "I hate this."

"Why can't you control the shadows?" I ask bluntly. "You're as powerful as Phoenix and me, but you need those bracelets to contain them. I don't get it."

Morpheus's dark gaze pierces me, leveling me with the weight of his hard stare. "Damn, Rufio. If I knew the answer to that, I wouldn't be sipping hot chocolate in my old bedroom at my parents' house."

He pushes the blankets away and throws his legs over the side of the bed. "Let's get out of here. The last thing I want is to bump into my father."

"He wasn't around when we brought you in," I say.

"That doesn't surprise me." Morpheus stands, wincing as he does.

"Need help there, buddy?" Phoenix makes a motion to grab his arm, but Morpheus hisses.

"If you touch me, you'll lose a limb."

Phoenix takes a step back, lifting his hands in a sign of backing down. "Jeez, I was just trying to help."

"Spare me."

"All right, then. Let's go." I veer for the door.

Morpheus is not completely recovered, that much is obvious, but I won't convince him to wait a little more. He's a big boy, and most importantly, the urgency to return to campus is overwhelming.

I need to know if Daisy is okay, as much as the thought dismays me.

"You're not getting any more warnings about the Norm, are you, Morpheus?" Phoenix asks when we're out in the hallway.

"Nothing as specific as to when I did last Saturday, but it doesn't mean shit. My gift is linked to these damn shadows, and now that the bracelets have been reinforced, I doubt I'll get a premonition any time soon."

A blanket of silence descends on our group. Too much has happened in only a few days, life-altering events, and I, for once, am clueless of what my role in this new reality is. I'm an Idol, taught to hate Norms, and sworn to destroy the weak. But when the call came, I ignored it.

We all should have listened to Morpheus when he said Daisy was bad news. There's no doubt now that he was right, and yet I don't care. The yearning and raw need I felt when I didn't know who she was at Unearthly Desires has only grown. There's a fine line between hating and wanting someone, and I've crossed that line with the Norm. It's like there was a vital piece of me missing all these years, and Daisy is it. The brutal truth is that if she's meant to be our destruction, I want her to wreck me.

2

DAISY

We're surrounded by several people, a mix of faculty and students. But the teacher who tossed me out of the window is not among the crowd, mercifully. Principal Fallon breaks away from the group and approaches us. Bryce holds me tighter, angling his body so he's protecting me.

"Miss Woods, are you okay?" she asks.

"She's fine now, but no thanks to you," Bryce snaps.

His harsh tone matches the energy I sense surrounding his body. Strangely, the sensation is different than when I felt his power before. It's more acute.

"I'm okay," I say.

Bryce turns to me, his eyes filled with savage intensity. I prefer the passion from before.

"Who threw you out the window?" he asks in a voice that's low and dangerous.

"I don't know his name. It was a teacher."

His nostrils flare and his eyes narrow. My body begins to shake, but it takes me a second to realize it's not me who's trembling. Bryce is.

"I'm going to kill him," he grits out.

"Mr. Rogers has been detained, and he'll be dealt with by the authorities," Principal Fallon says.

"We'll see about that." Bryce stares Principal Fallon straight in her eyes, and even though he's in a lower position, he still feels more threatening than her.

As for me, I'm confused as hell. I'm pretty sure I died, but somehow Bryce was able to heal all my injuries. That he could do that was a surprise, but not as astonishing as the fact that he *wanted* to save me. The earth-shattering kiss that followed was just the cherry on top.

Bryce slides his arms under my body and stands up. It feels amazing to be cradled against his chest like this, but I don't want to appear weak.

"Bryce, you can put me down now. I can walk."

He watches me closely for a moment, his eyebrows furrowed together. I reach for his cheek, something I'd never thought I would do to an Idol ever.

"Seriously. I'm okay." I smile a little to make my point.

The tension on his face eases a tad, but it's not enough for me. I get that he's worried, and the notion fills my heart with a powerful emotion that makes me giddy. Feeling bold, I brush my thumb over his lips. They part as he takes in a sharp breath. He brings his mouth closer to mine, but a throat-clearing halts his progress.

"Bryce, Daisy needs to see the nurse immediately," Principal Fallon says.

With a sigh, Bryce puts me down, but he doesn't let go of me. Circling his arm around my waist, he pulls me flush against his side.

The contact feels incendiary, but despite my crazy hormones, a new emotion takes hold of me.

Fear.

"What happened to Toby?" I ask Principal Fallon.

"He's in the infirmary. Broken arm."

"Let's go, then." I take a step forward, but it's hard to move when I have an over-six-foot guy attached to my hip. But Bryce seems hesitant to let go of me.

As one, we head for the main building, trailing after Principal Fallon. She warns the students to return to class, but people seem disinclined to heed her words. Everyone is too occupied with staring at me.

As I walk near some students, I hear one say, "How can she not have a scratch?"

"Maybe Bryce caught her before she crashed," someone answers.

The murmurs continue, but it's easy to push them to the background. They can gossip all they want. I have bigger concerns. A teacher tried to kill me. I've always thought the most dangerous individuals at Gifted Academy were the students, Bryce included. I was wrong.

When we move away from the crowd, I quicken my steps to walk side by side with the principal. "What's going to happen to Drusilla, Cherise, and Renata?"

Before Principal Fallon can reply, Bryce cuts in. "What did they do?"

Ah shit. Bryce is still riding his rage. Maybe I shouldn't have mentioned the dreadful trio in front of him. I don't want him to get in trouble on my account.

"They, uh, were picking on me just before Mr. Rogers decided to throw me out the window," I explain.

"Did they use their powers against you?" he asks.

"Yes."

There's no point in lying about it. There were plenty of witnesses, and I'm sure Bryce could find out the truth quickly.

"Those bitches," he says under his breath.

"Don't even think about going on a revenge spree, Bryce.

Those girls will be disciplined by me," Principal Fallon interjects.

Bryce makes a strange sound in the back of his throat, almost a roar. "What did they do to you, Daisy?"

I nibble on my lower lip. Bryce is a level seventeen. He could easily do some real damage to Dreadzilla and her friends. They deserve punishment, but I don't want him to be the one doling it out. They attacked *me*. *I* should be the one putting them in their place, but that's not likely to happen in this lifetime.

"Doesn't matter what they did to me. Renata broke Toby's arm though. Would that warrant her expulsion?" I ask Principal Fallon.

She doesn't answer until we're inside the building. Just like outside, the students here stare as we walk down the hallway. I wonder how many of them are disappointed I'm not dead.

"As I said, those girls will be punished, but that's not something you should worry about," she finally replies.

Her dismissive answer clues me in on one thing: whatever punishment they receive will be mild. And that knowledge pisses me off.

"With all due respect, Principal Fallon, those Idols tortured me and attacked my best friend. I'd say that makes it my concern."

I sense Bryce's stare, so I turn to him. "You disagree?" I ask him.

The corners of his lips twitch up. "No, not at all."

Principal Fallon, however, doesn't offer a retort. I want to ask again what she plans to do with those bullies, but we enter the infirmary next, and Drusilla and her posse are pushed to a corner of my mind for the moment.

The nurse is not at her desk but behind a curtain, which I can only assume is the treatment area. She's talking to Toby, and unaware that she has company, she continues the conversation.

"You're very lucky she didn't pulverize the entire bone, Toby. What were you thinking, charging an Idol like that?"

"I had to do something. Cherise was drowning Daisy."

Bryce presses his fingers deeper into my waist while his body becomes tenser.

"Ellen, how is Toby?" Principal Fallon asks.

The curtain is pulled to the side, and a tall woman with short, curly brown hair appears. Her expression is grave as she pulls off her rubber gloves.

"One broken bone. I suppose it could be worse, considering who inflicted the pain."

Her gaze switches from Principal Fallon to me. She gives me a quick once-over, and then she says, "I thought you fell from the third floor. How come you're standing there without a scratch?"

Bryce steps aside, letting go of my waist. I miss his proximity immediately and berate myself for it. Since when do I depend on anyone for comfort? I can't deny I've developed unfamiliar feelings for him, but whether I'm falling for the guy or not, it's no excuse for my weakness.

"I healed Daisy," he says.

The nurse arches her eyebrows. "I didn't know you could that, Bryce. It's a handy gift. Need a job?"

I can't tell if the woman is joking or not.

Toby joins us in the small reception area, his arm in a cast. Now he and Rosie match.

Son of a bitch. I hate bullies. An ugly feeling brews in the pit of my stomach. I want those bitches to pay for hurting him. Maybe I should let Bryce do whatever he wants to them since I can't.

"Daisy. You're alive." Toby breaches the distance between us and hugs me with one arm. "I can't believe it."

"Me neither." I'm careful not to hurt Toby further. After a moment, I ease off the embrace and turn to Bryce.

He's looking at Toby in a funny way. I hope he's not jealous.

"If you're done with Toby, I'd like you to check Daisy," Principal Fallon says.

"Of course." The nurse turns to Toby. "Take the medication I gave you if the pain is too much."

"No problem, Ellen." He shakes the plastic bottle with pills inside.

"Toby, we called your parents. They should be here shortly," Principal Fallon says.

"Why?" His voice rises to a shrill. "I'm fine."

"It's school policy."

He pinches the bridge of his nose, closing his eyes. "They're going to pull me out of Gifted Academy."

"Let's not worry about that now." Principal Fallon pats his shoulder, then steers him out the door.

Boy, that lady is cold.

Once he's gone, the nurse says, "What's up with you crazy Norm kids challenging Idols like that? Do you like to live dangerously, is that it?"

"Maybe we're just tired of being treated like dirt," I retort angrily. "Besides, I'm the only crazy Norm here. Toby is a Fringe."

"Where did you get that notion from?" The nurse's eyes turn rounder as if my statement is news to her.

"Wait? Are you saying Toby is not a Fringe?" Bryce asks before I can.

"No. Toby is a Norm," Principal Fallon replies, then turns to me. "Didn't I mention there was another Norm student on a scholarship here?"

"Yeah, but I didn't know it was him," I say, leaving out the fact that Toby has been pretending to be a Fringe this whole time.

I face Bryce, meeting his eyes. He's just as surprised as I am. I hope he can read in my gaze that I want to keep Toby's deception on the down low. If the other students find out Toby deceived them, it won't end well for him.

Please, Bryce, don't say anything.

He nods a fraction as if he actually heard my thoughts. If he did, it's not the first time. One more thing for me to worry about. If he can read my mind, what else does he know about me?

Heading for the small examination room, Nurse Ellen says, "Shall we, Daisy?"

3

BRYCE

As much as I want to stay close to Daisy, when my mother stepped out of the infirmary to make a call, I followed her. As soon as she puts the phone away, I grab her arm and turn her around. I'm done playing the respectful son.

"Mr. Rogers was one of the most levelheaded teachers in the entire school. Why would he try to kill Daisy all of a sudden?"

Mom looks left and right in a cagey manner. There are a few students roaming about, and they're throwing long, curious glances in our direction. I'm only feeding the gossip mill, but I'm way past caring.

"Now is not the time to talk about Daisy's attempted murder," Mom replies in a low tone.

I laugh without humor. "At least you're calling it for what it was."

"You think I'm the worst for what I did to Daisy, but one day you'll understand my reasons."

"Right. We all have a role to play on the game board of the gods. Such a load of crap."

"You know what's a load of crap? You. You stink. Where have you been?"

Shit. With all that happened, my ordeal at the hands of the Knights got pushed far back in my mind.

"Nowhere." I let go of her arm and step back.

"Go take a shower. And before you open your mouth to argue with me, I assure you Daisy won't be left alone."

"What, you're going to babysit her now?"

Mom lets out a heavy sigh. "I'll ask Ellen to escort Daisy back to her room once the examination is over. Does that mollify you?"

Not in the least. But now that she brought my attention to my stench, it's all I can smell. And I was all over Daisy, drenched in *Eau de piss*. Fucking great.

"Fine. But you and I aren't done yet. There's much to discuss."

I turn around and stride in the opposite direction. When I pass by a group of gossiping idiots who are dumb enough to point their camera phones in my direction, I fry their devices with a snap of my fingers. Asides from yelps, I don't hear a peep. Good. They still remember who's at the top of the food chain in this school.

I continue on toward the dorm building, but with each step I take, my muscles become heavier. A great sense of lethargy begins to take hold of me.

What the fuck. I'm never fatigued.

You were never held captive for over twenty-hours unable to tap into your powers either, you idiot. Maybe everything that happened this weekend is taking a toll on me.

After taking twice as long to reach my apartment, I push the door open and stumble toward my room. I yank my clothes off as if I'm drunk and head for the shower. I don't wait for the water to warm up, stepping under the freezing-cold jet stream.

The cold water should jolt me awake, but it has no effect on the bone-tiredness that's swept over me.

It's not until I begin to see double that I realize this is not merely a case of exhaustion. I'm light-headed, on the verge of passing out. I lean against the wall with my eyes closed, breathing through my mouth and nose. It's no use. My legs give out from under me, and I fall on the wet tiled floor with a loud thud.

What the hell is wrong with me?

DAISY

"I can't believe it." Nurse Ellen stares at me wide-eyed after she looked at me from all angles. "No broken bones, no signs of internal bleeding. Not even a scratch mark."

I'm down to my underwear, and to say I'm feeling exposed is an understatement. Never mind that the only thing providing privacy is a flimsy green curtain. Anyone can yank it open. I'm surprised Principal Fallon waited outside, though she has seen me wearing less.

Crossing my arms in front of my chest, I shrink into myself. "How can you tell? You only looked at me. Where's the X-ray machine?"

Shaking her head, she laughs. "Oh, child. I don't need machines to examine my patients. All I need is this." She points at her eyes.

"You have supervision? Like you can see through stuff?" I ask, not hiding my astonishment.

"Yup. That's why I wanted to be a nurse. It was either that or becoming a bank robber. There's no safe in this world that I can't breakthrough." She gives me a crooked smile.

"Why not become a doctor?" I ask.

Her smile is replaced by a scowl. "Doctors don't care about their patients. They're too concerned about beating the competition. It might be different among Norm doctors, but in my world, doctors are assholes."

"I'm surprised Idols need doctors," I say. "Aren't you guys indestructible?"

She snorts. "Nope. We get sick and hurt as often as Norms and Fringes. The only difference is that our diseases are a thousand times more devastating than yours. It's a good thing you're immune to most of them."

I can't believe she's telling me all this. Not even Dad's diary had so much information about Idols' illnesses. I erroneously assumed they didn't get sick.

"How about Fringes?"

"What about them?" She turns to the small desk in the corner of the room and retrieves a tablet device from it.

"Well, they aren't as strong as Idols, but they have godly powers in them. Are they immune to diseases that affect Norms too?"

"Unfortunately, no. And depending on their level, some of our diseases are fatal to Fringes. Their bodies simply can't handle them."

I bite my lower lip, thinking about Toby. He wants to become a doctor, but the best med schools are run by Idols.

"What's with that frown?" Ellen asks.

"Are there different paths in med school?"

"I don't follow."

"I mean, do Norm and Idol students learn different things?"

"In some institutions, yes. But the best med schools in the country have a unified curriculum. Why do you ask? Do you want to become a doctor?"

"No, not me. Toby does. He wants to attend Prism City University. I heard it's a top school."

"Oh yeah. And very competitive. It's harder for Norms to be

accepted, but not impossible. Since Toby attends Gifted Academy, he has a better chance than other Norm kids."

I wonder if that's why Toby lied about being a Fringe, not because he was afraid of being bullied but because he wanted to increase his chances of being accepted at his dream school.

"Well, I'm done here," Nurse Ellen tells me. "If you don't have any other questions, you're free to go."

I jump off the examination table and get dressed. My uniform is torn in places and stained with blood. Considering I no longer have the injuries to match, it looks like a Halloween costume now.

Principal Fallon stands up when Ellen heads for her desk.

"So, is she completely healed?" she asks.

"Yes, Jodie. Your son did a terrific job."

Wait a minute. Son?

The nurse sits behind her desk and begins to type away on her laptop. I turn to the principal with mouth agape.

"Bryce is your son?" My voice rises to a shrill.

The woman raises an eyebrow. "Yes, Daisy. Rufio too, if you're wondering."

Oh my God. Of all the things to find out, this revelation has me speechless. My brain is going at a hundred miles an hour.

Principal Fallon glances over my shoulder. "Ellen, I promised Bryce I wouldn't leave Daisy alone, but I have to handle the fallout of what happened to her. Would you mind escorting her back to her room?"

"Sure. I can do that. Let's hope no one else decides to toss a student out the window." The nurse winks at me.

Was that supposed to be funny? I'd be dead if it weren't for Bryce.

"I don't need a bodyguard," I grumble.

Now both women are staring at me like I'm crazy. Right. Two people have tried to kill me today, and one almost succeeded.

"You won't need one after I'm done with the culprits, but for now, indulge me," Principal Fallon says.

"Fine," I reply resignedly, but at the same time annoyed. I sound just like Rosie when she doesn't want to do something.

Shit. I hope Toby doesn't tell Rosie about what happened today. I can't have her worrying about me, not after I promised her I'd be safe here. Keeping information from my sister makes me guilty as hell, but I can't quit school now. Not because this is the opportunity of a lifetime, but because I sense a significant shift is about to occur in our world, and it will start here, at Gifted Academy.

4

———

DAISY

"You looked shocked to learn Bryce and Rufio Kent are Jodie's sons," Ellen says.

We already left the main school building, and there's no one around to eavesdrop on our conversation.

"No one bothered to tell me."

"I don't think the boys want to broadcast to the world that their mother is the principal. You know, they'd lose a few cool points if they did." The woman chuckles.

"Well, she should have told me."

We enter the dorm room building, but before we take the stairs to my floor, the nurse's phone rings.

"Nurse Carstairs speaking." There's a pause, followed by a frown. "All right. I'll see you in five minutes."

She puts the phone away and turns to me. "I have to get back to the infirmary. It seems today kids have decided to act extra stupid. Are you going to be all right on your own?"

"Yeah. I'll be fine."

With a nod, she heads out. I veer for the stairs. It's strange that, despite what happened, I'm not feeling jittery or anxious. I was attacked for crying out loud. Shouldn't I be suffering from PTSD or something?

I sprint up the stairs, though. There's no reason I should risk getting caught alone by a vengeful Idol.

As I approach my room, my eyes scan ahead, landing on the guys' apartment door. It's ajar. My stomach coils as apprehension sneaks into my heart. I'm feeling nothing about being almost killed, but the prospect of seeing Rufio, Phoenix, and Morpheus puts me on edge? That's insane.

Despite that, I tiptoe toward their apartment and look inside. It seems empty.

"Bryce?" I call out.

No answer. I should leave, but something tugs in my chest, almost as if there's an invisible line pulling me in.

I enter and then veer toward the direction I think his bedroom is. There are two doors. One is closed, but the second is open. The sound of a shower running warns me someone is home.

"Bryce, are you in there?" I walk in.

A queen-size bed takes most of the room, which makes the space a little cramped. The desk pushed against the window is covered with books and loose sheets of paper. On the floor, a trail of discarded clothes leads to the bathroom. The door is cracked open, but the pool of water leaking from under it makes me worried.

Without a second thought, I stride toward it and push the door in all the way. The bathroom is filled with steam, but I can still make out Bryce's legs sticking out from the shower stall.

"Bryce!" I yank the shower curtain open and drop to my knees.

His head is hanging low, and his long bangs are covering his face. I push them off and lift his chin.

"Bryce! Wake up." I shake him.

A moan escapes from his lips, but his eyes remain closed.

"Damn it." I rise again to turn off the shower. Now we're both drenched, but at least he's naked, unlike me.

I grab him by the shoulders and shake him harder. "Come on, Bryce. Wake up. You're scaring me."

His eyelids peel open, but only halfway. "Daisy? Is that you?"

"Yes, it's me. Come on. I have to get you out of here."

Crouching next to him, I drape his arm over my shoulder and try to lift him off the floor. But I have two problems: Bryce is as slick as butter, and he weighs a ton. *Damn all those muscles.*

"Bryce, please. You gotta help me here."

"I'm so tired."

"Well, can you crawl on your knees, then? Because I can't lift you and drag you out."

He rubs his face and then hits his cheek for good measure. "Okay, okay. Try to lift me again."

"All right, on the count of three. One, two, three."

I pump my legs up, straining my muscles to the max. Now that Bryce isn't a total deadweight, we manage to stand and get out of the wet stall. Slowly, I steer him to his bed. I have every intention to let go of him as he falls, but he pulls me with him, and I end up on top.

He chuckles. "I'm glad you found me."

He brings his lips to mine before I can reply, kissing me lazily as if he has all the time in the world—or doesn't have the energy to do more than that. Regardless, my body melts against his, and soon I discover Bryce is not that tired. His cock is very much awake, pressing against my pelvis.

With difficulty, I lean back, ending the kiss. "Bryce, I didn't come here to make out with you. You passed out. Shouldn't we call Ellen?"

Bryce reaches for my face and cups my cheek. "Nah. I'm beginning to feel better."

And I don't think he's lying. His eyes are way more alert

than they were before. His lids drop to half-mast as his gaze focuses on my mouth.

"How did you get in?" he asks in a husky voice.

"You left the door wide open."

He lifts his eyes to mine. "Is it still wide open?"

"Yeah. Why?"

He answers with a crooked grin before his bedroom door closes and locks by itself.

"Bryce, what do you think you're—"

He brings his lips to mine once more, and this kiss is anything but lazy. The hand cupping my cheek slides to the back of my head, keeping me in place as Bryce devours my mouth. He runs his other fingers down my arm before he sprawls them on my hip, digging in a little as he rotates under me. The movement moves his erection closer to my already throbbing clit, eliciting a moan from me.

"Bryce," I say between feverish kisses. "We shouldn't be doing this."

He stops suddenly, and I pull back completely, now straddling him, which only increases the friction between our bodies.

"Are you in pain or feeling ill?"

"No. Nothing like that. Ellen said I'm healed completely."

He grabs my hips, and then, with an expression that tells me he's up to no good, he slides his hands down until they reach the bottom of my skirt. I let out a gasp as my heart lurches forward. Without breaking eye contact, he slides his hands underneath my skirt, and with a smoldering caress, he skims back up until his fingers curl around the sides of my underwear.

"Bryce, what are you doing?" I breathe out.

"I want to make sure Ellen's assessment was correct."

Without releasing his grip on my panties, Bryce drops his

eyes to the front of my wet shirt. It must be completely see-through now. Slowly, the buttons pop open. If breathing was difficult before, now it's almost impossible. The fabric gets pushed down my arms by an invisible force until the shirt is gone. Bryce repeats the process with my simple cotton bra. He unclasps the back and peels the wet material off my body using his telekinesis while staring at me with the hunger of a starving man.

My breasts are now free, and immediately my nipples turn into small pebbles.

"Fuck. You're more breathtaking than I imagined."

I'm almost naked in front of him, and yet I don't feel exposed. I'm utterly enjoying his appreciative stare. I'm the meek Norm who can make Bryce, one of the strongest Idols I've ever met, go crazy with desire. It makes me feel powerful, invincible.

"Touch me," I say, surprising myself with my boldness.

I'm not a blushing virgin, but all my previous experiences were the garden-variety type. Nothing remarkable. But the fire burning bright in my core tells me that what I'm about to do will be more than extraordinary. It will be unforgettable.

When Bryce doesn't move fast enough, I grab his hand and bring it to one of my boobs. A hiss escapes his lips and his cock twitches. To torture him more—and also myself—I rotate my hips just a little.

Fast as a cobra, Bryce sits up and kisses me. As his tongue goes on a wild exploration, he tears my panties with one hard yank. I don't have the chance to protest before he flips us around. Now I'm the one at his mercy, trapped underneath his herculean frame.

"I don't want to just touch you, Daisy. I want to taste you. Here." He kisses the corner of my mouth. "Here." Then my chin. "And here." His mouth is on my neck now.

Holding his arms, I arch my back. His lips move to my breasts, and the kisses become wetter and hotter. Making lazy movements with the tip of his tongue, Bryce teases the area around my right nipple before sucking the nub in. *Fuck.* My toes curl inside my shoes, and the sound that comes from the back of my throat is hoarse and needy.

Bryce lets go of my nipple with a wet pop to continue his progress south. The closer he gets to where I so desperately need him to be, the greater the desire for him becomes.

When he reaches my skirt's waistband, he says, "This needs to go now."

Using both hands, he tears the fabric in two.

"Bryce! What am I going to wear now?" I ask, trying to sound indignant, but I'm too horny for that.

His lips curl into a lopsided grin. "Me. But first...." He parts my legs gently and brings his mouth to my pussy.

One swipe of his tongue against my clit sends an electric current down my legs that turns my blood into liquid fire.

"So fucking delicious," he says before having another taste.

With each stroke, he unravels me. I run my fingers through his hair, then yank the long strands by the roots. My hips buckle, a knee-jerk reaction when he inserts two fingers inside of me.

"Easy there." He chuckles, fanning hot air against my over-sensitive skin.

Forming coherent words is impossible when I'm trying my hardest not to lose myself completely too soon. I can only answer with a moan, which seems to motivate Bryce even more. He sucks my clit into his mouth as he begins to pump his fingers faster. With my free hand, I curl my fingers around the comforter, trying to hold on. But the feeling that I'm soaring through the sky doesn't disappear.

"Oh my God, Bryce. Please don't stop."

"I don't plan to, darling."

He returns to his torture, and not even a minute later, a jolt goes through me, and I cry out, arching my back. Bryce continues licking and sucking until I'm boneless and dizzy. Then he eases off me, places a kiss on the inside of my thigh, and jumps out of bed.

Leaning on my elbows, I'm about to ask what he's doing when I catch him with a condom wrapper in his hand. Sensing my stare, he sits on the edge of the bed, twisting his body to mine.

"I want this to happen between us, but if you're not sure or rea—"

"I'm ready!" I shout like a sex-deprived woman.

Bryce smiles from ear to ear. "Thank heavens."

He brings the foil package to his mouth and tears it open with his teeth. He looks so normal doing that, it's almost possible to pretend he's not an Idol with extraordinary powers. That notion flies straight out of my head when his eyes become brighter, almost molten gold.

Condom in place, Bryce cages me in with his arms and body. He's kneeling, hovering above me as he stares into my eyes.

"I've been craving you since I saw you wearing that microskirt and red cowboy boots."

"I can wear it for you again, I mean, if you want me to." Sudden insecurity rears its ugly head in my heart. This could very well be nothing but a onetime thing.

He lowers his body, bringing the head of his cock to my entrance. With a featherlight touch, he pushes strands of hair off my forehead. "Daisy, this is not a hookup. Now that I've tasted you, you're not getting rid of me that easily."

He slides in slowly, filling me in a delicious way. I close my eyes and clutch Bryce's back. He sears my lips with a torching kiss as he pushes all the way in. In a thoughtless action, I bring my knees up and cross my ankles together. Bryce groans in response, increasing the tempo of his thrusts. In this new angle, I can tell it won't take much for me to climax again.

But Bryce isn't satisfied; he hooks his arm under my knees and props my leg over his shoulder. Damn it. It feels even better now.

There is no need for words; the song of our bodies together is enough. Bryce's face is red as we lock gazes. His breathing is erratic when he rises to his knees, lifting me with him. With a firm grip on my hips, he doesn't miss a beat. The muscles on his neck and arms strain, and then Bryce becomes the epitome of the God of Sex.

The lights in his room start to flicker as light emanates from his body. It envelopes us both, right before he throws his head back and cries out. Closing my eyes, I follow suit a split second later, this orgasm even more intense than the previous one. It seems to last forever and not long enough.

A moment later, when the light begins to fade, Bryce lowers my body before he collapses next to me. I keep my eyes closed as I attempt to control my breathing.

He laces his hand with mine and says, "I think I should be rescued more often. This was amazing."

Opening my eyes, I turn to him. "I loved the outcome, but I'd prefer if you didn't scare me just so you can have sex."

He leans on his side and looks at me with a cheeky smile on his gorgeous face. God, he's even more beautiful all sexed up like this.

"Aw, you were worried about me. You're cute."

I hit his chest with the back of my hand. "Jerk. I learned today that Idols get sick too. So yeah, I got worried."

He scooches closer, bringing his face to mine. "I'm sorry that I scared you, but I like that you care."

His sinful mouth captures mine again, and by the way my

body immediately catches fire, I know a second round is coming.

Until the sound of Rufio's voice calling out Bryce's name just outside the room douses the fire in the blink of an eye.

Shit. The fun is over.

5

RUFIO

"Bryce?" I head for my brother's room.

On the way here, our phones were blowing up with news of the incident involving Daisy, which only made me drive faster back to campus. The problem with gossip is that nothing is accurate—each message we received told a different story—but the bottom line is someone tried to kill Daisy and nearly succeeded.

"Are you home?" I try the door, but it's locked.

"Yeah. One second," he replies.

I hear the sound of sheets being tossed and then a loud thump followed by a curse from Bryce.

"What the hell is going on in there?" I frown at the door.

"What? Is his door locked?" Phoenix stops next to me.

"Yup."

"Want me to unlock it?" Phoenix asks.

The door opens, but not completely, and Bryce sticks his head out. "What is it?"

His hair is a mess, and his skin is flushed and covered in sweat. One deep breath tells me exactly what Bryce was doing locked in his room.

"Who's in there with you?" I take a step forward, bracing my hand against his door.

"Not your damn business. Now tell me what you want or leave."

I watch Bryce closely. He never gave a fuck about protecting his hookups' identities before. A nagging suspicion makes itself known.

"Is Daisy in there with you?" I ask, my voice cold and hard.

Bryce's expression matches my tone. A muscle in his jaw twitches before he replies, "What do you want?"

Fine. He wants to be an ass about it, so be it. Summoning the dark power that lives underneath my skin to the palm of my hand, I turn Bryce's door into nothing but a pile of dust.

"You fucker." Bryce takes a step forward, ready to unleash his fury on me when Daisy slips past him and gets in between us.

And she's wearing nothing but Bryce's sheet around her body. Son of a bitch.

"Enough already," she says.

"What are you doing here? Didn't you almost die?" Phoenix asks with the tactfulness of a blunt knife.

She flinches before she turns to him, but her attention switches to Morpheus, who's hanging back. "You don't look well."

He shrugs. "I'm better now."

"Yeah, yeah. Morpheus is fine. But did you sleep with Bryce?" Phoenix's tone of incredulity matches his astonished expression.

"How is that your business?" She levels him with a glare, clutching her makeshift coverall tighter.

Even if she weren't naked underneath that wrap, I'd be able to tell. I can smell sex all over her. I wait for jealousy to spear my chest, but all I feel right now is a crazy desire to pull that sheet off Daisy's body. As if sensing where my thoughts have wandered, she looks at me. No guilt in her eyes. She fucked my brother only days after we fooled around, and she's not sorry she got caught. Strangely, that makes her even more alluring in my eyes.

"You're right. It's not, and I don't give a damn." Phoenix stalks away like a petulant child and plops on the couch. "Oh, by the way. A thank-you would have been nice," he says as an afterthought.

A hint of blush spreads through Daisy's cheeks; the first time I've ever caught that reaction on her.

"Why would Daisy need to thank you?" Bryce arches his eyebrows.

"Phoenix and Rufio saved me from drowning last Saturday," she replies.

"What happened?" Bryce looks at me.

"The weather turned bad, and Daisy got caught in the middle of it." I purposely give a vague answer. Just because Daisy has slept with my brother doesn't earn her the right to know everything about us.

"And you volunteered to save her?" Bryce asks.

"Can't make Daisy's life miserable if she's not around." I give the girl my best wicked smile.

With a shake of her head, she says, "You're such an ass."

"I'm still waiting for my thank-you," Phoenix pipes in.

Embarrassment returns to her eyes, mixing with the contempt. "Thank you for saving my life, despite the motives."

"You're welcome." Phoenix and I say at the same time. My answer is followed by a smirk.

"Ugh. I'm leaving." Daisy heads for the door.

"Are you walking out like that?" I ask.

She pauses with her hand on the doorknob and looks over her shoulder. "I have no choice. Bryce ripped the clothes right off my body."

With a grin, she slips out, leaving me staring at the door with my mouth agape. *What the actual fuck.*

Phoenix whistles. "Damn. Postcoital Daisy is even sassier."

The comment is meant to be a joke, but Phoenix's tone is off. He's trying to hide his true feelings on the matter. We didn't discuss in depth what our actions in the last forty hours meant.

Bryce stares at the gap where his door used to be, then turns a murderous glare in my direction. "You're fixing this, asshole."

"Now that Daisy is gone, can we talk without trading insults?" Morpheus approaches, still wearing more clothes than the weather asks for.

"Fine. Tell me exactly what happened on Saturday," Bryce replies.

"You'd better put your clothes on and have a seat. It's a long story." Morpheus heads for the couch.

BRYCE

An hour later, we realize our problems are bigger than we thought. I told the guys everything that happened to me since I disappeared. Well, almost everything. I didn't get into the details of the conversation between my parents. I don't think Rufio is ready to learn the whole truth about our mother. All he knows now is that she's the one who pushed for Daisy's scholarship.

The most troublesome part is the fact that the Knights were able to not only kidnap me but keep me captive for the entire weekend.

Between Mom's shady agenda and the Knights, there's Daisy—sexy and sassy Daisy—who proved to be a surprise in more ways than one. Just thinking about her makes my cock twitch. I push thoughts about sex to the side and focus on the other aspect of her that, for now, I'm keeping to myself as well. Her last name. Why would she use a fake one? What is she trying to hide?

Morpheus rubs his face. "I don't know what to think anymore. Why would Mr. Rogers try to kill Daisy like that? It doesn't make any sense."

"You're worried about him? What about the Knights' interest in Daisy? What do they want with her?" Rufio replies.

"Let's not forget your mother playing 'good cop, bad cop' with you two." Phoenix scoffs.

I don't want to focus on my mother's shenanigans, so I ask, "Did you really see the god's face in the sky?"

"I thought that maybe I was imagining things, but after what the bastard did to Morpheus, I'm sure." Phoenix leans on his elbows and stares me straight in the eyes. "But, man, you can heal people? That's huge."

"I suppose." I shrug.

"I can't believe you boned her before Rufio or I could. That's a plot twist I didn't see coming."

"Oh, for fuck's sake, Phoenix. Can you take your mind out of the gutter for one second?" Rufio snaps.

"What's with you? Are you jealous?" he asks.

"You know the god who wants Daisy dead won't stop, right?" Morpheus chimes in. "What are we going to do about that? She clearly has a big part to play in whatever's happening to our world."

I become tense in an instant. They might have saved Daisy at the beach, but they were dead set on destroying her before.

"I'm sorry you took the brunt of his wrath, but I want to make one thing very clear. No one is touching Daisy," I say.

"What's that supposed to mean?" Rufio lifts his gaze to mine.

"It means if you're still thinking about continuing your wicked games, think again."

I stand up, feeling bone-tired all of a sudden. Not the same lethargy that knocked me down earlier, but it's enough to make me want to lie down and not wake up until tomorrow. Unfortunately, rest will have to wait.

"Jeez, Bryce. Since when do you care about the chicks you fuck?" Phoenix asks.

I don't answer because I don't want to tell them. I never truly cared about anyone besides my brother, and even so, I had a hard time showing it. Emotion is not something I master well.

"You're not in love with her, are you?" Phoenix's expression turns somber, and when I look around the room, he's not the only one sporting a frown.

"Don't be an idiot. Of course not," I reply.

"I could have fucked her, you know?" Rufio says. His comment is sharp, meant to cut.

My brother is cruel, but never without reason. His remark only serves one purpose: to tell me he feels more for Daisy than he wants to acknowledge.

Phoenix turns to him. "When?"

"On the evening Bryce was hanging out with her." My brother leans against the couch, sprawling his arms over the backrest.

His smug smile is supposed to irritate me, and it's working. I left Daisy in a hurry to protect her from Rufio's anger, but all I did was leave her alone with him.

"She was high, easy prey. So tell me, brother, why didn't you?" I ask.

The smile vanishes from his face, replaced by a glare.

"Because I wanted her to remember when I do fuck her into oblivion. I did make her scream, though. It turns out she's quite sensitive around her nipples."

Watching Rufio through slits, I count to ten in my head to avoid doing something I'll regret.

Phoenix jumps off the couch in a hurry. "You know what? Fuck you two. Now I have a boner and am in desperate need of a cold shower." He stalks out of the living room, banging his door so hard that it rattles the picture frame on the wall.

"Son of a bitch." Morpheus rests his head in his hands. "I'm surrounded by idiots."

Ignoring Morpheus, Rufio stands from the couch as well. "I have zero interest in torturing Daisy now, so don't go getting premature wrinkles on your forehead, brother."

"Oh yeah? You're simply going to let go of all your hatred toward Norms?"

Rufio smiles ruefully. "No. I still believe Norms are vermin. But Daisy—" He pauses to lick his lower lip. "—is not a regular Norm. The Knights want her alive, and the god we're sworn to wants her dead. She may be a pawn, but I'm betting she's a queen, and I always fuck the queen."

With that statement, he walks out.

"It seems you got competition," Morpheus points out.

Narrowing my gaze, I reply, "Who says I'm playing?"

6

DAISY

Alone in my room, I allow myself to freak out completely. I can't believe Bryce and I got caught by those three. It was a herculean effort not to let Rufio know how guilty I felt. And the worst of all is that I don't have any reason to feel guilty. He's nothing to me, a blip in my life at Gifted Academy that I wish I could forget.

The thought that I was somehow betraying Rufio when I was in bed with Bryce didn't even enter my mind. So then why the hell do I feel dirty now?

Suddenly, my room seems confining. The walls are caging me in. I head for the bathroom and take the quickest shower known to man. Then, once I can no longer smell Bryce on my skin, I get dressed in a simple pair of jeans and a T-shirt. I'm heading out.

I stick my head out in the hallway first to make sure the coast is clear, then sprint toward the stairs and out of the building. On my way to the bus stop just outside of the campus gates, I call Toby. He was freaking out about his parents' visit, and I want to make sure everything is okay.

The call goes straight to voice mail. Crap. I hope he's okay.

I call Rosie next, but she doesn't answer. I remember then that she should still be in school. I park my butt on the bus stop bench and look out in the distance, thinking how my life has done a one-eighty on me.

A moment later, the sound of an approaching vehicle calls my attention to the road. A black SUV is approaching. The windows are tinted black, and I can't see who is inside. The car slows down when it passes in front of the bus stop, and I have the eerie impression that the driver is staring at me. I clutch my backpack tighter against my chest, using it as a shield.

The SUV speeds up again before stopping at the gates of Gifted Academy. In that precise moment, my bus arrives.

I pay for my ticket and veer for the closest set of empty seats near the front. I don't feel safe sitting in the back of the bus; more often than not, that's where bullying occurs. The bus is almost empty, and the few passengers are all adults. None of them bat an eye toward me.

The drive from Gifted Academy to the Saturn's Bay city center takes a little over an hour. During that time, I look out the window and take time to reflect on my predicament. A teacher tried to kill me, and I don't know why. I slept with Bryce, and it was the most exhilarating experience of life, which still doesn't diminish my attraction for his brother. Oh, and I also lost my lightning-glass dagger.

I nibble on my lower lip. That part worries me the most. Who found it? And whoever did, will they know what it is? I pull the thick tome the librarian lent me from my backpack. I haven't lost the place Bryce marked, the one where it explains what I must do to keep Phoenix from messing with my head. It turns out acting on it will be more difficult than finding the solution itself.

But I think maybe I should read the whole thing from start to finish. Bryce seemed very interested in the book when he saw it. What other important information about the Idols does it contain?

The lettering on the cover is faded, but even so, I angle my body so I'm concealing most of the book from the woman sitting across the aisle. I can't take any chances. By the time the bus approaches my stop, I've read roughly 10 percent of the book and found nothing that really jumped out. It doesn't matter. I'll keep reading until I'm done.

I stick the book back into my backpack and hop off the bus. It's warmer here than it is at Gifted Academy, probably because of the traffic, and soon sweat begins to trickle down my back and between my breasts. I walk fast, sticking to the side of the curb that's under the building's shade. Looking at my phone's clock, I see Rosie's school will be out in ten minutes. My former high school is just around the corner. I should be able to catch her before she takes the bus home.

When I round the corner onto the school's street, the first thing I see parked in front of the building is Toby's car—Purple Delight. As I get nearer, I catch sight of Toby's bright red hair. He's leaning against the car, facing the building. Students are already milling out. Before I can get to him, Rosie walks out. She lets out a squeak and runs into Toby's arms.

Whoa. When did they move from awkward side glances to that?

I slow my pace so I can observe them without being spotted. Rosie's chin dips. She must be looking at Toby's cast. She lifts her face a moment later and cups his cheek. I freeze, not wanting to be the older sister who interrupts a tender moment. Rosie rises on her tiptoes and kisses Toby on his lips. I don't know if that's their first time or not, but their lip-locking gets intense pretty quickly. Okay, now's the time to interrupt them.

With quick strides, I reach the side of Toby's car, but they're too engrossed in each other and oblivious to my presence. I clear my throat.

Rosie steps down and turns toward me with her face

flushed. Her eyes become as round as saucers when she sees me there.

"Daisy, what are you doing here?"

If it's possible, Rosie's cheeks are now redder than a tomato. Toby's face is not doing much better either.

"I had to get out for a while. So... when did this happen?" I wave my index finger between them.

Toby scratches the back of his neck and glances down.

Rosie pouts. "Just now, if you must know. Thanks for ruining the moment, by the way."

I shake my head. "Yes, it was totally on purpose." I turn to Toby. "I called you to ask how things went with your parents. It went straight to voice mail."

Toby pinches his lips, furrowing his brow. "I didn't feel like talking to anyone."

"Anyone besides my sister, you mean?"

Rosie slides closer to Toby and links her hand with his. "It's what good boyfriends do."

The frown disappears from Toby's face as he gazes at my sister. "I'm your boyfriend?"

"Well, aren't you?"

"Well, I-I guess so. That is, if you want me to be your boyfriend."

I turn my gaze skyward. "Boy, you're dense."

"More so than ever. I'm leaving Gifted Academy," he says.

"What?" Rosie and I say at the same time.

"Why? They didn't expel you, did they?" I take a step forward.

"Why would Toby be expelled?" Rosie looks from me to him.

Pinching the bridge of his nose, Toby says, "Can we go somewhere to talk? I don't feel like having this conversation standing in the middle of the street."

We slide into Purple Delight. Rosie takes the shotgun,

naturally. It feels strange that my baby sister now has a boyfriend. But a sense of unease is growing in my chest. I've come to care deeply for Toby in the few weeks we've known each other, but I still don't know anything about him, only that he pretended to be a Fringe for two years. How did he even pull it off?

"Where should we go?" Rosie asks.

"Anywhere but Poppy's Joint," I reply quickly. I can't deal with Poppy or Felicity right now. I'm still trying to process everything that happened.

Rosie turns around in her seat. "I never got to ask you how your surfing lesson went. Toby told me he took you to Echo Cove on Saturday."

"Uh, I...." I search for Toby's gaze in the rearview mirror. I can't believe he didn't tell Rosie what happened at the beach.

"It was a disaster," I finally reply. "I don't think I'm meant to be a surfer."

"Really? You're quitting after one lesson?" Rosie chuckles. "Did you expect to be a pro from the get-go?"

"No, it's not that. It just didn't live up to my expectations. I thought I was going to enjoy it more. It's not a big deal. At least I've done it. Besides, it's not like I'd have the time to practice."

Rosie turns to Toby. "Are you going to tell me how you broke your arm or not?"

"I got into a fight with an Idol."

"Toby! Are you crazy?" Rosie's voice rises to a shrill. "Why?"

"To defend me," I say. I don't want Toby to lie to Rosie on my account. "Some bullies were seriously hurting me."

Rosie's turns to me again, her blue eye blazing with fury. "I told you Gifted Academy would be dangerous."

"Oh, Rosie, we're Norms. Anywhere is dangerous to our kind," I reply.

"Not only Norms. Look what those bastards did to Toby." Rosie's gaze drops to his cast.

"Uh, Rosie, I actually need to tell you something," Toby says meekly.

"What is it?" Her voice becomes tight.

"I'm not a Fringe." Toby keeps his eyes glued on the road ahead.

"I don't understand."

"I'm a Norm, just like you and Daisy. I've been pretending to be a low-level Fringe for two years. Since I was accepted at Gifted Academy, to be exact."

"Why?"

Toby lets out a heavy exhale and spares a quick glance at Rosie. "For two reasons. One, I knew that being the only Norm student in a school filled with Idols and high-level Fringes would be a nightmare. And two, my dream is to attend the top medical school in the country. Do you want to know how many Norm students they accept each year?"

"I guess not many," Rosie replies in a small voice.

"Zero. There hasn't been a Norm student at Prism City University in over ten years. Ten fucking years!" Toby hits the steering wheel hard.

Both Rosie and I wince at his outburst. I've never seen him lose control like that.

He shakes his head. "I'm sorry. I didn't mean to scare you." He glances at Rosie apologetically. "It's just so damn frustrating that because we're Norms, we don't get the same chances as Idols and Fringes."

Rosie reaches over and covers Toby's hand with hers. "You don't need to apologize. We know more than anyone how unfair life is. I wish all Idols would be blown off the face of the Earth. I hate them like I've never hated anything in my life."

Rosie's confession is not new to me. I used to feel the same way. But she sounds way harsher now, as if her hatred for Idols has grown exponentially in the last year.

"You aren't mad that I didn't tell you the truth sooner?" Toby asks.

Rosie pulls her hand back. "A little, but you told me now."

"How did you manage to convince those Idols you weren't a Norm?" I ask. "They can sense our lack of powers."

"Science. The biggest challenge was masking the fact that I didn't possess any gift. I told you that my father works for one of the Idols who isn't hateful, right?"

"Yeah."

"Anyway, I asked him how he could tell the difference between Fringes and Norms. It's all in the energy surrounding the person. When you meet an Idol, the first thing they do is scan you. It's the same way for us. We know when we're in the presence of an Idol because their energy is too powerful to be ignored. Norms can't easily sense Fringes, especially if they're low levels."

"So, did you build an energetic field around yourself?" I ask.

"Sort of."

We stop at a red light, and Toby lets go of the steering wheel to pull a necklace from under his shirt. "This pendant is actually a magnetic field generator. It emits waves that mimic the energy a low-level Fringe exudes."

"Wow, ingenious," Rosie says.

"And they never wondered what your gift was?" I ask.

"I knew that at some point, I'd have to demonstrate what I could do. So I picked the time and place where there would be enough students around."

"What did you do?" Rosie asks.

"I made some drinks explode in the cafeteria. I placed special cups among the regular ones. They had a fake bottom, and inside I hid a mechanism that would pump pressured air against the liquid via remote control."

"That's impressive. I wish I could've seen it," I say, bitterly remembering when Drusilla dumped orange juice over my head in the cafeteria.

I wonder what's going to happen to the odious girl and her friends. In a perfect world, they'd be kicked out of school, but there's no such a thing if you're an Idol.

Distracted by the conversation, I don't realize where Toby is going until he turns on a familiar street. Rosie looks out the window and says, "Oh, I thought you wanted to do something."

"I can't. I'm sorry. I wasn't supposed to go anywhere. My parents are freaking out about what happened to me. Well, mostly my mother, but she's the loudest. It's the reason I'm not returning to school."

"Wait, are they pulling you out? How is that fair?" I ask.

"It's not, but my mother doesn't think a diploma from Gifted Academy is worth losing my life, and my father doesn't have the cojones to go against her wishes. He's whipped."

"Where are you going to go now? Maybe you can enroll in my school?" Rosie's tone becomes hopeful.

Toby parks the car in front of our house and lets out a heavy sigh. "I wish. Unfortunately, I live outside your school zone."

"That's too bad."

Toby unbuckles his seat belt and leans over to Rosie's side. She does the same and they meet in the middle for, damn, more kissing.

"My eyes, my eyes! Could you please wait until I'm out of the car?"

I slide out in a hurry and veer for the front door. My landlord opens it before I can fish my key out of my bag.

"Daisy. What a surprise." The woman hugs me tightly, making me tense in an instant. She's never done that to me before, and only on a few occasions with Rosie. What gives?

"Hi, Mrs. Wilmot. How are you?"

"I'm well, child." Her gaze travels past my shoulder. "Is that Rosie?"

"Yeah, she'll come in a minute."

Mrs. Wilmot is now sporting a frown as she stares at Purple Delight.

"So, what's new?" I ask her.

"Same old. Oh, I almost forgot, a package was delivered for you earlier today."

She turns on her heels and walks in. On the small desk by the entry hall, there's a courier envelope waiting for me. Strange. Who would send me anything?

I immediately scan the sender's address. My blood runs cold. It's a PO Box address from Hawk City.

"Aren't you going to open it?" Mrs. Wilmot hovers too close to me.

"Yeah, later." I stick the package in my backpack, not missing the glint of disappointment in her eyes.

Rosie comes in then, all flushed.

"Did Toby leave?" I look out the door. Shit. He's gone. I wanted to talk to him more without Rosie around.

"Yeah, he said he had things to do, like sort out his academic stuff."

Rosie heads for our bedroom, and I follow her.

"Can I get you girls anything to eat?" Mrs. Wilmot offers. "You must be starving."

We both turn to find her right behind us. What's up with her today?

"Uh, no. We're good," I reply.

The woman just hangs in the hallway with the look of a dog that just lost her bone. I shut the door, but I know she'll hang around to eavesdrop.

"Has Mrs. Wilmot been acting weirdly lately, or is it just today?" I ask.

Rosie sits on the bed, resting her back against the headboard. "She's been nicer to me, for sure, but I just assumed it was because you were gone."

I bite my lower lip. If she had started acting friendlier a few weeks ago, I wouldn't have thought much about it. But now, after everything that's happened to me, I can't help the worry that fills my heart. Mrs. Wilmot is a Norm, but that doesn't mean she can be trusted.

7

BRYCE

It doesn't take long for me to discover who Daisy is. All I have to do is type in 'Hawk City' and 'Rodale' in the search engine. The first article that pops up is about the murder of her parents, Paul and Anna Rodale. Paul was the editor of the *Hawk City Gazette*, a newspaper known for controversial articles. They weren't afraid to poke the powerful Idols in Hawk City.

I click on the link, which is surprisingly not from the newspaper he used to work for. It's from a more traditional publication, *Hawk City News*. It says Daisy's parents died in a tragic fire in their apartment, along with their children, Daisy and Rose. I lean back against my chair, rubbing my chin.

Daisy didn't want me to know anything about her past. It was Rosie who told us her parents had been murdered. It happened seven years ago, which begs the question: Where did Daisy and her sister go after those events? I get the impression that she doesn't have any other family, but again, she could be withholding that information as well.

Despite her deceit, I can't bring myself to be angry at her. No, the feeling that's swirling in my chest is the opposite of anger. I won't dare give a name to it yet, but just thinking about her makes me want to see her again. Damn it. Weren't cravings supposed to stop once you got what you wanted?

There's a knock on my doorframe. "Can I talk to you?" Morpheus asks.

I close my laptop and swivel my chair around. "Sure."

A quick once-over tells me Morpheus is not back in top shape yet. His skin is too pale, and there are dark circles under his eyes. He's shed some of the layers of clothing, but he's still wearing a cashmere sweater and woolen beanie.

Morpheus closes the door and shoves his hands into his jeans pockets. "It's about Daisy."

My spine becomes rigid in an instant. Of all the subjects I want to avoid, Daisy is at the top of the list.

"If you're here to give me a sermon about how foolish I was for hooking up with the Norm, you'd better—"

"It's not about that," Morpheus cuts me off. "It's about what I saw while that asshole was in my head, torturing me."

"You had another vision?" I lean forward, eager all of a sudden.

"Yeah. I didn't realize at the time it was a vision. I was in too much pain to pay attention. But once that motherfucker got out of my head, my thoughts became clearer."

"What did you see?"

"Daisy and you next to her. You were in a white void of sorts, and there was a line of power linking each of you to other people."

"Other people? Who?" I narrow my eyes to slits.

"I don't know. I couldn't get a clear visual of them. They were blurry and see-through, almost like ghosts." Morpheus shakes his head. "I honestly have no clue what it means. The sense I got is that you were separated from those ghosts by a great space, time maybe."

I lean my elbows on my knees and let my head dip between

my shoulders. "Were Daisy and I linked in any other way in your vision?"

Morpheus makes a disgruntled noise in the back of his throat, prompting me to meet his gaze again. "What?"

"There was an infinity band circling your wrists."

I inhale sharply. Son of a bitch. "Are you sure?"

"Yeah."

Running my fingers through my hair, I straighten up in my chair. The infinity band is the ultimate vow two Idols can make to each other. It's like marriage on steroids. Unbreakable.

"Daisy isn't an Idol. Even if I was crazy enough to even consider it, we could never form an infinity band. She'd be killed in an instant."

"You're concerned about that?" Morpheus's eyes widen. "How about the fact that you were bonded by an eternal vow in my vision? An infinity band doesn't only link you in one lifetime. It's forever."

"I know that. Jeez, Morpheus. Chill out. I'm not worried about it because it's never going to happen, and not because Daisy is a Norm. I'd never do something stupid like that."

"Fine. Whatever. But we still need to figure who you two were connected to in my vision. If it's someone from the past, you should start with your bloodlines. Daisy's will be trickier. Do we even know where she's from originally?"

"Hawk City," I reply.

"Damn. There must be thousands of Woods in that metropolis."

"Her last name isn't Woods." I turn to my laptop, opening it once more. There's no sense hiding what I learned from Morpheus, not after what he told me. "Her last name is Rodale, and her parents died in a fire seven years ago. Her father was the editor of the *Hawk City Gazette*."

"Shit. Isn't that newspaper known for inflammatory articles?" Morpheus moves closer to my screen.

"Yeah."

"Wait, her father was the infamous Paul Rodale?" Morpheus's tone rises in pitch.

"What about him?"

"Dude, he stirred a lot of feathers in the Idol community prior to his death. He wrote a controversial article stating that Idols were initially created to protect the weak, but instead we turned into tyrants who terrorize the people we were supposed to protect."

I snort. "So, the guy was a wacko."

"Pretty much. And it doesn't stop there. He ended the piece by saying that if Idols couldn't be bothered to uphold their purpose, then what does the world need them for?"

"So, basically he was calling for our destruction," I say.

Morpheus nods. "I'm not surprised he was killed."

Pieces of the puzzle are slowly becoming clearer. I just don't know how they fit together yet. My mother doesn't hate Norms, but what happened to her in the past that made her hate her own kind? What if she's part of the Knights? I can't believe that possibility never occurred to me until now.

"What's on your mind?" Morpheus asks.

Meeting his gaze, I say, "If word gets out that Daisy is his daughter, she's as good as dead."

Morpheus turns his back to me and begins to pace. "What if Daisy shares her father's ideas about Idols?"

His suspicion makes my blood run cold. What if I allowed myself to care about someone who wanted me dead all along? No. I don't believe Daisy is duplicitous like that.

"I don't think she does."

Morpheus whirls around. "How can you be so sure?"

"I'm not sure. But what if she does share the same ideas as her father? She's a Norm, Morpheus. Powerless. She can't kill us by just wishing us dead."

"But she could be working for the Knights, and *they* aren't powerless."

I run a hand through my hair. They could have easily killed me, but they didn't.

"My own mother could be a Knight, which is way more troubling than Daisy's possible connection to them," I say, but my words are empty. They lack conviction. Morpheus's argument has filled me with doubt.

He stares at me without blinking for a moment. "Do you seriously believe that?"

"It would explain a lot."

He shakes his head. "But it doesn't explain why that powerful god would want Daisy gone."

"Maybe it has to do with your vision. Maybe Daisy isn't the problem, but her lineage is."

His expression twists into a frown, making me wary.

"You don't think we should obey his wishes, do you?" I ask.

He glances away. "If you'd asked me this a few weeks ago, I'd say fuck yes. But now, I don't know."

"So why did you spend the last minute trying to convince me Daisy is the bad guy?" I snap.

Morpheus meets my gaze once more with arched eyebrows. "That's not what I was doing. But we can't simply ignore her past."

"You hated her from the very beginning," I point out.

"I didn't hate her like Rufio did. I knew she was dangerous. I still believe she is, but now I'm not so sure if the danger she presents is to us or to the god with the leash around our necks."

"If she can somehow help us get rid of him, that's one more reason to keep her safe."

"I know."

"So what's up with the scowl?" I ask. *Seriously, I can't guess what he's thinking.*

"We need a specialist in Idol bloodlines and history to dig further into your past and Daisy's, someone we can trust."

"I see. I'm sure we can find someone who qualifies."

"That's not the problem. I already have someone in mind."

"Who?"

"My father."

8

RUFIO

Away from the guys, I can finally let the rage coiled tight in the pit of my stomach loose. It spreads through my body like wildfire, tinting my vision red. School is still in session—a murder attempt on a Norm wouldn't be enough reason to cancel classes.

The students I encounter on my way to the principal's office recoil away from me. I'm projecting my destructive nature to the max, and they can sense it.

I barge into the office's reception area like I own the place. My mother's assistant lifts her gaze from the computer and opens her mouth, but I ignore the old hag completely and march straight into my mother's office.

"I'd like to have a—"

My statement is cut short when I see she has company. Her visitors—two suits, a man and a woman—turn around when I enter. My mother stares hard in my direction.

"Rufio, what's the meaning of this?" she demands.

"I came to talk. Didn't know you had company."

"These are Agents Sylvia Hawthorne and Greg Bauer. They came to ask a few questions about Mr. Rogers."

"You called the cops on him?" I ask in disbelief.

Sure, Bryce told me Mom was the one who got Daisy a scholarship and that she doesn't hate Norms like she'd led us to believe, but I'm still shocked.

"Of course I called the cops. What Mr. Rogers did was inexcusable."

Agent Hawthorne chuckles. "You don't need to keep up the pretenses around us, Principal Fallon."

"What's going to happen to him?" I ask.

"Well, he's detained for questioning, and then, well, who knows?" The second agent shrugs. "Wait for trial—that is, if he's indicted."

I can't remember the last time an Idol was charged for attempting to kill a Norm, or even succeeding in killing one, but the agent's answer doesn't sit well with me. The fury hovering above my skin increases tenfold.

"Are you saying he can go free?" I ask through clenched teeth.

Both agents regard me with surprise.

"I think I've answered all your questions, agents," Mom chimes in. "I'd like to be informed when Mr. Rogers is released. He's banned from the school grounds, of course, but without knowing his motives for attacking Daisy Woods, I can't rule out that he'll try again."

I don't know if Mom's statement was meant to get a reaction from me or not, but my stomach clenches painfully. If Mr. Rogers gets near Daisy, I'll kill him. The thought should alarm me; after all, I'm vowing to kill an Idol over a puny Norm.

Understanding Mom is dismissing them, the agents stand up and shake her hand.

"We'll inform you, naturally. We understand this situation is less than ideal for you and this institution's reputation," Agent Bauer says, "but perhaps it can also serve as a lesson."

"A lesson?" she asks with a frown.

"Norms have their place in society, and it's not among Idols."

My mother narrows her eyes. She grabs a random item from her desk, a dark stone paperweight in the shape of a pyramid, and runs her thumb over the sharp edge.

"Are you trying to teach me how to do my job?" she asks in a hard, dangerous tone.

The window behind her desk bursts open and a gust of wind comes through. Mom is a level fifteen Idol, and her gift is elemental—air, to be exact. She can summon the nastiest storms. I saw her do it once when I was very young, maybe five. She was having an argument with my father then, but I can't remember what it was about.

"No, not at all," Agent Hawthorne amends quickly. "Forgive my partner."

Both suits hastily make their way out of my mother's office, leaving the door wide open. With an annoyed grunt, Mom flicks her finger, and the door closes. She drops to her seat and massages her temple.

"Morons."

"I don't know why you called the cops. You know their investigation won't go anywhere," I say.

"I didn't call them. Mr. Amaro did. Now we'll just have to deal with them." She stares me straight in the eye. "What do you want? If it's to bitch about something, I'm not in the mood."

I grapple with my emotions, which are bouncing all over the place. Anger is dominant, but the reasons for it are the problem. They contradict. I'm angry that Mom made me her puppet, angry at Bryce for sleeping with Daisy, and furious at myself for caring.

"You lied to me," I say.

"About what?" she asks like she doesn't know.

"Cut the bullshit, *Mother*. Two weeks ago you called me here to make sure Daisy wouldn't last a week at Gifted Academy, but you were the one behind her admission. I want to know what kind of game you're playing."

"I'm going to say the same thing I told your brother. I did what was necessary."

"Necessary for what?" I raise my voice. "What's so special about Daisy?"

Mom narrows her eyes. "Don't tell me you don't know. I gave you one simple task: unleash your worst on the girl. But you couldn't do it, could you? You held back, and when she was in mortal danger, you chose to save her. Why is that, Rufio?"

I yank my hair at the roots. "Fuck! I don't know. If I did, I wouldn't be here."

"The world is in constant motion, and there's a big shift coming our way. You either embrace the change or you perish," she says.

"What's that supposed to mean?"

"Our kind has been dominant for centuries, but it hasn't always been this way. The universe works in cycles, and we're on the verge of an era where Idols are no longer at the top."

"You mean Norms are going to take over, and you're planning on siding with them?"

I can't believe this. It's one thing for me to crave Daisy knowing she's not ordinary. Quite another to completely betray my kind in favor of beings I've been taught to despise my entire life.

Mom leans against her chair and stares at me intensely, still clutching the paperweight. "I don't know if that's going to happen, but make no mistake, Rufio. Change is coming."

I approach her desk and sprawl my hands over it as I lean forward. "Do you think I buy this load of crap? You're hiding something, and I *will* find out."

Before she can spew more half-baked stories, I leave her office, but the desire to unleash my fury and level this building to the ground is immense. By a miracle, I manage to keep my power bottled in. But I can't return to my apartment and be that close to Daisy.

I head for the treehouse where we keep our stash of Silver-voltage. Tomorrow, I'll figure out my next move. Tonight, only oblivion will do.

9

DAISY

I had hoped that I would feel better after I saw Rosie, but I'm feeling more wretched than before thanks to the conversation I had with Toby. It's horrible that his parents are pulling him out of Gifted Academy because he defended me. It's not fair.

My heart is heavy, and my mind is whirling as I take the bus back to campus. The mysterious package from Hawk City is burning a hole through my backpack, but I won't open it until I'm in my room. Not knowing who sent it or what it contains, it would be a bad idea to find out in public.

About fifteen minutes away from my stop, the bus's engine begins to sputter. The vehicle loses speed until the driver pulls off the highway.

"What's going on?" a woman sitting across the aisle asks.

Grumbling, the driver heads out to check the bus's motor. A few minutes later, he returns, fuming and cursing.

"All right, folks. This bus is not going anywhere. You all have to wait for the next one."

Distressed murmurs erupt among the passengers. I look out

the window and curse in my head. The next bus won't come for another hour. I'll get back to school faster if I walk.

One by one, the passengers file out of the bus. I hoist my backpack over my shoulder and follow them. Together, we head toward the next bus stop, which is half a mile from where we are. They all stay there, but I continue on. The afternoon sun is hot on my back, but the walk is not unbearable. I'm glad I'm wearing my comfortable sneakers.

About thirty minutes up the road, I hear the sound of a car approach. Without changing my pace, I glance over my shoulder. An old station wagon slows down until it stops next to me. I'm wary in an instant, even if the occupants of the vehicle are an old couple.

"Hello there," the woman says with a smile. "Are you okay?"

"Yeah, I'm fine."

"Where are you headed in this heat? Do you need a ride somewhere?" the man asks.

I shake my head. As tempting as it is not to have to walk all the way to campus, I know better than to accept rides from strangers, no matter how friendly they seem.

"It's okay. I'm not too far from my destination."

"It's no big deal, sweetheart. We're headed in that direction anyway," the woman insists.

"No, really. I'm okay." I begin to walk faster.

"Nonsense. We can't simply let you walk all by yourself. It's not safe. I'd feel horrible if we just left you behind."

They're too pushy. I don't sense power coming from them, which means they're Norms, but even so, that doesn't mean I can trust them. Norms can be bad too. Maybe I should run back to the bus stop and wait for the next bus to come.

"No offense, but I don't know you, and I was taught to never get into a car with strangers," I say, ready to bolt.

The smile wilts from the woman's face. "I understand. But I *must* insist."

Something strange happens to me. My mind becomes foggy, and I start to see the friendly couple in an entirely different light. I can't remember now why I shouldn't accept their offer.

"Okay," I reply.

"Good girl. Hop in, Daisy. We'll get you back to Gifted Academy in no time."

I open the back door and slide into their car. They know my name and where I'm going, but that doesn't alarm me at all.

"You're so lucky we saw you on the side of the road. It's not safe for a pretty girl like you to be walking by yourself in the middle of nowhere," the old man says.

"Yes, I'm very fortunate. Thank you," I reply.

In less than five minutes, the gates of Gifted Academy loom on the horizon, but instead of heading straight for it, the driver stops the car just before the campus entrance.

"Why are we stopping here?" I ask.

"Oh, honey, it wouldn't be convenient for us to be caught on your school's security camera," the woman replies.

"Why not?" I ask.

"Trust us on that, sweetheart. Before you go, can I ask you something?"

"Sure."

"Do you like cake?" She turns in her seat, holding a pink box.

"Who doesn't?"

"Oh, goodie. Here, take this. I'm an enthusiastic baker, and I always end up baking more cake than my husband and I can eat."

"Thanks." I grab the box. "What kind of cake is it?"

"Vanilla with a surprise filling. You'll love it," the man replies.

Still bewildered by this strange couple and my reaction to them, I exit their car. They drive off before I get to the gate. It's not until I return to my room that the strange fog lifts from my brain.

Holy shit. I don't know who those people were, but they scrambled my thoughts. Which means they weren't Norms like I thought they were. Suddenly, the pink box feels like a ticking bomb. What the hell is inside? Placing it on my desk, I open the lid slowly. Relief washes over me when I see it's indeed a round cake with vanilla frosting. But the guy said something about the filling.

Afraid to stick my fingers in the cake, I grab a pencil from my desk and push it through the top. Halfway in, I feel resistance. There's something hard inside. My heart is pounding hard as I destroy the top layer of the cake. I suck in a breath when I discover the surprise inside.

Another lightning-glass dagger.

I take a step back, trembling. My chest feels tight as panic sets in. Seeing a replica of the weapon I lost earlier works as a gate opener. The emotions I should have felt earlier, the fear that gripped me when I fell out the window, finally come forth. Like an avalanche, it runs me over, burying me alive.

I sit at the edge of my bed with my head in my hands and cry. Sobs rack my body, coming out loud and pitiful. Even when the tears are gone, I continue to shake. I get up and head for the bathroom to wash my face when I see my backpack discarded by the foot of the bed and remember the mysterious package from Hawk City.

After finding the dagger in the cake, I'm even more cautious about opening it, but I can't simply ignore it. I'm already a mess anyway; whatever it is, it can't make me feel worse. I yank the cardboard envelop out and rip it open. Inside, I find a single sheet of paper. A black-and-white photograph, to be precise, of my father when he was a teen standing between two men and a woman. One of the men I don't recognize, but the other two people I do.

It's Mr. X and Principal Fallon.

Son of a bitch.

∼

MORPHEUS

I try to rest because I know I'm not entirely recovered from my ordeal, but I only manage to catch an hour of restless sleep before my eyes fly open. An acute pain spears my chest. I'm not shivering, and a quick glance at my wrist tells me the shadows aren't too blame for the crushing weight threatening to cave in my rib cage.

With a gasp, I sit up. As fast as the pain came, it goes away, but my breathing is still erratic. *What the hell was that?*

I get out of bed and head for the kitchen. The apartment is quiet. A soft glow coming from Bryce's room tells me he must still be glued to his laptop. Knowing how strained my relationship is with my father, he's going to do as much research about his bloodline as possible before I turn to the man who loathes me.

I'm on my way to the fridge when some strange tug draws my attention to the front door. I've never felt a hunch before that didn't involve my shadows wreaking havoc, but maybe, thanks to the bracelets' reinforcements, the shadows can't manifest.

Ignoring the pull is not only unwise but not something I can do. I stride out of the apartment and, surprise, surprise, the strange tug leads me to Daisy's door. What am I supposed to do now? I place my sprawled fingers against the hard surface and wait for... I don't know what. A sign that I should knock? Fuck, where is this bout of uncertainty coming from?

I wait for several beats until I realize I'm acting like a fool. I curl my hand into a fist, ready to knock when Daisy opens the door. Her eyes are red and puffy. Worry immediately hits me.

"Are you okay?" I ask.

"No. What are you doing here?"

A rush of embarrassment goes through me. "I... well, I came to check on you. How did you know there was someone at your door?"

She bites her lower lip and fidgets where she stands. "I don't know."

I sense the lie, so I ask, "You didn't ask Principal Fallon to give you access to the security camera feed, did you?"

Daisy snorts. "Right. Like that would help me much. If any of you wanted to break in, a security camera wouldn't stop you."

"Actually, we couldn't break in," I say.

"Come on. A door wouldn't deter any of you."

"I guess Principal Fallon forgot to tell you that all dorm doors are reinforced. No amount of Idol power could break through them."

Daisy's eyebrows arch. "No, she didn't tell me."

"Why were you crying?" I blurt out, unable to stop myself.

She lowers her gaze. "I guess the shock from my ordeal has finally worn off. I got hit by all the emotions at once."

"I'm sorry."

It's a heartfelt statement, and it catches me by surprise. I *am* sorry about what Daisy went through, not only today but also at the beach. Talk about a flip.

Daisy lifts her chin to meet my gaze. "Because you almost lost your tutor."

"No, that's not the reason."

She frowns but thankfully doesn't question me further on that. "Well, as you can see, I'm a mess. You can report that back to your buddies. I'm sure Rufio and Phoenix will be ecstatic to know."

I could remind her that they risked their lives to save her, but in all honesty, I don't know their true feelings concerning Daisy. Hell, I don't know my *own* feelings toward the Norm.

"So, will I see you tomorrow at school?" I ask.

"We don't have any classes together tomorrow."

"Right, but I missed math class today, and, well...."

Daisy crosses her arms over her chest. "Are you trying to ask me if we can resume tutoring tomorrow? Is that it?"

I honestly don't give a fuck about math right now. I'm more interested in finding out everything I can about the girl before I talk to my father.

"Yes," I lie.

She lets out a resigned sigh. "Yes, Morpheus. We can resume your lessons tomorrow. I'm going to bed now, and you should do the same. You still look like crap."

I smile despite myself. "See you tomorrow, Daisy."

She closes the door softly, and I find myself frozen, staring at it like a fool with a stupid grin on my face.

10

DAISY

I'm out of bed bright and early, before sunrise, ready to face the day. I cried myself to sleep, especially after seeing the old photograph with my Dad in it. When I ran away with Rosie, I brought nothing with me, no memento to remember my parents. Whoever the person who sent the picture to me is, I thank them, despite their shady motives.

So my father, Mr. X, and Principal Fallon knew each other when they were younger. It explains why the duo took an interest in me, but it doesn't begin to reveal the mystery of their connection.

Silly as it may be, I hid the photograph inside my pillowcase and pretended Dad was watching me sleep like he used to when I was little. But the time for crying is over. I need to get ready for battle. I'm healed, but that doesn't mean the Idols here will stop gunning for me. I have to maintain my stamina.

I change quickly into jogging clothes, but today I'm heading out with an extra accessory. The dagger. I wrap it in a piece of cloth and tuck it behind my shorts' waistband. I'm never going anywhere without it now.

After a quick stretch, I head for my usual course around

campus. My muscles strain more than usual in the beginning since I've been neglecting my morning jogs, but I push through the pain, knowing it will get better eventually.

It takes me longer to complete my run, but I still have plenty of time to get ready for school. I can't wait to see the looks of surprise on my hateful classmates' faces. I bet they don't think I'll stick around after a teacher tried to kill me.

I have a big smile on my face when I round the corner. This is the final stretch before the dorm building. But then, all of a sudden, I feel a tug pulling me off the path. It's the same strange sensation I felt when I discovered Bryce passed out in his bathroom and when I found Morpheus planted in front of my door. A punch of worry hits me. Did Bryce do something to me other than healing?

Curious to see where this pull will take me, I veer off onto a dirt track that leads to a thicker part of the woods surrounding the campus. I didn't have the chance to explore the area before. The farther I go in, the faster my heart beats. If someone were to ambush me, no one would hear my cries for help. To be safe, I pull my dagger out.

After a minute or so, I reach a clearing. On the other side is a massive tree with a treehouse on top. My jaw drops of its own accord. Why would anyone build a treehouse on school property? The impulse to check it out is immense. I should head back, but in this moment, it seems common sense has vacated my brain.

I cross the remaining distance on soft feet, not wanting to alert anyone of my approach. Standing under the tree, I tuck the dagger behind my waistband again so I can climb up the ladder. The steps creak loudly as I put my weight on them. So much for being inconspicuous. At the top of the ladder is a hatch door that's already open. Slowly, I stick my head inside. The place is cozy, a perfect hideout. The floor is covered with a plush carpet, and there are beanbags and blankets spread about.

And one of them is occupied by Rufio.

He's sprawled across it as if he passed out like that. I should run in the opposite direction, but instead I go in. The wooden boards groan, but Rufio doesn't even flinch. On light feet, I approach him. He must have spent the night here. He's clutching something in his hand, a small glass bottle. Alcohol, maybe? Although, drinking from a miniature bottle would have no effect on him. Not even Norms can get drunk on such a small amount of booze.

I crouch next to him and take a moment to appreciate the beauty of his face. It should be illegal for a guy to have those high cheekbones and full lips. I still remember what his lips taste like, even though I was high at the time.

His long bangs are covering his right eye, and like an idiot, I push them off. Rufio stirs in his sleep and then blinks his eyes open. *Shit.* I try to jump back up but end up falling on my butt.

"Daisy? What are you doing here?" He sits straighter on the beanbag.

"I, uh, found this place by accident."

Rufio doesn't reply to my statement for a couple of beats, just keeps staring at me with an unreadable expression. Finally, he stands up and offers me his hand. I make the second mistake of the day and accept it.

When he pulls me up, he also makes sure I'm flush against his body. A shiver of anticipation runs down my spine. I keep my eyes glued to the hollow of his throat while I try to calm the fuck down. I can't allow him to trap me in his blue gaze.

"You were running. Would you like something to drink?" His voice is low and smooth, like whiskey poured over ice. It sends more tingles down my back.

I let go of his hand and take a step back. "No, I'm fine."

Rufio clamps his jaw tight and frowns. "Ugh. My mouth

tastes like ashes." He tosses the small glass bottle on the beanbag and pulls a pack of gum from his jeans pocket. "Want some?" He extends his hand with the offer.

I shake my head, unable to form words. What's going on here? Why is Rufio acting like we aren't mortal enemies?

He sticks one piece of gum into his mouth, then whirls around. Wary, I keep watching him. I don't understand why I don't just leave. Why can't I force my legs to move? He veers for a mini fridge that was tucked into a corner and pulls a can of soda from it.

"I'd better go," I finally say. With effort, I turn toward the trapdoor, but I don't make it two steps before Rufio reaches me and wraps his arms around my waist.

Tension spreads through my body like wildfire, sending my already agitated heart into overdrive.

"Don't," he whispers. Then he rests his chin on my shoulder and takes a deep breath. In an instant, I become pudding, puny in his arms. Shit. I'm a moron.

"What's this?" Rufio's voice changes. I'm too slow to understand the meaning of his question. Damn stupid hormones. Then Rufio pulls the dagger from my waistband, and just like that, my desire changes into fear.

I pivot around and stare wide-eyed at the lightning-glass dagger in his hand. My throat is unbearably dry now, and my tongue is stuck in my mouth. I'm shaking, but the longer it takes me to answer his question, the more suspicious he'll become.

"Protection," I say. "Give it back."

"This is a strange dagger. What is it made of?" Rufio runs his hand over the smooth surface of the blade.

"I don't know," I lie.

It seems he doesn't know about lightning glass. The Idol I killed didn't recognize the material either.

Rufio finally lifts his face to meet my eyes. "Do you think you're still in danger?"

I was expecting anger and distrust in his gaze, not the worry I see shining there. His change of attitude toward me is making my head spin.

"I'm not stupid. I don't think. I *know*," I reply.

I'm actually pretty stupid. I should have run back to my room the moment I saw Rufio was in here.

Instead of returning my dagger, he sets it on the small table near him. "You don't need to walk around campus armed."

"Oh yeah. Why is that? Are you offering me your bodyguard services?" I hug my middle, a gesture I know shows weakness, but I can't help myself. I *am* afraid of so many things right now. But mostly I'm terrified of the desire that's slowly returning. Rufio should only ignite fear in me, not this absurd craving.

He steps closer. "Maybe I am."

"What?" I squeak like a silly girl while my heart decides to take Rufio's statement at face value. It's now doing the cha-cha in my chest. *Traitor*.

Rufio invades my space and reaches for my arms. Slowly, he uncrosses them without breaking eye contact. My breathing is coming out in bursts now, and an enormous lump gets stuck in my throat.

"What are you doing?" I whisper.

Without answering my question, he drops his gaze to my chest. I'm only wearing a sports bra, no T-shirt. Rufio leans forward and places a kiss right between my breasts. My skin immediately breaks out in goose bumps. He moves lower, bypassing my girls to place another kiss in the middle of my belly. I close my eyes because I'm getting dizzy already.

Rufio reaches my waistband, but instead of kissing under my belly button, he bites the fabric and tugs it down a little, exposing my cotton panties. With a gasp, I reach for his shoulder, trying to remain standing. My legs soon won't be able to support me, for they've turned into jelly.

He lets go of my arms to run his fingers down the backs of my legs. I open my eyes and glance down. The protest on the tip of my tongue is forgotten when Rufio's intense gaze connects with mine. Pure lust shines in his blue eyes.

"You're shaking. Do I frighten you, Daisy?"

"No," I croak. I'm so full of shit.

He rewards me with a knowing smile before he begins to pull my shorts down slowly. A moment of clarity hits me finally. *What the hell am I doing?* I grab his hands, halting his progress before I step back.

"I didn't come here for this," I say.

Rufio unfurls from his crouch as his expression darkens. "Why did you come here, then?"

Not having an answer, I simply turn on my heels and head for the trapdoor. But it's wishful thinking on my part to believe Rufio would simply let me go. His strong arms wrap around my middle, and my back connects with his front. I let a yelp, my heart thundering in my chest.

He brings his mouth close to my ear and whispers, "You didn't answer my question."

I struggle against his hold, which only makes him squeeze me tighter. "Let me go."

"Is that what you really want, Daisy?" My name rolls off his tongue like honey, and his warm breath fanning against my neck only serves to make me melt in his arms.

"Yes," I breathe out.

"You're such a bad liar." He kisses me softly just below my ear, a gentle action that's at complete odds with his dark nature.

A moan escapes my lips, which prompts Rufio to run his tongue down my neck. Desire shoots down my spine, curling around its base. A mild throbbing between my legs is the warning that if I don't escape soon, it'll be too late.

He runs his right hand down my belly and then cups my sex. Game over. My legs buckle beneath me. If it weren't for Rufio holding me tight, I would have collapsed.

"We have unfinished business, Daisy." He strokes my clit through the layers of clothing, sending a zing of pleasure down my limbs.

"That night was a mistake," I say without conviction.

"The only mistake about that night is that I didn't fuck you."

There's a hint of anger in his reply, which excites me more than makes me scared. But it also makes me suspect that he's pissed I slept with Bryce.

"Because that means your brother got there first?"

With a groan, Rufio twists me around, and before I can react, he crushes his lips against mine. The kiss is savage and angry, but it's also electrifying. I try to fight him off for a hot second, a lost cause. I'm powerless to stop him. A heated frenzy takes over both of us. It's like we've been secretly lusting after one another despite all the hatred, and now the dam has broken loose.

We only break apart to remove the pieces of clothing separating our bodies. Rufio peels my sports bra off first, tossing it to the side. His hungry gaze drops to my breasts, but before he can bring his lips to them, I reach for the bottom of his T-shirt. With impatient hands, I yank it off, messing up his hair in a sexy way.

Rufio is on me in the next second, capturing a nipple with his eager mouth. He sucks it hard until it hurts, but the pain only intensifies the pleasure. Clutching his hair by the roots, I arch my back. My mind is spinning out of control, so it's no surprise that I don't notice the moment we change positions until I open my eyes and am staring at the ceiling. Rufio's lips are on the move, going down until he finds my shorts. They vanish in the next moment, along with my panties. Then he's between my legs, licking and sucking while he fucks me with his fingers.

Oh my God. What's up with the Kent brothers and their tongues?

I'm moaning and panting like a cat in heat. It's not a shocker when Rufio sends me over the edge faster than I could have imagined, and I cry out as my hips buckle. Rufio sprawls his fingers over my belly, keeping me still while he mercilessly teases my clit until the tremors running through my body cease.

I keep my eyes closed while my breathing comes out in spurts. Time has no meaning anymore. But if I thought Rufio was done with me, it was a mistake. I hear the sound of a wrapper being torn just before he rolls me over on my belly. He then pins me to the floor with his body. The tip of his cock is at my entrance, and his mouth is at my ear again.

"You're mine now, Daisy."

"No I'm not," I say through clenched teeth. "I belong to no one."

"I beg to differ." With a precise thrust, he sheaths himself inside of me.

He feels too good. And he's right. In this moment, he owns me completely. Rufio covers my hands with his, linking our fingers together while he fucks me hard from behind. A delicious pressure begins to build again between my legs, and it feels like my body is operating at a hundred degrees.

"Damn it, Daisy. Your pussy is so tight," he grunts in my ear.

My body starts to tingle, and I'm so hot, I know I have a fever. My thoughts are all scrambled as though I'm high. As crazy as it may sound, I want—no, I *need* Rufio to punish me, to give me his worst. It's like he brings out the dark side of me.

"Harder. Fuck me harder," I urge.

With a groan, he increases the tempo, but it's not enough. As if he's reading my mind, Rufio bites my shoulder hard enough to inflict just the right amount of pain to send me over the edge.

We both cry out at the same time. A strange energy surrounds our bodies, leaving traces of heat and ice over my skin. Such nonsense. I must have lost my mind to orgasmic bliss. I keep my eyes shut because the room is spinning.

Rufio gives one final, shuddering thrust, and then he collapses next to me. And that's the last thing I remember before oblivion takes over.

11

RUFIO

It takes a couple of minutes for my breathing to return to normal. Hot damn. That was the most intense fuck I've had in my life. I shouldn't be surprised that sleeping with Daisy would be an experience, but I had no idea it would be like that. Shit, I'm not giving this up.

I told Drusilla I never go for seconds, but hell, I'm breaking my own rule. And I'm doing it for a Norm. I rub my face. If someone had told me this would happen to me, I'd laugh my ass off.

I turn to Daisy. She hasn't moved since I slipped out of her. Does she regret giving in so easily? Is she thinking about Bryce? A sharp pain spears my chest. Then anger takes its place. Is this what jealousy feels like? I've never cared about any girl before, so the feeling is unknown to me.

I prop myself on my elbow and push her long hair off her face. "Daisy?"

No answer. *What the hell. Did she fall asleep?*

I shake her shoulder. "Hey, Daisy. Wake up."

Nothing. Not even a moan. Fuck. Did I accidentally kill her?

I'm gripped by panic for a second, then realize she's not cold. On the contrary, she's burning up. I roll her over so she's lying on her back. Her eyes are closed, but she's breathing, albeit a little shallowly. Her hair is matted against her clammy forehead.

I shake her harder. "Daisy. What the fuck? Wake up!"

She's out cold. Shit. This is not normal.

I jump back to my feet and go in search of my cell. I don't think twice before calling my brother. I'm not even doing it on purpose to rub it in his face that I fucked his darling. He's just my go-to person when the shit hits the fan, no matter how hard we fight.

He answers on the second ring. "What?"

"Bryce, I have a problem." I run a hand through my hair.

"What did you do?" His tone is harsh, and it rubs me the wrong way. He always assumes the worst about me.

"I'm not sure. It's Daisy."

There's a pause. "Rufio, I swear if you hurt Daisy in any way, I'll forget you're my brother."

Considering the tone of his voice has gone ten degrees cooler, I believe him.

"I didn't hurt her. Could you please come to the treehouse ASAP?"

"What is she doing there with you?"

I pinch the bridge of my nose and begin to pace. "She got here on her own."

I hear the sound of Phoenix's voice in the background, then Morpheus's. Great. Now they're all gonna tag along.

"I'll be there in a minute," Bryce replies before the line goes silent.

I toss my phone on the nearest beanbag and search for Daisy's discarded clothes. I don't want them to find her naked like that. Considering how fast Bryce and the others can run, I know they'll be here in less than a minute, so I forgo Daisy's panties and just put her running shorts back on. The sports bra is a little trickier.

Ah, fuck it. I can already sense my brother. Running out of time, I simply cover Daisy's torso with my shirt. A second later, Bryce is coming up the ladder. Morpheus and Phoenix join him, all in partial states of dressing. They literally dropped everything they were doing to check on Daisy.

Bryce spares me one fleeting glance before he runs to the girl lying on the floor. He pulls her tangled hair off her face and cups her cheek.

"Daisy, sweetheart. Wake up."

Sweetheart? What the hell? When did he start calling her by cute nicknames?

"What did you do to her?" Morpheus watches me through slitted eyes.

"Isn't it obvious?" Phoenix interjects. "He fucked her."

Bryce looks over his shoulder, eyes spitting fire. "If you forced her—"

"Don't you dare finish that sentence." I point at him. "I'd never do that to anyone."

"But you guys hooked up," Morpheus replies.

"Obviously. Look at the evidence." Phoenix points at the used condom I didn't have the chance to toss in the trash.

"Yeah, we fucked, but she wanted it as much as I did. I didn't ask you here to grill me about what went down between Daisy and me." I switch my attention to her. She's in Bryce's arms now, and he has his hand pressed against her forehead. "What are you doing?"

"She has a fucking fever, and she's unresponsive. What do you think I'm doing?" he snaps.

"Are you healing her?" Phoenix asks.

"I'm trying. Now everyone shut up." He glances at her again. His hand begins to glow and the light spreads throughout her body next, enveloping her whole.

I squint, raising my arm to shield my eyes. When the light fades, I have to blink a couple of times.

"Daisy?" Bryce calls softly.

She moans before opening her eyes partially. A wash of relief runs through me.

"What's going on?" she croaks, then hisses. "Everything hurts."

"Damn it, Bryce. I thought you had healing powers." Phoenix takes a step forward, his face scrunched up in worry.

"I haven't gotten the hang of it yet. I just discovered I have it."

"Is she still running a fever?" Morpheus asks.

Bryce nods. "Yes."

With a swift movement, he's back on his feet.

"Where are you taking her?" My voice rises, laced with worry.

"Back to her room. Then I'm calling Ellen."

Before I can say anything, Bryce heads for the window and jumps with Daisy in his arms, disappearing from view. If Bryce is willing to involve the school nurse, then he's truly freaked out about Daisy.

In truth, so I am.

BRYCE

Ellen uses her hands to scan Daisy's feverish body, and I don't like the frown she's sporting now one bit. I rub my face, then rip at my hair. *Fuck*. I wonder if I didn't truly heal Daisy but only delayed the inevitable.

Once the nurse finishes her perusal, she sighs loudly and then turns to Rufio, who's standing off in a corner in Daisy's room. At first, Ellen wanted to kick all of us out, but seeing how adamant we were on staying, she decided it wasn't worth the waste of time and went to work on Daisy right away.

"I don't understand. There's nothing wrong with her besides this high fever. I saw no traces of infection or flu," she says.

"So, my healing is not reversing?" I ask.

She shakes her head. "No. All her bones are intact, and there's no internal bleeding either."

"You don't think too much sex could do that to a Norm, do you?" Phoenix asks earnestly.

We all turn to gawk at him.

"You're serious," Morpheus finally replies.

He shrugs. "What? I've never hung out with Norms after I fu—I mean, after I slept with them."

Ellen stands back from Daisy's bed and pulls a plastic bottle with pills inside from her bag. "There's nothing for us to do besides wait for her fever to run its course. Just make sure it doesn't go over 100 degrees."

The nurse gives a couple of pills to Daisy, who is completely out of it. She at least manages to swallow the medication with a little water.

"Do you want us to check on her?" Rufio asks.

She turns to him with an eyebrow raised. "You're her neighbors, and you asked me not to tell the principal the details of what happened to Daisy prior to the fever, so yeah, I'm asking you to keep an eye on her."

Rufio shuts his pie hole, glancing away.

"I can stay with her," Morpheus offers.

"You're going to ditch class for her? Why?" I ask, narrowing my eyes.

"Because I'm the only one who hasn't or doesn't want to bone her." Morpheus switches his attention to the nurse. "Sorry, Ellen."

The woman simply shakes her head. "Don't worry about

my ears, kid. I've heard worse." She hoists her bag over her shoulder. "I'll come back later to check on her."

Once the woman leaves, Daisy makes a disgruntled sound in the back of her throat.

"Morpheus, you can't skip class on my account," she croaks, trying to sit up.

"Hey, what are you doing there, girlie? Lay back down." Phoenix motions to her bed, stopping halfway as if he realizes something.

"I'll stay with you," I offer before Rufio or Phoenix decides to volunteer.

From the corner of my eye, I catch Rufio open his mouth, but Daisy replies before he can.

"Okay." She sinks farther into her pillow and closes her eyes.

My brother's stare is practically burning a hole through my face. I turn to him. "What?"

"Nothing," he grumbles.

"Go on, then. You're already late."

Rufio strides out of Daisy's room with angry steps, followed by Phoenix and Morpheus. Morpheus stops by the door and looks over his shoulder. "Text me if she gets worse."

He finally steps out, closing the door with a soft click. I pull the desk chair closer to Daisy's bed and stare at her. Her eyebrows are slightly furrowed, and her facial muscles are tense. I believe she's sleeping now, but she's in discomfort. I wish there was something I could do, but it seems I can't summon my healing powers at will yet.

Daisy starts to mumble incoherent words. I lean closer, trying to make out what she's saying. She's repeating the same thing over and over again, and after a moment, I can make it out.

"Repellam te."

It sounds like Latin, but why would she be dreaming about

a phrase in Latin? Morpheus's vision comes to the forefront of my mind again. I won't deny I've been obsessing about it since he told me. I care about Daisy more than I ever have about anyone in my life, but the infinity band is forever. I can't imagine what would propel me to make that kind of commitment to anyone, no matter how much I loved them.

He also said Daisy was linked to someone from the past. I sit up straighter in my chair and glance around. I'm in her room, and she's out cold. There won't be a better opportunity to look for clues about her past, since, thanks to the protection on all dorm room doors, we can't break in.

I'm gripped by a momentary feeling of guilt, but it vanishes quickly. The stakes are too high for such sentimentalities. Too many powerful players want something from Daisy. I have to find out what.

12

MORPHEUS

Going to class is pointless. I can't pay attention, so now I not only have to worry about math but everything else too. Fucking great. My brain can only latch on to one thing, my vision of Daisy and Bryce. What the hell does it mean?

I skip lunch and head to the library. I need a word with Mrs. Wilkins. Maybe she has a book that explains the line I saw connecting Daisy and Bryce to the ghost figures. I couldn't find anything online, but growing up in a scholar's house taught me that a lot of important knowledge never made to the web. I believe that's thanks to the snobbish nature of people like my father. The man isn't even an Idol, but he has the ego to match one.

I'm on Mrs. Wilkins's shit list after the stunt I pulled in the library, which proves that I'm at the end of my rope. I wouldn't seek her help if I had any other choice. Well, I have another choice, but facing her is easier than the alternative.

The library is not empty. Gifted Academy houses a lot of nerds, and the library is their natural habitat. Several heads turn my way when I push through the double doors. The girl manning the front desk looks startled by my presence. I don't know who she is, but she knows who I am, hence the deer-caught-in-headlights expression she's sporting now.

"Is Mrs. Wilkins in?" I ask.

"Yeah, she's in her office." The girl points in the right direction, like I don't know where it is.

"Thanks."

The door to the office is closed but not the blinds on her window, which faces the library floor. She's at her desk, eating a salad for lunch. I knock, and then I wave at her.

She scrunches her eyebrows and pinches her lips together. *Great. She's already annoyed.* Her expression doesn't improve when she opens the door.

"Is there a problem, Mr. Malek?" she asks.

"I'd like to ask you a question."

"I'm taking my lunch break now. Come back later." She begins to close the door in my face, but I press my hand against it, holding it open.

"Please, Mrs. Wilkins. This is important." I put extra emphasis in my tone as I let my power ebb freely from my frame. The shadows, which have been fairly quiet since my ordeal, become agitated. They lick my wrists, turning the skin around my bracelets cold.

Her gaze narrows as she focuses on the shadows peeking from underneath my jacket. I'm sure she can also sense my power since I'm not doing anything to reel it in.

Students are forbidden to use their powers against teachers and school personnel. But she also knows I'm dangerous and unhinged with a penchant for bad temper. Finally, with a sigh, she relents and lets me in.

Walking back to her seat, she asks, "What do you want to know? Better make it quick." She sinks her fork in her salad.

"I want to know if you have any books here on past lives."

She pauses with her fork halfway to her mouth. "Past lives as in reincarnation?"

I shove my hands in my pockets and shrug. "Something like that."

I honestly have no clue what I'm looking for. Maybe the line connecting Daisy to the other being means a link connecting her to her former self. Or it could be something completely different like what I had originally thought—the line represents her connection to a descendant. Since it's unlikely this library has anything on the bloodlines of Norms, I'm going with the reincarnation possibility.

I also can't tell Mrs. Wilkins about my vision. We can't trust anyone outside our inner circle.

"If you want a book that covers that particular topic, it would be in the religion section."

I groan in my head. Whatever those books contain, it's not something I can't find online.

"I was wondering if you have a rare tome on the subject. Something you wouldn't display with the other books."

Mrs. Wilkins's eyebrows arch as she stares at me intensely. "All our books are out there." She points out the window. "Now go and let me eat my lunch in peace."

Clenching my jaw, I whirl around and walk out of her office. What a fucking waste of time. I should have known the bitch wouldn't help me. I'm also an idiot. My father's library probably has what I'm looking for, but by trying to avoid the man, I let Mrs. Wilkins know about my strange interest. I bet an arm and a leg she'll run to tell Principal Fallon.

Son of a bitch. Bryce will be pissed.

BRYCE

I looked everywhere in Daisy's room, but I didn't find anything that shed a light on her past. I even checked her text messages and computer files. They were password protected, but bypassing them was child's play. With my ability to manipulate energy, hacking is second nature.

She's still sleeping like the dead, but her fever is under control. It hasn't gone down, but it hasn't gone up either. I stand at the foot of her bed with my hands on my hips as I scan the small room. I must have missed something.

Think, Bryce. Think. If you had to hide something, where would you? Daisy turns around, lying on her side now. The bed is the only place I didn't look—more precisely, the mattress.

I drop onto my back and slide under the frame. Using my phone, I illuminate the bottom of it so I can see through the rows of wood boards. Right down the middle, I find what I'm looking for: a cut in the mattress. Sticking my fingers inside, I brush against something solid, a book maybe.

It would be easier to remove the hidden object if the mattress was flipped, but with some bending and twisting, I manage to pull a leather-bound notebook from the opening in the foam.

Once out from under the bed, I open what looks to be a diary. The handwriting is difficult to decipher, and it definitely doesn't match what I've seen from Daisy. After looking at a few pages, I realize whose diary's this is: Paul Rodale's, Daisy's father.

I sit back in my chair and begin to read from beginning to end. The further I get, the more disturbed I become, until I reach one of the last pages and my blood runs cold. I scan the page twice to make sure I'm not seeing things.

No. I'm not.

I rub my face. *Son of a bitch.* If other Norms have this information, then it's the end of our society as we know it.

"Bryce?" Daisy asks from her bed.

I lift my chin, meeting her gaze. I don't know what she sees in my eyes, but after a few seconds, she drops her stare to the diary in my hands and gasps.

"So, this is why you wanted to come here?" I ask, my voice low and hard.

Anger swirls in the pit of my stomach. How could I have been so blind? All this time I believed Daisy was an innocent Norm thrown in shark-infested waters. But she's far from innocent. In hindsight, I was fucking stupid. She and her sister survived alone on the streets for seven years. She wouldn't have accomplished that if she weren't ruthless.

"You don't understand." She throws her legs to the side of the bed and attempts to stand up. Her legs are wobbly, so she braces her hand against the wall to remain standing.

"Oh, I understand. Your father discovered a weapon that can kill Idols, and he was killed for it. Do you want me to believe you ended up in Gifted Academy by chance?"

"Your mother offered me a scholarship. I didn't seek it out."

"My mother is an Idol-hating woman, just like you." I spit the words out like they're poison. And it does make me ill. The pain in my chest feels like someone stabbed me there.

I head for the door, carrying the diary with me.

"Bryce. Where are you going?"

I don't stop until I hear a thump behind me. I turn around and find Daisy sprawled on the floor. Her hair is a mess, she's probably still feverish, and she's looking at me with tear-filled eyes. My heart shatters completely at the sight. I want to help her, cradle her in my arms, and say everything is going to be okay. But it's not going to be okay. She's been lying to us since she got here. My vision becomes blurry, and I curse her. She's going to make me cry again.

No. I'm stronger than these fucking emotions. She won't trick me with her pathetic weakness. Holding on to my anger, to the sense of betrayal, works in the moment. The rage keeps me in my place. I won't let my feelings cloud my judgment again.

"Back to my apartment. If I were you, I'd pack my shit and leave. You don't want to be around when I show this"—I shake the diary in my hand—"to the guys."

"Please, I'm begging you. Let me explain."

Another crack and the fissure in my heart expands. *Fuck. I gotta get out of here.* I walk out the door without another glance back. I'm afraid if I look at Daisy's pitiful expression again, I'll give in.

Damn Daisy to hell for making me fall in love with her.

13

———

DAISY

Through the haze of the fever, I get up. There's a tear in my heart, a pain so sharp that it makes breathing harder. But the feeling is competing with the immense fear that's occupying the same space. I stumble around my room, searching for my backpack. My legs feel like jelly, and staying upright is a tremendous effort. There's no time to collect all my belongings, so I focus on the things I can't leave without: my wallet, the book I got from the library, and my phone. Bryce took my most precious possession with him, and I'll probably never get it back.

The dagger. What happened to the dagger that odd couple gave me? I spin around, which in hindsight wasn't a good idea, as it almost sends me to the floor. I grip the edge of my desk and wait for the dizzy spell to pass. Then I search for the dagger, but I see nothing. Foggy memories emerge. *Shit*. Rufio took it from me in the treehouse, and after we slept together, I don't remember what happened. When I came to, I was in my room.

Damn it, Daisy. How could you have been so stupid? You lost two Idol-killing weapons in a matter of days and when you need them the most.

I can't believe Bryce didn't kill me just now. He could have crushed me like a bug. But I believe him when he said Rufio and the others won't be so merciful. I look out the window. The sky is dark thanks to the ominous clouds that are fast approaching. A storm is coming to Saturn's Bay, and I know I won't make it to the bus stop in time before it hits the school campus.

Whatever. I'll take rain anytime over facing four vengeful Idols.

I'm only wearing a tank top and panties. I shove my legs inside the first pair of jeans I find, put on a hoodie, and grab other random clothes that I come across. With a deep, steadying breath, I amble toward the door, afraid I'll collapse any second. Something red catches my attention in the corner of the room. Rosie's cowboy boots. My stomach is in knots, and I don't know if I'll pass out or vomit first, but still I make the effort to collect them. Bryce took a part of me when he stole Dad's diary, but hell if I'm going to leave these boots behind. I clutch them to my chest and make it to the door.

It's my bad luck that I hear a group of seniors about to turn the corner into my corridor. I'm in no shape to bump into anyone; one look at me and they'll know I'm easy prey. I stride in the opposite direction as fast as I can, then take the stairs. My heart is pounding by the time I reach the building's side exit.

No sooner do I step outside than the booming noise of thunder sounds in the distance. Shit. It's coming down soon. I continue on my painfully slow progress, clutching Rosie's boots as tight as I can, hoping they'll somehow give me the strength I need to make it to the bus stop. I'm about halfway from the school's gate when the sky opens in a shower so thick it creates a gray curtain around me.

Worse, my legs are about to collapse, and black dots are

appearing in my vision. I can't pass out in the middle of the sidewalk. Using the bit of strength I have left, I inch toward the cluster of trees nearby, not going much farther into the forest now that I know about Rufio's secret hideout. I find the biggest tree nearby and lean against its trunk, sliding down until my butt hits the muddy ground.

Hugging my knees, I rest my forehead against them and close my eyes. I could easily fall asleep here and never wake up. I must be delirious. I'll just wait until the storm is over and then say goodbye to Gifted Academy.

But my body doesn't want to make things easy for me. There's the fever, then the pain. Excruciating, white-hot pain that knocks me down to the cold ground and brings forth a yell from deep in my throat that's mercifully muffled by the pounding of falling rain. It's like I'm being electrocuted. I'd thrash on the ground if I could, but the agony is too great for me to move.

It recedes after a minute, leaving me panting. My heart is hammering in my chest while I try to grasp what the hell is wrong with me. But my reprieve doesn't last long. Another wave of torture hits me, stronger than before. It also lasts longer, making me wish for death.

Whatever is happening to me soon becomes a pattern. The pain comes at intervals, and each time is more devastating than the last. My jaw is sore from gritting my teeth so hard. I can't stay here like this. I need help.

When I catch a break, I roll onto my belly and reach for my backpack. It's completely soaked and, unfortunately, not water-proof. Fuck. I hope my phone still works.

With trembling fingers, I fish out the device. The screen is lit, giving me hope. But when I flip the phone open, another wave of agony comes, and I drop it in the mud. This torture spell seems to last much longer than the other ones. When it finally retreats, it doesn't do so completely.

Breathing hard, I look for my phone. It's almost completely buried into the ground. My heart sinks when I see the screen is black.

No!

Fat tears stream down my face as my heart sinks. There's no calling for help. A great sense of doom descends over me. There's no escaping my fate this time. I'm going to die helpless and alone.

14

RUFIO

I lost count of how many times during the school day I wanted to bolt out of class and run back to Daisy. I got what I wanted. I fucked her senseless, something I'd been jonesing to do since I saw her in Unearthly Desires. She more than met my expectations. If I'm being honest with myself, she blew all my other sexual encounters out of the water.

The need to repeat what we did is messing with my head. She's a Norm. I should hate her. But everything I've done recently is at odds with what I believe. *Taught* to believe, to be exact. She has a power over us. Phoenix and Morpheus aren't immune either. Even after the punishment Morpheus received from the god who owns our asses, he didn't turn against her.

I didn't text Bryce for updates because I don't want him to know I'm whipped. But as soon as the last class of the day is over, I'm cruising through the hallway like a race car. I ignore the stares and gossip. From the corner of my eye, I catch sight of Drusilla and one of her minions, Renata. Cherise, the Fringe who tried to drown Daisy, was expelled, or at least that's what the rumors are saying. Only my mother can confirm that, but I'm avoiding the bitch at all costs.

The sky has opened up with one of the worst storms I've seen in a while. I run through the quad toward the dorm building, getting drenched in a matter of seconds. Once inside, I shake my head and push my wet bangs back. There are other students hanging out in the entrance hall, some clustering close to the vending machine. They all turn to stare at me. Fuckers.

"What are you looking at?" I bark, tired of all the ogling.

I forgo the elevator, opting for the stairs. Taking two steps at a time, I reach the landing of my floor in less than a minute. My heart feels tight all of a sudden, and I can't fathom where the feeling is coming from. I stop in front of Daisy's door and knock hard.

"Bryce. Open up," I say.

There's no answer. What's he doing? I pull my phone out to call him, but before I press the button, the door to our apartment opens and Bryce appears.

"Get in here, Rufio," he says with an expression that matches the bad weather outside.

I keep the angry retort bottled up until I'm in our living room and the front door is closed again. "What the fuck is going on? I thought you were supposed to keep an eye on Daisy."

Bryce opens his mouth to reply, but in that precise moment, Phoenix and Morpheus walk in.

"Whoa, what's with the scowls? Did something happen to the Norm chick you guys are sharing?" Phoenix jokes, but I sense an underlying anger in his comment.

"Bite me, asshole," I snap.

"Great, you're all here. It saves me the time of repeating the same story," Bryce grumbles.

"You look positively wretched, Bryce." Morpheus frowns.

"While I was in Daisy's room, I decided to do some investigation and found this." Bryce picks up a leather notebook from the coffee table.

"What's that?" I ask.

"A diary from Daisy's father." Bryce stares meaningfully at Morpheus.

"I take it that whatever you discovered didn't comfort you," Morpheus says.

My brother shakes his head and offers him the diary. "Read the last entries."

I intercept the object before Morpheus can and, with eager fingers, flip to the last pages. I scan the text fast, and by the time I finish, my stomach feels as tight as a coiled spring. *Son of a bitch.* Daisy's father must have been one of the Norm rebels my father used to talk about at the dinner table.

I lift my head to meet Bryce's eyes. "You think Daisy was sent here to kill us?"

Phoenix lets out a snort. "Come on, guys. Daisy is a fucking Norm. How could she kill us?"

"Her father discovered a weapon that can kill Idols. If this knowledge is widespread among the Norm population, how long until we have a fucking war on our hands?" Bryce replies.

"Even if they have a weapon, we have the power. We can obliterate them with a snap of our fingers," Phoenix retorts.

"God, Phoenix, you're dense," Bryce snaps. "I was kidnapped by the Knights, and they were able to void my powers for hours. Combine that with a weapon that can kill us and the fact that there are way more Norms than Idols...." Bryce stops to laugh ruefully. "We're fucked."

"Can I have the diary now?" Morpheus extends his hand to me.

"Does the diary say what kind of weapon?" Phoenix asks.

"No." Bryce shakes his head.

My nostrils flare when the realization hits me. I go to my room and retrieve the dagger I got from Daisy yesterday. When I return to the living room, I catch the end of Morpheus's reply.

"... your mother must have known about Daisy's past."

I can't offer a response to that. Mom is too smart, and her interest in Daisy is obvious. She doesn't do anything without a purpose.

"So what? She hates Idols," Bryce replies.

Phoenix's eyebrows arch. "Why would she hate her own kind?"

"Because she fell in love with a Norm, and our father killed the son of a bitch."

Bryce's reply feels like a punch to my chest. "You're joking," I say.

"I wish I was. I heard from Mom's own mouth." Bryce's gaze drops to the dagger in my hand. "What's that?"

"This, I believe, is an Idol-killing weapon. Daisy had it on her yesterday."

Bryce takes the object from my hand with care. He inspects the handle and the peculiar blade, his eyebrows scrunched together. "I've never seen anything quite like it."

"Where's Daisy?" Morpheus asks suddenly.

Bryce lifts his gaze to Morpheus. "I told her to pack her shit and leave."

"You sent her out while she was burning up with fever?" Morpheus's voice rises until he's almost shouting. "Are you fucking crazy?"

Bryce's expression turns into a scowl. "Why are you giving me a hard time? You've always said from the beginning she was bad news. And then you had that vision of yours."

"What vision?" I ask.

Bryce whirls around and walks toward the window. "Never mind."

"That's what's eating you. You're afraid of what I saw," Morpheus replies.

"For fuck's sake. What did you see?" Phoenix asks, clearly exasperated. I share his sentiment.

"Daisy and Bryce standing side by side, bound by the infinity band."

My eyes widen of their own accord while a deep-rooted pain takes hold of my heart. The infinity band is the ultimate promise an Idol can make to a lover.

"Come on now. You guys must know that vision is bogus. Daisy is a Norm. Only Idols can be bound with an infinity band," Phoenix contests.

"My visions have never been wrong before," Morpheus replies through clenched teeth. "Also, may I remind you that if Daisy wanted to kill either Bryce or Rufio, she had ample time to do so."

Morpheus looks meaningfully at me and my brother. I hear exactly what he's not saying. Bryce and I slept with her; she could have easily plunged the dagger into our hearts while we were distracted.

"When did this happen?" Phoenix asks.

"Maybe half an hour ago." Bryce runs his hand through his hair. He seems torn.

Phoenix pulls his phone from his pocket and places a call.

"Who are you calling?" I ask.

He holds a finger in front of his mouth and then speaks. "Joseph? Phoenix here. Can you tell me if Daisy Woods left the campus grounds?" A pause, and then he continues. "Are you sure?" Another pause. "Okay, thanks, man."

He turns to us. "So yeah, Daisy hasn't left campus."

My eyes immediately veer toward the window and the pouring rain that's coming down so quickly it's created a gray film, making visibility hard.

"She must have got caught in the rain," I say.

Morpheus takes his uniform jacket off and grabs a hoodie that was draped over a tall chair.

"What are you doing?" Phoenix stares at our friend.

"What does it look like? I'm going after Daisy." He doesn't wait for our reply before he strides out.

Phoenix curses and rubs his chin. "Morpheus, wait up." He runs to catch up with him.

Fuck. I want to look for her as well, but my ingrained hatred for her kind keeps me rooted to the floor.

"You're not going after her?" Bryce asks without looking at me.

"No. I'm surprised you're not out there. You saved her from certain death, after all."

He turns to me, crossing his arms over his chest. "I don't know what to think anymore, Rufio. What if we made a mistake by saving her? What if she played us all?" Bryce chokes up at the end.

Son of a bitch. The impossible has happened. My brother, the coldest motherfucker I've ever known, has fallen in love.

"What's scaring you the most, brother? The possibility that Daisy is a two-faced bitch or that you're fated to bond for all eternity with her?"

Bryce's eyes narrow to slits. "I'm scared of both in equal measures. How about you, Rufio?"

"What about me?" I frown.

"Which one of those scenarios pisses you off the most?"

I know exactly what he's doing. Does he think I'm in the same boat as him? Lusting is a far cry from loving someone.

"I just fucked the girl. I'm not an idiot to fall for her."

Bryce laughs without humor. "Whatever lies make you feel better."

I'm pissed about his implication, and naturally, I can't have him have the last word.

"Sick as she was, Daisy can die out there. Are you okay with that?"

The lights in our apartment start to flicker. Bryce's jaw twitches, but it's the agony I see shining in his eyes that should give me a sense of satisfaction. Only it doesn't. The jab hurt him, but I got caught in the whiplash too.

"Damn everything to hell!" I whirl around and head for the door.

"Where are you going?"

"After her."

Outside in the hallway, I hear several pops and the shattering of glass. A second later, Bryce is by my side. I could say several things to provoke my brother now, but no comment from me would make him suffer more than he already is.

Remorse is a bitch.

15

PHOENIX

As soon as the first droplets of rain hit my face, I question my reasoning for coming out. Water is falling down so fast and furious that I'm drenched to the bone in a few seconds, yet here I am, looking for Daisy, a Norm who could very well be working to destroy us all. Besides lusting for her more than is normal, I'm not whipped like Bryce and Rufio are. Morpheus's motives are still a mystery to me.

But I know why I'm out here in the storm. If Daisy can kill an Idol, she can maybe set me free. I'd betray my entire race for that.

Morpheus takes the path leading to the gym building, but if I were trying to get the hell away, that's not the direction I'd go. I glance at the forest skirting the path and tap him on the shoulder, halting him.

"Yo, maybe she decided to take cover in there."

Morpheus nods and wordlessly changes course. We scout the perimeter closer to the curb and leading toward the gate, but there's no sign of Daisy.

"Maybe she went back to the treehouse," Morpheus says, not waiting for me to follow.

This could possibly turn into looking for a needle in a haystack, especially with this storm. The problem with Daisy being a Norm is that she doesn't have a gift signature. Her lack of power is working against us now.

When we arrive in the clearing, Rufio and Bryce are coming down from our secret spot.

"She's not there," Rufio states the obvious.

"You decided to join the hunt, huh?" I smirk at him despite the grim look he's sporting.

"Shut up, Phoenix," Rufio barks, then turns to his brother. "Are you sure you can't sense her at all?"

"Why would Bryce be able to sense her when we can't?" I ask.

"Maybe because he saved her life," Morpheus replies.

Okay, that's a stretch and, based on Bryce's expression, obviously not the case.

"Damn it. She could be anywhere." Rufio glances around. "Fuck!"

"Why are *you* here?" I ask Bryce, which in hindsight wasn't the smartest decision to make. The guy is about to blow.

I'm proven right when he lets out a roar and releases an electric bolt, zapping a tree nearby. The smell of charred wood immediately fills my nostrils.

"What the fuck, Bryce! Now is not the time to throw a temper tantrum," Morpheus yells, but then he seems to freeze. His expression turns from aggravated to anxious.

"What is it?" I ask, taking a step closer to him.

"I don't kno—aargh!" He presses the heel of his hand against his forehead.

"Fuck! Is the god back in your head?"

Morpheus's eyes fly open. "Rufio, watch out!"

In that moment, a lightning bolt shoots from the sky, straight where Rufio was standing. Only it doesn't hit him but Bryce instead. He must have pushed his brother out of the way.

Vises of electricity wrap around his body. All his muscles go tight, his face twists into a scowl of pure agony, and his hands are curled into fists as he absorbs a helluva lot of raw energy.

The electric current vanishes after a few seconds, sending Bryce to his knees with a loud grunt.

"Holy shit!" I run to him, ready to help, but Rufio holds me back.

"Don't touch him unless you want to fry too."

"What?"

Bryce lifts his face, still showing signs of pain. "This is not the first time I've been hit by lightning. Touching me will be like sitting in an electric chair."

"How long until you're safe?" I ask.

"A minute or two."

"That wasn't ordinary lightning." Morpheus approaches us.

"Let me guess, our asshole god struck again," Rufio replies.

"No. It wasn't him this time."

We all trade worried glances.

"If it wasn't him, then who?" Bryce slowly gets back to his feet.

"I don't know who, but definitely another powerful god." Morpheus's face is solemn.

"Are you fucking kidding me?" I throw my hands up in the air. "Wasn't dealing with one jerk deity enough?"

"That doesn't make any sense. The gods left this plane many millennia ago. It was already strange that we met the one on the island of horrors, but now there are two? Does that mean they're all coming back?" Rufio poses the question that's also on my mind.

"If it was another god, why did it want you dead?" Bryce grits out, bracing his hands on his knees.

Another lightning bolt lights up the sky, but at least it didn't hit anywhere near us.

"We really have to find Daisy. If one god wanted her dead, this one must too," I say.

"Let's split up. We can cover more ground faster," Morpheus suggests.

We all go in different directions, and I decide to return to the area closer to the road. She was sick out of her mind the last time I saw her. She couldn't have walked far.

When I near a tall bush, I stop. Morpheus and I came through here, but we turned right instead of left.

Visibility is horrible, and I see nothing but the shape of a tall tree a little ways ahead until my eyes catch something red sticking out from the mud. I walk faster toward it, and then I hear a loud scream.

"Daisy!" I run in her direction, only to be stopped by a lightning bolt that strikes right in front of me, missing me by a hair.

I jump back, adrenaline kicking in. Daisy continues to scream as if she's in unbearable pain. Fuck. I need to get to her. My legs tense to run, but a succession of lightning strikes blocks the path to her. Damn it. Whoever is behind them doesn't want me to help Daisy at all. But it also doesn't want me near her. What's going on?

It doesn't matter. I won't let Daisy suffer alone like that.

I prepare to make a run for her when I'm hit. I cry out while the most excruciating pain ravages my body. It seems all my nerves are frying at once. Before I can recover from the blow, a vortex of light surrounds me, making me dizzy as fuck. I'm lifted off the ground until I don't know which way is up. I close my eyes as the spinning intensifies, then black out.

"Phoenix, what the hell. Wake up!" someone shouts in my ear as they shake me.

My eyelids feel like they're glued together, but with some effort, I manage to peel them open. Morpheus is glaring at me.

"What?" I grumble.

"You fucking bailed on us last night."

I sit up, feeling light-headed. Shit. I don't remember how I got back to my room.

"Did you find Daisy?" I ask him.

"No, asshole. We didn't find her. We searched for her the entire night. Rufio and Bryce are beside themselves, and when they found you passed out in your bed, it took a miracle to keep them from kicking your ass."

I run a hand through my hair, finding bits of dried mud stuck in them.

What the fuck happened to me?

"We have another problem, Morpheus. I can't remember how I got here," I admit.

"What do you mean? Did you get drunk somehow during Daisy's search party?"

"I don't know." I rip at my hair. "Shit, there's a big black hole in my head, as if part of my memories was scrubbed."

Morpheus arches his eyebrows. "Scrubbed on purpose by someone?"

"Yeah."

He looks away, tenser than before. "This is bad, Phoenix. Really bad. Daisy is MIA, Rufio and Bryce are both about to blow, and you can't remember a thing."

"Aren't you getting any visions?"

"No, and you shouldn't ask for them. Rarely do I see something that's not disastrous."

I stand up and the room begins to spin. Pinching the bridge of my nose, I close my eyes for a second.

"What time is it?" I ask.

"A little past seven."

"Shit. I need to get dressed."

"Wait. Are you going to class?"

I look Morpheus in the eye. "Damn straight. We looked for Daisy everywhere, right? And we couldn't find her. That means it's possible she made it off campus after all."

Doubt shines in Morpheus's eyes, but in the end, he lets out a resigned sigh. "You're right."

He heads for the door but stops in the threshold and looks over his shoulder. "Is it me or are you also feeling a heaviness in your chest like you can't breathe right?"

His question catches me by surprise. Morpheus has never been one to talk about personal shit.

"Nah. I'm good."

A big fat lie, but no one will ever know that. I'm the master of deceit, after all. I've being doing it my whole life.

16

DAISY

When I open my eyes, the air is dry and the sky is clear. I left my room in the afternoon, so by all accounts it should be nighttime, unless....

Holy shit. Did I spend the night in the forest?

I sit up fast, immediately noticing the dry mud caked all over my clothes and in my hair.

What happened to me? I had a fever and then the relentless pain that leveled me completely. I don't remember how long the torture lasted, but oddly enough, I've never felt more refreshed and full of energy than I do now.

I spy my backpack, discarded nearby with Rosie's cowboy boots. My heart sinks when I take in the state of the footwear. No leather can withstand so much water dumped on it. The last thing I spot is my cell phone, which is now completely useless. Cursing, I collect everything and head back toward the dorm building.

Yesterday, Bryce scared me enough to make me want to run away, fever and all, out in the rain. Today, as strange as it sounds, there isn't an ounce of fear left in my body. Instead, the only thing coursing through my veins is determination. I'm Daisy Rodale. I won't allow any Idol to intimidate me.

With chin lifted high, I enter the dorm through the main door. It's early, maybe not even seven yet, and the common area is quiet. I don't take the stairs this time, aiming for the elevator —just because I'm not trembling in fear doesn't mean I want to come across anyone.

As I near my room, I have a mind to continue on and knock on Bryce's door to demand my father's diary back. But I don't want him or the others to see me in this state, so I slip into my room and head for the shower.

I take my time under the hot jet, and the water runs brown around my feet for several minutes. I have mud in places I didn't know could get dirty. Yuck.

Half an hour later, I finally get out. The mirror is completely foggy. I wipe it off and stare at my reflection. There's no visible difference in the way I look. I expected to resemble a wraith after the ordeal I went through, but no. I actually look healthy.

Whatever. It's time to get ready for school.

***

THE DAISY from before would have made sure to arrive before anyone else. Today, I spent extra time getting ready. I even blow-dried my hair and put makeup on. Garnering plenty of stares as I walk toward class, I honestly feel like I'm in a romantic comedy where the underdog character receives a makeover and her peers can't believe she's the same person.

I don't think the red lipstick I'm wearing qualifies as a makeover. And I know they aren't staring because of that.

That's right, assholes. You can't get rid of me that easily.

Taking my time to get ready paid off. When I enter math

class, Phoenix, Rufio, and Morpheus are already there, looking worse for wear. The corners of my lips twist upward. My amusement grows by leaps and bounds when they see me standing in the front of the room.

I look each one of them in the eye, but my gaze doesn't linger. They aren't worth my attention. It's like my protective shield got an upgrade.

No sooner does my butt hit the seat than Phoenix leans forward. "Where the hell have you been? We've been looking for you all night."

"I went out."

"Bullshit. You didn't leave the campus grounds," Rufio pipes up.

"Why do you care where I went? Didn't Bryce tell you what he found in my room?" I keep staring straight ahead.

"Yes, he did. We thought you had run away," Morpheus replies.

I'm tempted to glance back so I can level the three assholes with a glare. But the girl who sits in front of Cherise's old chair enters the room and balks at my presence. It's comical to witness her expression go from surprised to furious in a matter of seconds. Fuming, she strides toward me.

Pointing an angry finger my way, she says, "What are *you* doing here? Haven't you learned your lesson?"

I open my mouth to put the bitch in her place, but Rufio beats me to it. "The question is, haven't you learned *yours*? Where's your friend Cherise?"

The girl switches her attention to him, her face becoming paler before she juts out her chin in defiance. She swallows hard before she replies, "Are you her knight in shining armor now? I thought Bryce was the one screwing her."

I sense Rufio's fury roll out in waves toward the Idol girl. I haven't had the chance to figure out what level she is or what she can do, but she clearly thinks she can take Rufio. Or maybe she's like Cherise and lacks in the brain department.

Mr. Atkins enters the room in that moment, interrupting what I'm sure was going to be a showdown. Throughout class, the magnificent trio tries to get my attention, but I ignore them all. I wonder what they're planning. No way they're just going to brush aside the fact that my father was part of a conspiracy to get rid of all Idols.

Aware they'll try to corner me the moment class is over, I prepare to bolt as soon as the bell rings. Unfortunately, I had forgotten that Phoenix has telekinesis powers, so while the students file out of the room, he keeps me glued to my seat.

"Let me go," I say through clenched teeth.

"Not until you tell us where you went," Phoenix replies.

"I don't owe you an explanation." I struggle against the invisible hold.

Rufio and Morpheus walk around my desk, blocking Mr. Atkins from my view. They tower over me, each sporting a different expression. Morpheus seems curious, whereas Rufio is downright pissed, if his scowl is any indication. He crosses his arms and stares hard at me.

"Where did you spend the night, Daisy?" His voice is low and dangerous, but all it does is send a lick of desire down my spine. Stupid hormones.

"Fine, if you must know, I spent the night under a tree."

Phoenix takes the position right in front of me with eyebrows furrowed. He doesn't say a word, just keeps staring as if he's trying to read my mind.

"You slept in the forest? We searched every inch of it," Morpheus retorts.

"Must have missed a spot," I reply.

He narrows his eyes and says, "You look different."

"I feel different. You got your answer. Can I go now?"

"No," Rufio says at the same time I manage to get up. Did Phoenix simply let me go?

Mr. Atkins is still in the room, and when our gazes connect, he asks, "Is everything okay there?"

"Yup, peachy." I stride toward the door.

Before I'm out of earshot, I hear Rufio say to Phoenix, "Why did you let her out?"

"I didn't," he replies.

He's lying. He must have released his power over me or I wouldn't have been able to move at all. I've witnessed firsthand what he can do.

Thanks to their impromptu interrogation, I'm late for class. The hallways are already empty. Fucking great. I break into a run. The class is on the third floor. This feels like déjà vu. Two days ago I was also running, but at least my reason is different.

Before I can reach the stairs, someone grabs my arm and pulls me inside the janitor's closet. I let out a yelp and that's quickly muffled by a large hand covering my mouth. My heart leapfrogs to my throat, getting lodged there.

It takes me a few seconds to recognize Bryce's scent, but the knowledge doesn't comfort me. It makes me even more nervous. The light turns on at the same time Bryce lets go of me. I whirl around, but in the confined space, that only brings me flush against his chest.

"What the hell, Bryce!"

"You're still here."

"Really? You almost gave me a heart attack to make that idiotic observation?" I step back, which only makes me hit my shoulder blades against the metal shelf behind me. I'm still too close to him.

His eyes drop to my feet and then travel up my body until his stormy eyes meet mine again. "You're in one piece."

"Yes, no thanks to you. But if you want to obliterate me, now's your chance. Go ahead."

Bryce narrows his eyes to slits. "I was worried sick about you."

A bubble of crazy laughter goes up throat. "You're something else, Bryce Kent. You're the one who kicked me out in the pouring rain while I was running a fever!"

Rage fills his eyes, colliding with the worry I also see there. "And look at you now, hotter than a California summer day."

My heart does a backflip at the compliment, even if it was said with venom. Stupid organ.

"Something is different about you," Bryce continues.

I throw my hands up in the air. "Oh my God. Not you too. I'm wearing makeup. Big fucking deal."

He steps forward, crowding my space. "Who noticed the change?"

"Morpheus. Now if you excuse me, I'm already late for class." I try to push him out of my way, but it's like trying to move a boulder. He won't budge.

He grabs my wrist and pulls me flush against his chest. I have to tilt my head back to glower at him.

"You didn't leave campus, and we searched for you everywhere. Where did you spend the night?"

Fury crackles above my skin, making me see red. "It's not your damn business where I spent the night. You didn't care one bit that you sent me packing while I was sick."

"You lied to me!" His eyes flash gold.

"I didn't lie to you. Since when is it a crime to not disclose every single detail of my life to everyone?"

"Since the information makes you a traitor to my kind."

"I'm not a traitor!" I pull my arm from his grasp, hitting my elbow against the metal shelf. White-hot pain shoots up my arm. "Son of a bitch." I rub the sore spot while I maintain my scowl at Bryce.

"How did you do that?" He frowns.

"Do what?"

Bryce blinks a couple of times before he replies in a tight voice, "Break free."

I open and shut my mouth like a fish out of water. Rufio asked the same thing just a moment ago. Finally, I reply, "You must be losing your mojo."

We don't speak for several beats. Thanks to the argument, my heart is thundering in my chest and my breathing is coming out in bursts.

"By the way, I want my father's diary back," I demand.

Bryce snorts. "Fat chance of that happening."

"That's the only thing I have left of him. How can you be so hateful?"

He flinches, and the reaction catches me by surprise. I didn't expect him to care at all about what I think of him.

"I—" His answer is cut short when the door bursts open and the janitor appears at the entrance.

"What are you doing here?" he asks.

"Nothing. I was just leaving."

I'm finally able to push Bryce out of the way. Looking at the clock mounted on the wall, I see it's too late for me to go to class. I don't think anyone is expecting me anyway, so I make a beeline for the school library.

17

DAISY

I miss Toby. I wish his parents would reconsider their decision to pull him out of Gifted Academy. He worked so hard for two years; it's not fair that he doesn't get to graduate. Growing up, I wanted to do well in school so I could have the chance to do something I loved when I finished, but I never knew exactly what I wanted to do. Toby is one of the rare teenagers who has a clear goal. No. I can't let this injustice happen to him without trying to help.

When my lunch break comes, I head to Principal Fallon's office, determined to make my case with her. If she was able to convince the council to give a scholarship to me, I'm sure she can persuade Toby's parents to reconsider their decision. However, when I arrive at her office, I find the door locked. Shit, they must be out for lunch too.

I drag my ass to the cafeteria. I'll just grab a juice. I'm not really hungry. Thanks to my detour, when I enter the room, it's buzzing with loud conversation. A lot of heads turn in my direction, and now I bet I'm the current topic of gossip. Ignoring the stares, I veer toward the vending machine.

I'm in a crouch, reaching for the dispenser at the bottom,

when I sense a presence behind me. The hairs on the back of my neck stand on end. Clutching the cold bottle tighter, I unbend my knees and turn around. No surprise when I come face-to-face with Drusilla and Renata.

"You have some nerve coming back here," Drusilla sneers.

"Fuck off. I'm not in the mood for your antics." I move forward to cut through the two bitches, but Drusilla pushes me back by the shoulder. I hit the vending machine with a loud bang.

"I don't care who your protectors are. Thanks to you, Cherise was expelled, and Renata and I got detention. You're going to pay, bitch."

"I guess you're seeking expulsion, then," I reply.

Drusilla throws her head back and laughs. "You're such a stupid whore. Principal Fallon can't touch me or Renata. Our families are too important, and we pour a lot of money in this school. You could say we own it."

"Well, I don't give a fuck about your connections. Get out of my way, or I'll show you how Norm kids handle fucktards like you."

I don't know where my bravado is coming from, but it's not a front. Before I was all bark, no bite. Now I'm not bluffing. *Did the fever addle my brain?*

Renata grabs my arm and squeezes so hard, I know she'll shatter my bones like she did with Toby. On reflex, I pull my arm back, and surprisingly I'm able to escape her clutches. Her eyes widen as if she can't believe it either.

I'm still staring at Renata when, from the corner of my eye, I see Drusilla's punch coming in my direction. By a miracle, I move out of the way, and her hand smashes through the vending machine's glass. She lets out a yell, but obviously there's no blood on her hand. She's a powerful Idol, so regular glass won't cut her. *Only lightning glass will,* I think bitterly.

One of the guys serving food runs in our direction. "Is everything all right here?"

Drusilla whirls around, clutching her hand. "Mind your own business, Fringe."

A small crowd has gathered around us, and closer to me, there's Morpheus, alone. Our gazes connect, and it's almost like he's asking if he should intervene. He's done so before without asking for permission; why did he hold back now?

Jeez, Daisy. Maybe because he also thinks you're here to kill them all.

Principal Fallon enters the cafeteria in that precise moment.

"Drusilla and Renata. I'm not surprised," she says. "In my office. Now!"

Renata twists her face into a remorseful look, but Drusilla stares at the principal with a defiant rise of her chin. "As you wish, *ma'am.*"

She walks off, but not before sparing me a glance that says this isn't over.

Since there was no blood—aka mine—the crowd disperses, but not Morpheus. He walks in my direction instead.

"Are you okay?" he asks.

"In one piece, as you can see."

"That was a pretty impressive move."

I frown, not understanding his remark. "I didn't do anything. Drusilla hit the vending machine all on her own."

"The way you moved out of the way was impressive."

"I guess I have good reflexes." I shrug.

"Sure. Let's call it that."

Morpheus continues to stare at me in a peculiar way.

"Can I ask you a question?"

"Sure," he replies.

"Why aren't you trying to kill me?" I uncap the juice bottle and take a sip.

"Do you want me to try?" He raises an eyebrow.

"You almost choked me to death for simply defending your former tutor. Now you know about my father, and yet I'm not getting any murderous vibes from you, Rufio, or Phoenix. So what gives?"

"I can't answer for Rufio or Phoenix, but maybe I don't want to give up my last chance of passing math. If you're staying at Gifted Academy, I'd like to resume our tutoring sessions."

My mouth drops of its own accord. I sure didn't expect this from him. There must be a catch.

"I stunned you into silence. That's a first." He chuckles, showing me a glimpse of his adorable dimples. *No, Daisy. Don't be lured by them.*

"I've missed a lot of classes. I need to catch up," I say.

"You can start catching up in math and helping me in the process."

Something strange is happening to me. I'm getting butterflies, and Morpheus is the cause. He's the perfect mix of cute and sexy when he's not glaring at me.

"Okay, fine. We can study for an hour after class. But only if you convince Bryce to give my father's diary back."

The easygoing smile vanishes from his face. "Why do you want it back?"

I pinch the bridge of my nose while letting out a loud sigh. "Jeez, maybe because my father is dead and that's the only thing I have that belonged to him?"

"I can't make any promises."

Well, that's better than nothing.

"Hey, Morpheus. Are you guys into sharing now?" the guy with bright blue hair—can't remember his name—says as he walks past us.

"Excuse me?" Morpheus's eyes narrow while his aura becomes darker.

The idiot who addressed him snorts, clueless to the beast he's about to unleash. Doesn't he know who he's speaking to?

God, one look at Morpheus at his worst is enough to put the fear in the hearts of many.

"You two look pretty chummy, and if I'm not mistaken, Bryce was all over the Norm a couple of days ago." He turns to me and gives me a leery once-over, making my skin crawl.

Morpheus steps in front of me, and I actually see a dark miasma erupt from his frame and zap into the guy. It's different than the shadows that usually concentrate around his wrists.

The blue-haired Idol gasps as he clutches his chest. His eyes widen, and he seems to be having trouble breathing.

"What's the matter, Pietro?" Morpheus asks in a taunting way.

The guy begins to wheeze as he lifts a supplicant hand toward Morpheus.

"Morpheus, let it go. He's not worth it," I say.

I can't have another student getting in trouble on my account, even if it's Morpheus and the likelihood he will suffer any consequence is slim. But I have been the subject of his wrath before, and it's no picnic.

The miasma I saw zap into Pietro comes out and evaporates into thin air. The guy bends over, resting his hands on his knees and taking deep breaths.

Morpheus leans forward and says near the guy's ear, "Let this be a reminder of who owns this school, asshole. If I hear you say anything about us or Daisy again, I won't be merciful."

18

BRYCE

After a quick remise, I end the match with one powerful lunge, hitting my opponent right where his heart is. With a grunt, he falls on his ass.

He removes his mask angrily and snarls. "What the fuck, Bryce? Are you trying to kill me?"

I pull my mask back and turn around. "If you can't handle the play, maybe you should spar with the Fringes."

This is a free period, so there aren't any teachers regulating what we do. A sudden heat comes from behind. I whirl around in the speed of light and block Nate's fireball with my own energy missile. His ball fizzles, but not before I'm on him, holding him by his neck.

"Do you think you can win against me, motherfucker?"

I throw him across the room, and he's lucky that's all I do. He hits the wood-paneled wall with a loud crack and doesn't get up.

"Whoa. I thought this was the fencing room," Morpheus proclaims from the entrance.

I glance at him briefly before heading for the bench. "What are you doing here? Don't you have class?"

"It's art class, the only subject I can afford to skip." Morpheus fixes his gaze on Nate, then sits next to me on the bench. "I have to talk to you about Daisy."

"Ah fuck no." I get up, not in the mood to talk about her. I'm frustrated that I can't make up my mind about her. I have every reason to distrust her, and yet I want to believe her innocence.

"I think you jumped the gun yesterday," Morpheus continues.

"Are you kidding me?"

Nate moans from the floor. He's not out, so we shouldn't be having this conversation here. I hoist my duffel bag's strap over my shoulder and head out. Morpheus is right behind me. In the hallway, we don't speak. Too many people around. It's not until we're on the path back to the dorms that Morpheus restarts the convo.

"I'm serious, Bryce. All I can think about is the vision I saw. You were bonded with her. She's not out to destroy us."

I clench my jaw but don't answer right away. I've been wrestling with the knowledge of Morpheus's visions and what I learned about Daisy's father all night. It didn't help that she decided to pull a disappearing act. I helped look for her not because I wanted to make sure she was gone but because I was fucking worried. But seeing her this morning, looking like a million bucks, rubbed me the wrong way.

"You can't know that. Maybe she's going to brainwash me or something."

"Shit. Are you listening to yourself? How could a Norm brainwash you?"

"I don't know. Maybe she's working with the Knights and there are some powerful Idols among them."

I push the door to the building open with too much force, breaking it off its hinges. It falls with a smash of glass breaking. Fucking great. My mother will have a cow. I forgo the elevators and aim for the stairs. Once in our apartment, I'm relieved that Rufio and Phoenix aren't around.

"I'm seeing Daisy later," Morpheus tells me. "She's going to keep tutoring me."

"Whatever. Do what you want." I make a beeline to my room. I'm done talking about her.

But Morpheus seems keen on pestering me. He follows me, stopping at the threshold. My idiotic brother hasn't fixed my door yet.

"I want the diary."

I turn around. "What?"

"You heard me. We've both read it from beginning to end. We don't need it."

"Did she ask you to do this?"

"What if she did?"

I shake my head. Daisy is dangerous. I should have listened to Morpheus when he wasn't under her spell. "Damn, Morpheus. Are you fucking her too?"

I know it was a shitty thing to say. And it also sounds like I'm jealous. He narrows his eyes and curls his hands into fists by his sides. Shadows leak from underneath his bracelets.

"Unlike you, Rufio, and Phoenix, I don't think with my dick," he replies.

He stomps away, and now I feel like an asshole. I sit on the edge of my bed and stare into nothing. I lived all my life numb, unable to feel emotion. I thought I was missing out. But Daisy managed to break the wall around all my suppressed feelings, and now I don't know what to do with them.

I hate her, crave her, miss her.

But one thing is clear. I have to make up my mind about her. I can't keep playing this game of push and pull. Maybe I should have let her explain instead of condemning her based on her father's sins. I promised her I would protect her at all costs, but it didn't take much for me to go back on my word.

Damn everything to hell.

RUFIO

Not in the mood to face the crowd, I blew off lunch and spent the time in the treehouse with Phoenix. We were both in need of some Silver-voltage. I know what my problem is. His is a mystery. But fuck if the first thing that popped into my head when I went through the trapdoor wasn't my time with Daisy here. My dick gets hard just replaying the memories.

"You're not thinking about her, are you?" Phoenix asks, guessing what's on my mind.

"No," I grumble.

"Riiight." He heads for the cupboard where we keep our stash of Silver-voltage and retrieves two vials.

I adjust my pants and drop onto the beanbag, my gaze fixed on the rug in front of me. I can almost see the imprint of Daisy's body on the soft rug. I groan out loud.

With a shake of his head, Phoenix tosses me one of the vials and then takes a seat on the beanbag opposite mine. "I don't know what Daisy was doing all night, but man, she looked good this morning." He whistles.

"Shut up." I dump half the vial's contents on my jacket sleeve and bring it to my nose. The strong fumes go straight to my head, and a few seconds later, the tension in my body begins to dissipate.

We don't speak for several minutes. Silver-voltage is actually the only thing that can make Phoenix shut his pie hole for more than a few seconds. But of course, the drug can do only so much, and he's the one who breaks the silence first.

"All jokes aside, didn't Daisy seem different today?"

I rub my face and curse Phoenix in my head. Why does he have to keep bringing her up?

"Different how?" I ask just to be antagonistic. I also noticed a peculiar vibe coming off her.

"I don't know. Norms' auras are usually dim, unremarkable. But Daisy's was megabright today."

"Did you seriously just use the word aura?" I chuckle, though only to hide my discomfort.

Shit. I shouldn't be feeling anything but bliss right now, but I can't ignore Phoenix's assessment. He was dead-on. It wasn't only Daisy's confidence and lack of fear that caught my attention today. It was exactly what Phoenix said. She was surrounded by this strange energy that made her even more magnetic to me.

Phoenix scoffs. "Whatever. But you know what I'm saying, right? I wonder what Morpheus makes out of it."

"He's probably going to spill the same kind of nonsense you did."

"Jeez, what crawled up your ass today? Do you need another hit of Silver-voltage?"

I run a hand through my hair. "I don't want to be completely baked."

Aggravating techno music pierces through the peace and quiet of the woods. Phoenix lets out a curse as he stares at his phone's screen.

"Are you going to get that?" I ask.

"It's my mother. She's been hounding me about dinner on Friday."

"Fucking parents. Just say you'll come and be done with it. Then you won't have to perform your son duties for another month or so."

Phoenix flinches, and I can't understand why. Neither of us has a good home life, but it's only fucking dinner, not the end of the world.

Instead of answering, he sends the call to voice mail. "She's gonna kill my buzz. I'll deal with her later."

PHOENIX

Ignoring my mother's call didn't work. The reminder that I'll have to see my father in only a few days brings bile up my throat. He won't make me 'perform' my son duties on Friday, not with my mother around. But I bet he'll come calling later, demanding a vision.

I stare at the tattoo he branded me with. I've searched high and low for a way to remove his damn mark from my body and haven't found an answer. As long as the tattoo is on my skin, that bastard has control over me.

"Bryce said the Knights were able to neutralize his powers. What do you think they used?"

Rufio turns to me with eyes that are already glazed. "Beats me. Maybe the same material used in Daisy's special dagger?"

I can tell there isn't deep thought in Rufio's comment, but what he said makes sense. "Her father's diary said lightning glass, whatever that is."

"Can we not talk about her for a second? I came here to relax."

I swallow my angry retort. Maybe Rufio doesn't truly believe the dagger can kill us, but if there's a remote chance that it's lethal to our kind, I'll take it. I won't be able to strike my father myself, not while I have the tattoo, but maybe a Norm with a thirst for revenge can.

19

———

DAISY

I'd like to believe my change in attitude is what's keeping the sharks at bay. But I know too well the reason Gifted Academy's student body is leaving me alone is their mortal fear of the Magnificent Four. Despite the fact that Bryce, Rufio, and Phoenix are ignoring me, it only takes one school king to take an interest in me to grant me immunity.

Today is my second tutoring lesson with Morpheus. We're back in the library because I will not step foot in his apartment and risk bumping into his roommates. It's bad enough we have class together.

After only ten minutes in his seat, he can't stop bouncing his leg up and down while he stares at the math equation he's working on. I decided to let him try to solve it without me butting in while I work on my own homework. We have another quiz next week, hence why Morpheus is more agitated than ever.

With a groan, he drops his pencil on the table and yanks his long hair back. "Gah, why is this so hard?"

"Are you done?" I peer at his paper, and then, seeing he has indeed solved the equation, I pull his notebook toward me.

"It's probably all wrong," he grumbles, folding his arms.

It takes me a few seconds to scan through his work. "No, actually, this is correct." I lift my face to his. "You did it, Morpheus."

His eyes widen as he leans closer so he can look at his own work again, which brings him all over my personal space. The scent of cinnamon and oranges fills my nose. I'm not sure if it's Morpheus's aftershave or his shampoo, but it makes me want to take a deeper whiff of the scent.

I clear my throat. "Uh, stop stealing my air."

He leans back and looks at me sheepishly. "Oops, sorry."

"Are you ready to tackle the next one?"

He sucks his lower lip in while he ponders my question. My eyes stay glued to his mouth, and I wonder if his lips taste like cinnamon and oranges too. *Whoa. Where did that thought come from?* Isn't it enough that I slept with Bryce and Rufio? *Jeez, I never knew I was a nympho.*

I sense someone has walked up, so that forces me to peel my eyes off Morpheus and his kissable mouth. Mrs. Wilkins is standing there.

"Miss Woods, may I have a word with you?"

It's strange to hear people call me by my fake last name in front of the guys now that they know my real name is Rodale.

"Yeah, sure."

I leave my things, guessing this conversation won't last long, and follow the librarian to her office. As I walk, I sense Morpheus's stare at my back, so I glance over my shoulder. His demeanor has changed. He's frowning now, but at least the glower isn't aimed at me, I think. He did say Mrs. Wilkins hates his guts now.

Once inside the woman's office, she gets straight to the point. "Have you found the answer you were looking for in that book I lent you?"

"Yes, I did."

"Good. I'd like it back."

My eyebrows arch. "Already? I haven't had the chance to read everything."

"That book is a priceless relic. I can't let a student keep it for an indefinite amount of time."

"Oh, okay. Can I keep it over the weekend at least?"

Her forehead wrinkles. "Fine. But I expect the book back first thing Monday morning."

"All right, then."

She turns her gaze to the window, and I can guess who she's staring at now. Our table is within her line of sight. "How is everything going with Mr. Malek? Is he behaving?"

"Yes. I haven't had any problems with him."

"Good. Let me know if he does return to his usual ways. Don't be fooled by his good disposition. That boy is the epitome of darkness. Anything can set him off."

"You don't like him very much, do you?" I cross my arms and pinch my lips.

Mrs. Wilkins watches me closely for a moment. "Would you like a nightmare personified? You felt his power before. How was that?" She arches an eyebrow.

A shiver runs down my spine at the memory. It was awful. Some of the worst seconds of my life. But I'm not going to give her the satisfaction.

I'm not sure why I'm feeling all protective of Morpheus. He was horrible to me when I started here, but now I think I'm finally seeing the real him. The way our society is built with Idols, Fringes, and Norms all hating each other turns us blind to the person behind the race. My father hated Idols with a fervor. To him, it was black and white. Idols needed to go. It's no wonder Bryce automatically assumed I shared my father's sentiments. He doesn't know Dad always protected Rosie and me from the ugliness of the world. I didn't know what he was up to until his death.

"Not great," I reply.

"I rest my case." She walks around her desk and takes a seat. "You have until Monday, Daisy. I hope you're a speedy reader."

Dismissed, I simply nod and walk out of her office. Morpheus has his head down toward his notebook, engrossed in what he's doing. He lifts his face when I approach the desk. He's no longer glowering, but his eyebrows are scrunched together.

"What did she want?"

"She lent me a rare book the other day, and she wants it back."

I see no sense in lying about it since Bryce saw the book already.

"Son of a bitch." Morpheus leans back and sets his pencil down.

"What?"

"I came here the other day asking if she had any rare books, and she lied to my face."

"Well, maybe that's the only rare book she has."

"When do you need to return it?" There's a new glint in his eye now.

"Monday, but don't get any ideas. I haven't had the chance to read that damn bible yet."

"We can photocopy it."

"It's over a thousand pages," I reply exasperatedly and earn a few shushing sounds from the students nearby.

"Fine. Let's do a read-a-thon together this weekend." He begins to collect his stuff and shove it in his bag.

"A what?" I squeak.

"I'll come by later, and we can read the damn bible together." His lips curl into a crooked grin.

Okay, now I'm speechless. I so do not want to spend a weekend hunched over a book with Morpheus. That's dangerous territory in more ways than one.

"Who says I don't have plans already?" I ask.

"Do you?" He lifts an eyebrow.

I could lie, but I'm sure he would be able to tell. "No."

"It's settled, then. I'll bring dinner. See you at seven?"

He's already up and ready to leave.

"Fine. Seven, but only if you bring a certain diary with you." I have not forgotten about our deal, even though I took pity on him and already restarted our tutoring sessions.

He twists his face into a grimace. "I'll try, but Bryce is stubborn as fuck."

"Let me put it this way. No diary, no read-a-thon."

I stare hard at him, trying my best to portray a stern expression. Not that I think I would scare the likes of Morpheus with my I'm-not-joking face.

"I'll see you at seven." He smiles, but it doesn't comfort me. He doesn't believe I'll follow through this time.

It's all your fault, Daisy. You shouldn't have succumbed to his cute face.

Fucking dimples get me every time.

20

DAISY

Since I no longer have a working cell phone and I don't own a laptop, I stay in the library a little longer to check my emails. There are only a few desktop computers that pretty much collect dust since everyone has their own.

I read Rosie's email first. She already knows I can't be reached by phone from my previous email, so her message is pretty lengthy. Apparently, our landlord is still acting strange, pestering Rosie with questions about me. I reply quickly, asking Rosie to keep evading the lady. Maybe I should look for another accommodation for her. If Mrs. Wilmot is fishing for information, she can't be trusted.

Next I send an email to Toby asking him how things are going. There's also an email from Felicity in my inbox. She broke up with her hippie boyfriend—shocker—and she's on her post-breakup week where she's sworn men from her life. Next week will be the I'm-single-let's-whore-out phase. I send her a quick update, leaving out all the juicy details.

By the time I'm done, it's already past five and the library will close soon. I collect my things and hastily walk out. The hallways are empty, which is to be expected; it's Friday afternoon, and I'm sure everyone has better things to do than hang out at school after classes.

I'm a minute away from the senior dorm building when Drusilla walks out from behind a tree and stands in my way.

With a groan, I ask, "What do you want now?"

"What do you think? You managed to get away from us, but there's no one around to save your ass from us this time."

I should be afraid—she's an Idol, and I'm still very much a Norm—but I'm feeling a bunch of stuff. Annoyance. Anger. But no fear. Did Bryce erase my ability to feel the emotion? Maybe I should ask Morpheus to test it out. He's a fearmancer, after all.

"You're seriously pathetic. It's so easy to show bravado when you have extra powers in your arsenal. You wouldn't last a minute if you had to fight with your muscles."

Drusilla's eyes flash with pure hatred. "There's only one pathetic being here, and it's you."

I make a motion to walk around her, but she continues. "You're not going anywhere."

Sure as shit, I lose my ability to move. Damn the bitch and her words.

"What are you going to force me to do? There's no crowd around. Humiliation is your thing, isn't it?"

She narrows her eyes to slits, and her lips curl into wicked smile. "I'm done playing childish games. I'm getting rid of you for good."

I sense someone approach me from behind, and then my nose and mouth are covered with a handkerchief laced with cheap perfume. The strong fumes burn my nostrils and go straight to my head. Almost immediately, the world begins to spiral out of control. Shit. It feels like I'm drunk. The handkerchief vanishes, but not the effects of the substance on it.

Renata appears in my line of vision. Actually, there are two of them now. Great.

"What the hell did you do to me?"

"Just giving you a taste of living as an Idol. You just took a big whiff of Silver-voltage," Drusilla replies with glee. "Oh shit. But that stuff is lethal to Norms, right?" She bites her nail and makes a phony guilty face. "Too bad."

"You bitch!" I yell, but my voice sounds wrong. I really underestimated her. "You were the one behind the deaths of the Fringe girls."

"I had nothing to do with that, but good riddance." She turns her attention to her minion. "Come on, Renata. Our work here is done."

"How long do you think she'll last?" Renata asks.

Drusilla shrugs. "Don't know. Don't care."

She sashays away, flipping her long red hair back like she's on a catwalk. I try to move, and to my surprise, I'm able to take a step forward. But coordination has left the building. I only manage to wobble like a drunk person for two seconds before I fall just off the path. I'd laugh if the situation wasn't grave. Toby warned me about Silver-voltage, and I've seen firsthand what it does to Fringes. How long until I start to convulse and bleed from my nose? There's gotta be an antidote. If only I could get to the infirmary or had my phone.

Damn it. I'm really screwed this time.

No, Daisy. You can get out of this. You're not going to die like a stupid junkie.

Clenching my jaw, I push myself off the ground. I'm super dizzy, but at least the world has stopped spiraling. I lean against the tree behind me and take deep breaths.

Surprisingly, with each inhale of fresh air, my head clears a little. My legs don't feel like they're boneless anymore. I can get help.

I begin my trek back to school while random thoughts pop in my head, too fast for me to latch on to any of them. The front door of the main building looms in front of me, just a few paces away, but I can't remember why in the world I came back here. I have my backpack with me, and my room keys are in my pocket.

I shake my head and spin around. *Man, I must be losing my mind.*

Sudden euphoria hits me, and crazy laughter bubbles up my throat. Like a silly girl, I skip the rest of the way toward the dorm building. I wish I had a car. It's a great day to go out dancing. Maybe I can convince Toby to come get me with Purple Delight. Oh, wait. I don't have a phone anymore. Damn it.

I'm about to pull the main door open when Phoenix walks out, looking and smelling like a million bucks. My eyes travel the length of his yummy body as my mouth waters.

"Daisy? Are you just coming from school?" He gives me a once-over.

"Yup. I had to check some emails. Where are you going? Hot date?"

Phoenix chuckles. "I wish. What's up with you?" He leans closer. "Your eyes are red. Are you high?"

"Me?" I place my hand over my chest. "I don't think so. At least, I don't remember taking anything."

"Really?" His eyes take on a dangerous glint. "What are you doing right now?"

"Nothing really. I'm probably going to grab something to eat at the vending machine and call it a night."

I have a vague memory that I was supposed to do something else, but I can't remember.

"You can do better than junk food. I'm going to my parents' for dinner. Want to tag along?"

I cock my head to the side and squint. "That sounds like a trap. Aren't your parents awful?"

Phoenix's smile wilts a little. "One more reason for you to come. You can save me from a torturous evening. Be my hero."

"Heroine," I correct him.

He chuckles. "Heroine. Fine. So, is that a yes?"

I shrug. "Sure. I have nothing better to do."

PHOENIX

Daisy's definitely high. She would never have a conversation with me like I'm an old friend of hers. And the fact that she didn't think twice before accepting my invitation just convinced me she took something. But what? Her eyes are red, so my guess is pot. I don't really know much about drugs Norms take since they don't affect me at all.

Well, pot meet kettle. I wouldn't have extended an invitation if I wasn't also high. I took a dose of Silver-voltage before heading out. It's the only thing that will help me endure an evening with my folks. And I have extra in my glove compartment for the way back.

"So, where do your parents live?" Daisy asks as she follows me to the garage.

"Near Echo Cove," I reply, giving her a side glance.

Her red lipstick is gone, but her bee-stung lips are a temptation I'm not sure I'll be able to resist. Now that I know who her father was, my fascination for her has grown. There's still the old hatred and suspicion though, lying just underneath the surface. I can't forget the time Daisy spotted my black eye and I ended up unleashing the beast on her. But since saving her from drowning, I can easily forget these feelings. Maybe Bryce was right to send her away. She does have a crazy power over us.

"Oh, do they have a beachfront mansion?" she asks.

"Naturally."

Nothing less will do for Mr. Westbrook. My white Porsche SUV comes into view. The back lights flash as I near the driver door.

"Oh, nice wheels. It fits you," she comments.

"Thanks."

The sound of tires screeching catches my attention, and a second later, Pietro's sleek sports car comes flying into view. On instinct, I pull Daisy out of the way, which means flush to my side. The idiot doesn't slow down until he reaches the garage's gate.

"Where is he going in such a hurry?" Daisy asks.

"Who knows? The guy is a moron."

It's an effort to step away from her, but I must if I intend to get into my car. I wait until she walks around the vehicle to slide behind the steering wheel. I don't share Daisy's enthusiasm over my *nice wheels*. It was paid for by my father and is therefore tainted. I'd rather live in poverty instead of being shackled to the monster.

We don't speak for a moment, but once we pass the academy gates and hit the highway, I glance at her. She's looking out the window, and for the first time, she doesn't have the usual edge I've come to associate with her. Her guard is down. Maybe I can satiate my curiosity about her.

"What happened after your parents died?" I ask.

She turns to me with a frown. "What do you mean?"

"The newspapers said you and your sister died in the fire, but that's obviously not true. So what happened to you?"

She lets out a heavy exhale. "I don't want to talk about it."

"Why not?" I push. She's trapped in my car; she's not going anywhere.

She leans back against the headrest. "We lived on the streets for a while, if you really must know."

"Really? What was that like?"

I sense her stare burning a hole in the side of my face. "What do you think, pretty boy?"

"Pretty boy?" I raise an eyebrow while the corners of my lips curl upward.

"Oh come on. You know how you look."

I don't know if Daisy is trying to change the subject or if her drug-addled brain can't focus on one thing for too long. My ego wants her to keep talking about how I look, but my curiosity wants to know everything about her. Maybe I can discover if she's working with the Knights after all. Or get a clue to what happened to my memories on the evening she went missing.

"You can talk about how attractive you find me later. So, what was it like living on the streets? Brutal, I suppose. Can't imagine how two Norm kids could survive unscathed."

"Who says we didn't get hurt?"

The most awful scenarios come to my mind. A pretty girl like Daisy would have been the target of the foulest predators. Bile pools in my mouth, and my knuckles turn white from holding the steering wheel too tight.

"What happened?"

"I said I don't want to talk about it. It was hell, but we lived to tell the tale."

"But you're not telling the tale."

"Meh, it's depressing. How about some music?" She reaches for the radio, and on instinct, I bat her hand away.

"Don't. You're going to mess up all the stations."

"Jeez, you're one of those guys, huh?" Daisy smirks.

"What guys?"

"The guys whose cars are an extension of their penises."

I chuckle. Who knew junkie Daisy was funny? "Baby, don't be talking about my penis unless you want it to come out and play."

"Oh my God. I just barfed in my mouth."

"Whatever. So, what radio station do you like?"

"How about The Freaks?"

"That's a Norm station, right?"

"Well, it's run by Fringes, but yeah, they play songs from Norm artists."

I use the voice-activated control to find the station. An unfamiliar pop song fills the interior of the car.

"I love this song!" Daisy proclaims, then begins to bob her head in sync with the melody.

Traffic is heavy at this time of the day, so I can't take my eyes off the road too much to stare at her. But every time I do, my dick twitches in my pants. When I take the exit to my parents' neighborhood, my temporary good mood evaporates. I also don't have to worry about a hard-on. Nothing good survives when I approach my father's domain.

Despite the Westbrook mansion being inside a high-security gated community, my father deemed it necessary to install another checkpoint to his property. My car is equipped with the remote control to the wrought iron gates, so with the push of a button, they open.

"Wow. Your house is pretty badass," Daisy says in awe.

"It's not my house," I reply harshly.

The modern mansion is a masterpiece in architecture and has been featured several times in lifestyle magazines. It's all about angles, cleans lines, and lots of glass.

I park the car right in front of the stairs leading to the front door on the second level, then pause a moment.

"Phoenix? Are you all right?"

"I just a need a minute." I take deep breaths, steeling myself to deal with my father. I always get sick to my stomach when I have to see him face-to-face.

Daisy covers my hand with hers and squeezes. I turn to meet her eyes, which are rounder and no longer red. "Whatever demons you're battling, you'll be okay."

I never wanted to kiss a girl as badly as I want to kiss her now. I'm actually on the verge of breaking the distance between us and crushing my lips to hers, but I sense a third presence not far from us. With difficulty, I peel my gaze off Daisy's face and look ahead. My mother is standing on the ledge, looking down on us.

"We've been spotted. We'd better get going." I open the door and slide out of the car.

I walk around the front of the SUV and meet Daisy halfway. I'm an asshole, but I won't let Daisy walk into the lion's den without protection.

I grab her hand and lace our fingers together. I sense a slight tension from her and a question in her gaze.

"My mother probably thinks you're my girlfriend. It'll be easier if we let her believe that."

"Why?" Daisy whispers.

"You'll find out soon enough."

21

DAISY

My head is still fuzzy, and there are crazy butterflies in my stomach. I'm pretty sure those were awakened by Phoenix. But when he laces his hand with mine, a zing of pleasure shoots up my arm, heightening all my current emotions.

Overwhelmed by my reaction to him, I float up the flight of stairs and only come back to Earth when a throat clearing ahead draws my attention. A gorgeous blonde woman is staring at me as if I'm an alien. Her green eyes are narrowed to slits, her lips pinched in a thin flat line.

"Phoenix, I didn't know you were bringing a guest," she says in a cold voice.

Yikes. I'm sensing major hostile vibes from her.

"It was a last-minute thing. I didn't know if Daisy could make it. She's a very dedicated student," Phoenix replies in a smooth voice that sends tingles down my spine. He's not even addressing me. I can't imagine how my body will react when he does.

The woman gives me a once-over that clearly says she finds me lacking. Whatever. I don't really care about what she thinks about me. In reality, I'm not even annoyed that she's been so rude.

"Well, I suppose I can ask the maid to put an extra plate on the table." She turns on her high heels and strides back into the house.

"Your mother is a bit uptight, huh?" I say.

"You have no idea. Are you ready?"

I sense Phoenix's stare, so I turn to meet his gaze. "If you had asked me any other day, I'd say forget about it. Not today though. So yeah, I'm ready."

Phoenix's lips curl into a lopsided grin. "What did you take before I found you?"

"What do you mean? I didn't take anything."

"Daisy...." He trails off while staring meaningfully at me.

"Phoenix," I mimic his tone.

With a shake of his head, he laughs. "Fine. Don't tell me. This evening ought to be interesting."

We finally follow Phoenix's mother into the house. The modern theme from outside continues seamlessly into the front foyer. The first thing that strikes me is Phoenix's parents' obsession with white. My eyes hurt from the brightness.

"Damn, what do your parents have against color?" I ask.

Phoenix chuckles.

A man in a pristine dark suit appears to greet us. "Mr. Westbrook. Hors d'oeuvres have been served in the patio area."

"Thanks, Vargas."

"You have a butler?" I ask.

The man in question makes a sourpuss expression as if he just sucked on a lemon.

"My parents have a butler," Phoenix replies.

We follow Vargas to the outside area just in time to catch a gorgeous sunset. Phoenix's mother is speaking in hushed tones with a woman in uniform before turning her attention to us.

"Where's Father?" Phoenix's asks.

"In his office. He'll join us shortly."

Phoenix heads for the wet bar and pours himself a double dose of whiskey. He drinks the full glass in large gulps before he refills it. All the while, his mother is watching him with a disapproving expression on her marble-statue face.

"So we're starting early," she says, to which Phoenix doesn't reply.

With a clicking of her tongue, she turns to me. "Would you like something to drink, Daisy?"

"No, thank you."

A sliver of dread runs down my spine, and the small hairs on my neck stand on end. A powerful Idol just stepped foot on the patio. Phoenix and his mother stand stiffly, both looking over my shoulder. I turn around and come face-to-face with a tall and imposing man dressed to the nines in a sharp suit and tie. There's absolutely no resemblance between him and Phoenix, but I know without a shred of doubt that the man staring daggers in my direction is Phoenix's father.

"What the hell is this Norm doing here?" he growls.

Suddenly, Phoenix is next to me and wrapping his arm around my waist. I don't know how he moved so fast from the other side of the patio, but I'm glad he did. Even in my current easy-breezy state, I still feel the wrath of his father.

"Daisy is my date for the evening," Phoenix replies.

"How dare you bring a filthy Norm to my house?"

I flinch and tense on the spot. Phoenix's hold on me tightens.

"You'd better treat my girlfriend with more respect," he hisses.

What is he doing? His father is about to blow a fuse.

"Your *girlfriend*?" The man's glower switches to a point behind us—his wife is my guess. "Leticia, did you know about this?"

"Of course not."

"I don't know what kind of idiotic games you're playing, boy, but Westbrooks don't date Norms. We don't even fuck them."

Okay, this is seriously pissing me off, and he's totally killing my buzz. I open my mouth to tell him what I think about his race when Phoenix speaks.

"Well, *this* Westbrook does. It's high time I break away from your disgusting traditions. Come on, Daisy. We're out of here." He begins to guide me toward the front of the house.

"Don't you dare walk away from me, boy," his father shouts.

"Watch me."

A high shrieking noise pierces my eardrums. I cover my ears with my hands and wonder what the hell is going on. Phoenix pushes me forward and says, "Run, Daisy."

He doesn't need to say it twice. I bolt toward the front door, but sensing Phoenix didn't follow me, I halt and whirl around in time to see all the window panels explode into shards of glass. Phoenix is standing with his feet wide apart, arms tense by his sides. The pieces of broken glass never touch him, stopping midair as if there's an invisible shield in front of him.

A hand on my shoulder makes me jump on the spot. It's Vargas, the butler. "You need to leave, miss. *Now.*"

"I can't go without Phoenix."

As if I summoned him with my words, Phoenix appears next to me. Without a word, he steers me out the door and to his car. Only when we're inside his vehicle and out of his parents' property do I dare to speak.

"What the hell was that?"

"My father showing how pissed off he was."

"Did you know that was going to happen when you decided to bring me over?"

Phoenix doesn't reply for several beats. His jaw is tense, and I see a muscle twitch.

"You did, didn't you?" I continue. "I can't believe you used me to provoke your old man." I cross my arms and look out the window.

"I'm sorry. I wasn't thinking. I just couldn't face dinner with the man alone."

"I'm glad to be at your service," I spit back.

My stomach decides to grumble just then, loud as fuck. I'm starving all of a sudden.

"I truly *am* sorry. I didn't think he was going to use his powers against us."

"What was that, anyway?"

"My father can control sound, among other things."

"Yikes. He almost made me deaf." I rub my right tragus.

"That was his intention. Again, I'm so sorry. Let me make it up to you. What do you fancy eating?"

I hug my middle. It feels like I haven't eaten in days. "I'm really in the mood for the greasiest cheeseburger you can find."

"Man, I could eat several. I know just the spot."

Phoenix drives us to the beach, and involuntarily, my body becomes as stiff as a board. It's too soon since my almost-drowning incident. I don't say anything though. The spot he was referring to is a food truck that, by the sheer volume of people waiting their turn, must serve pretty amazing food.

"Stay here," he tells me. "I'll be right back."

Instead of getting in line, he heads to the back of the truck, disappearing from view. I don't have a phone, and Phoenix forgot to turn on the radio. Remembering how he prevented me from touching the controls, I don't even try. Pissing off one Idol is enough for today.

After five minutes or so, Phoenix returns carrying several brown paper bags. When he enters the car, the delicious smell of burgers and french fries fills my nose, making my mouth water. With greedy hands, I reach for one of the bags. A moan escapes my lips when I take a deep whiff of my dinner.

Phoenix groans.

"What?" I look at him. He's watching me with hooded eyes.

"Please don't make that sound, Daisy, unless you want me to attack your mouth."

Heat spreads through my cheeks, and I avert my gaze. "Control yourself and eat your food."

"So bossy."

I'm halfway into my ginormous meal when Phoenix makes a disgruntled sound in the back of his throat. Thinking that he's again making lewd noises, I glower at him. But he's not looking at me, and his face is twisted into a grimace. He's also holding his right wrist tightly.

"Phoenix? What's the matter?"

"My punishment," he grits out.

"Your punishment?" My eyes widen when a glowing light comes from his wrist. Without a second thought, I reach for it.

"No, Daisy. Don't touch me." Phoenix pulls away, but he's not fast enough for me. Another alarming detail.

I push the hand covering his wrist away and stare at the glowing tattoo. "What is this?"

"It's... his mark." Phoenix throws his head back on the headrest with eyes closed.

On an impulse, I cover his tattoo with my hand. A zap of energy goes up my arm at the same time Phoenix jolts in his seat.

"Daisy? What are you doing?"

"I don't know."

Slowly, the glow diminishes until it's gone. Sensing Phoenix's stare, I lift my eyes to meet his.

"How did you do that?" he asks, staring at me oddly.

"I didn't do anything besides touch you."

He doesn't break the connection, and a strange energy is exchanged between us. My heart is beating madly inside of my chest, and I'm all too aware of Phoenix's presence. It's like he's everywhere. My mouth goes dry, and I find myself at a loss for words. He inches closer, his eyes once again filled with desire. He's going to kiss me, and I don't have it in me to stop him.

He humiliated me, tortured me, and yet I'm still on the verge of succumbing to the crazy sexual tension between us.

But the sound of his phone ringing breaks the charged moment and also serves as a wake-up call. I pull away.

He looks ahead, rubbing his face. Then he glances at his phone on the storage compartment between our seats. It's a call from Bryce. My mood plummets completely.

Finally, Phoenix reaches for the device and presses the green button. "What's up, Bryce?"

"Is Daisy with you?" I hear his question loud and clear. He sounds agitated.

"Yeah. Why?"

"Is she okay?"

Phoenix glances at me, eyebrows furrowed. "She seems okay. What's going on?"

The sound gets muffled then, and I can't make out Bryce's answer, but whatever he said makes Phoenix widen his eyes. "Daisy, what did you take before I found you?"

"I already told you. I didn't take anything."

Phoenix reaches over and opens the glove compartment. He pulls out a clear vial. Still on the phone, he says, "Bryce, I'm going to have to call you back."

He tosses the phone away and opens the vial in his hand. He extends his arm, placing the vial close enough to my nose so I can smell its contents.

"Is this scent familiar to you?"

I only need to take one whiff of the clear liquid to trigger my memories.

"That's Silver-voltage," I whisper, thanks to the huge lump lodged in my throat. "Drusilla and Renata forced me to take it."

Fury and fear mix in Phoenix's gaze. He throws his half-eaten burger aside and puts his car in Drive.

"Motherfucker. I'm going to kill those bitches," he says through clenched teeth.

He peels his car out of the parking lot like he's running away from the devil.

"Where are we going?" I ask.

"To get you help."

I nibble on my lower lip while I fight the growing desperation in my chest. It's been at least a couple of hours since I encountered those nasty Idols.

"Shouldn't I be dead by now?" I murmur.

"Yes, Daisy. You should."

22

BRYCE

I've been staring at Daisy's father's diary for an indefinite amount of my time, trying to figure out what to do about it and her. There hasn't been a moment when she hasn't plagued my mind. And the more I think about her, the more I agree with Morpheus's assessment. It wasn't the diary that made me shun her. It was his vision and what it meant.

Loud whistling from the kitchen distracts me from my turbulent thoughts. The only person prone to busting out tunes is Phoenix, but he's out. Curious, I head out of my room and find Morpheus is the one responsible for the music. In all the years I've known him, I've never heard him make any sound besides derisive ones.

Rufio walks out of his room as well, wearing nothing but boxer shorts and holding a towel in his hand. He stares at Morpheus with his mouth agape.

"Who are you, and what have you done with Morpheus?" he asks.

Morpheus stops whistling and stares at us. "What?"

"You're in a good mood," I say.

Morpheus widens his eyes slightly, looking hella guilty. The question is, guilty about what?

"Is that a crime?" he asks.

"No, but it's weird as fuck. Keep the volume down." Rufio returns to his room.

"Don't worry, I'm heading out." Morpheus grabs a bag of chips from the cupboard and a couple beer cans.

"Where are you going?" I ask.

Again, the guilty glint in Morpheus's eyes. A nagging suspicion takes hold of me. "You're going to see Daisy, aren't you?" I continue.

Rufio runs back into the living room. "You're going to see Daisy?"

"Yes, if you must know. She still has the rare book she got from the librarian, and we're doing a read-a-thon before she has to return it on Monday."

"A what now?" Rufio asks.

"And do you have to go to her room?" I ask, unable to hide my annoyance or jealousy.

"It was her condition. She doesn't want to see either of you." Morpheus looks pointedly at Rufio and me.

"What did I do?" My brother arches his eyebrows innocently.

"Maybe she thought you were bad in the sack," I answer perversely.

"Bite me, Bryce. You're jealous that she didn't put up a fight with me."

"Okay. I'm out of here." Morpheus heads for the door, but I beat him to it.

"Bryce, what do you think you're doing?" he asks.

"I'm going to clear the air once and for all."

I knock hard on Daisy's door before Morpheus can stop me. We wait, and when there's no reply, I look at him. "Are you sure she agreed to meet with you?"

"Yes." Morpheus frowns.

"Uh, guys." Rufio joins us in the hallway. "I just received a text message from Drusilla. She's asking about Daisy."

The cold touch of dread runs down my spine. Daisy isn't home, and Drusilla is asking about her. That can't be good.

Rufio already has the phone glued to his ear. "Come on, bitch, pick up already."

After a moment, he gives up. "She's not answering."

There's a ping from his phone, announcing a new text message. Rufio reads it quickly and then raises his gaze to mine. "She's saying that if I want to know what happened to Daisy, I have to head down to her impromptu party by the pool."

The lights in the hallway flicker, my power leaking from me automatically. I whirl around and head for the stairs with Rufio and Morpheus right behind me.

If Drusilla touched one hair of Daisy, she's as good as dead. I don't fucking care about the consequences.

RUFIO

Bryce is going to explode. He went from a guy who felt nothing to a short-fused one. I used to be the hothead in the group, but Bryce is giving me a run for my money.

As soon as we hit the sidewalk outside the building, he takes off at breakneck speed. He can probably outrun a cheetah. Morpheus and I struggle to keep up. Bryce has always been the fastest among us, which used to piss me off. Still does. I love my brother, but the rivalry between us is strong.

I can hear the upbeat techno music from outside the gym, plus laughter. Bryce has already disappeared inside. In his current state, he's probably going to start blowing shit up first and asking questions later.

The music cuts off suddenly, and Morpheus curses under his breath.

"Here we go," I say.

I push the double doors to the pool area open with enough force to command the attention of those nearby. But most of the partygoers have their gazes glued to Bryce, who is striding toward the bitch of the hour. Drusilla.

The idiot has the audacity to stare at my brother with a smug grin on her face. Either she's gone completely crazy, or she has a trump card up her sleeve. She's a powerful Idol, but she's no match for Bryce. At least her friend Renata has enough brain cells to look fearful.

"Bryce, what an ho—" Her stupid speech is cut short when a waterspout erupts from the pool and curls around her neck, lifting her off the ground as it chokes her.

Damn. Bryce has amped his telekinesis game.

"What have you done with Daisy?" he asks in a low and dangerous tone.

Drusilla's face turns beet red, and it's obvious she can't answer while Bryce is crushing her airway.

"Bryce. She can't talk like that," Morpheus points out.

It takes another couple of seconds for Bryce to release Drusilla. She drops to her knees and wheezes.

"Talk, bitch," Bryce growls.

Drusilla lifts her chin in defiance. "You're too late. Your Norm whore is probably already dead."

"What did you do?" I take a step forward, curling my hands into fists in a futile attempt to control my anger. Bryce is not the only one who can do some serious damage.

Drusilla slowly rises from her crouch. "We gave her a taste of Idol life. She wanted to try Silver-voltage so badly. We couldn't say no."

With a roar, Bryce unleashes his fury on Drusilla, but the energy bolt he sends her way misses the mark.

What the hell. How did she move so fast?

She laughs from the bleachers. "Oh, Bryce. You're no longer the hottest ticket in town. I've been blessed too." She pulls the neckline of her shirt to the side, revealing a lightning bolt–shaped mark. The same mark the guys and I have.

Son of a bitch.

Morpheus lets out a groan and clutches his head between his hands. *Ah hell. Don't tell me our deity godfather decided to make an appearance in his head.* The shadows on his wrists are darker and writhing as if they want to escape the bracelets' bindings.

A high-out-of-his mind Pietro comes stumbling forward. "What are you guys fighting for? It's a parteey." He raises his fist up in the air. "Besides, Drusilla is totally lying."

Pietro smirks at her, and she glowers. There's no lost love between the two. He came on to her, and she shut him down hard, more than once.

"She's not lying. I gave Silver-voltage to the Norm myself," Renata replies.

Drusilla might have acquired extra juice, but I don't sense anything extra about her stupid friend. I'm on the girl before Bryce can reach her, grabbing Renata by her neck and squeezing tight. "You'd better be lying."

Dark veins appear in my hand. I'm one second away from turning Renata into dust.

"Dude, chillax," Pietro says. "She's totally lying. I saw Daisy with Phoenix like an hour ago. She was fine."

Without letting go of Renata, I turn to Bryce. He already has his cell phone out.

"Is Daisy with you?" he asks Phoenix. After a pause, he continues. "Is she okay?"

"Dude, what's going on with Morpheus?" Pietro asks.

He's definitely not looking too good right now. He made his way to the bleachers and keeps holding his head in his hands. Fuck. We don't need this right now.

I let go of Renata and walk over to my friend. Before I reach Morpheus, I catch Bryce fry his phone with an energy blast.

"What the hell did you do that for?" I ask.

"Phoenix hung up on me."

"But Daisy is okay?" I take a step in his direction.

"She's alive, which means she didn't take Silver-voltage." Bryce turns his attention to Drusilla.

"I told you she was lying." Pietro sneers.

"Shut up, asshole!" she commands, and at once, Pietro shuts his cake hole. By the way he's turning red, she used her compulsion power on him.

Morpheus lifts his head, his face pale now. "The god told me she isn't lying," he whispers so only Bryce and I can hear him.

I trade a glance with my brother. "What now?"

I can't mistake the regretful expression on Bryce's face. "We find Phoenix and Daisy and hope for a miracle."

23

PHOENIX

The street and cars flash by in a blur. I push my SUV to the limit because I don't know how much time Daisy has left. I've never met a Norm who was dumb enough to take Silver-voltage, but if even Fringes are dying like flies, it's only a matter of time before Daisy succumbs to the drug.

Today, I broke the record of stupid shit I pulled. First, inviting Daisy to meet my parents and thus putting her in my odious father's path. Second, not suspecting what was wrong with her. I've taken Silver-voltage plenty of times; I should have been able to read the signs.

The navigation system tells me I need to make a left, but I'm going too fast.

"Hold tight, Daisy." I yank the wheel, the tires screeching violently as I make the sharp turn.

She yelps, but I can't risk peeling my eyes off the road for one second.

Finally, the damn robotic voice tells me Nurse Ellen's home is coming up. Last year, we hacked into the school's system and got everyone's addresses just because we could. It's finally being useful. She lives downtown on a narrow street, which at the moment has no parking spots available. Screw it. I'm parking in the middle.

I slam on the brakes, and Daisy's body lurches forward. I'm glad she's wearing her seat belt. I'm out of the car and by her door in a split second. She's still buckled to her seat when I yank the door open.

Using my telekinesis, I free her from the strap and pull her out.

"Ouch, Phoenix. You don't need to tear my arm off."

I don't stop or offer a comment. I'm running on pure adrenaline. I ring the doorbell, but only because I sense the nurse's front door is protected against break-ins. When she doesn't answer right away, I pound on it.

"Ellen, open up!"

I hear footsteps coming down the stairs. A second later, a distraught woman opens the door. She's not Ellen, and she's a Norm.

"Who are you?" she asks.

"Who is it, Fatima?" Ellen asks from inside the apartment.

"It's Phoenix. And Daisy."

Ellen finally runs down the stairs wearing comfy sweatpants and a T-shirt.

"What happened?" she asks with wide eyes.

"Daisy took Silver-voltage," I reply.

"What?" both women exclaim.

"I didn't take it willingly. I was forced to," Daisy supplies.

"Oh my God. Come on in. Quickly." Ellen urges us in with her hand.

In single file, we hurry up the stairs. As soon as Daisy reaches the landing, Ellen grabs her by the hand and sits her down on a high stool.

"How are you feeling? Dizziness, nausea, headache?" The

nurse fires one question after another while staring intently at Daisy's face.

"I was dizzy when the drug entered my system. And my legs were numb for a while. But after that, I felt euphoric and relaxed."

"That's the effect of the drug on Idols," I say.

"Stay still, Daisy," Ellen tells her. "I'm going to scan you."

Daisy's panicked gaze switches to me for a fleeting moment. I want to tell her everything will be okay. I should be strong for her. But I'm freaking out myself. At least my father left me alone for now, which in itself is a bizarre occurrence, especially after the stunt I pulled at dinner.

Ellen closes her eyes and stretches her hands in front of Daisy. I faint light emanates from her palms. Whatever she's doing takes about a minute. Then the nurse lowers her arms, but she doesn't speak at all.

I walk to Daisy's side. "So?"

"I can't find any trace of the drug in her body."

"Are you sure?" Daisy and I ask at the same time.

"Positive. Is it possible that this was only a prank?"

"We're talking about Drusilla here. It's not her MO to brag about something she didn't do," I say.

"If she truly had given Daisy Silver-voltage, that would be murder," Ellen's Norm friend says.

"Like Idols care about that." Daisy leaps off the stool.

Both women make a face, then glance at each other.

"We're not all bad," I say, but my words are hollow. Not too long ago, I wouldn't lose a night of sleep if someone I knew had killed a Norm. They were bugs to me. But not anymore. Well, at least one of them isn't.

"I don't begrudge your point of view about Idols, Daisy, but not all of us are evil." Ellen looks affectionately at her Norm friend.

Holy shit. I'm dense. The woman is only wearing a long T-shirt and socks. She must be Ellen's *girlfriend*, not a friend.

"Poppers is a similar drug to Silver-voltage but not lethal to Norms or Fringes," the girlfriend says. "It's no longer popular among Norm kids, but if someone wants it badly enough, they can get their hands on it."

"So your theory is that Drusilla gave Daisy Poppers and told her it was Silver-voltage instead?" I ask.

Daisy shakes her head. "I'm not so sure. You didn't see the glee in her eyes when Renata dosed me with whatever it was. She was ecstatic."

"It's the only logical conclusion, Daisy," Ellen says.

"I've seen kids dying of Silver-voltage overdose. It happens quickly, a few minutes after they take the drug," the girlfriend says, and Ellen nods in agreement.

"That's right. This was a terrible prank, no denying that. But be glad they didn't use the real deal," Ellen adds.

Daisy looks pensive, and as she does so, she bites her lower lip. Hell and damn. Now that a tragedy has been averted, my cock is all too aware of how much it wants her. Her nibbling on her plump lips is not helping my case.

"I guess we should go back to campus, then," I say with a voice that's a little rough.

"Thanks for seeing me," Daisy says. "And sorry for the trouble."

"Don't mention it, hon. I'm glad everything turned out okay." Ellen smiles.

"Yeah, thanks a bunch," I say.

Ellen walks us to the front door and then peers over my shoulder. "I can't believe you parked in the middle of the street and no one called the tow truck on you."

"I guess it was a lucky evening all around," I quip, but there isn't humor in it. It wasn't a fortunate evening at all. I defied my father, and I'll pay for it. With blood.

Daisy is quiet on the way back, so after a long stretch without a word from her, I break the silence.

"A penny for your thoughts?"

She turns her face to mine. "I can't believe Drusilla tricked me like that. I honestly thought she had given me Silver-voltage."

"Well, maybe she's not as savage as we thought."

Yeah, even I'm not buying that horseshit.

Once we're on the move again, I call Bryce. By the sheer number of missed calls and text messages not only from him but from Rufio as well, I know they must be losing their minds. But I get his voice mail instead, so I call Rufio. He answers on the first ring.

"What the fuck, Phoenix. Finally!" he screams in my ear.

"She's fine. It was a false alarm. Drusilla lied. She didn't give Daisy Silver-voltage. We suspect they used Poppers."

I look at Daisy, finding her frowning. It's almost like she's upset that Drusilla didn't try to kill her.

"Son of a bitch. Get your ass here as fast as you can. There's been new developments," Rufio barks.

His tone is ominous. Great. More problems are exactly what we need.

"I'll be there as soon as I can," I tell him.

"How is she?" he asks in a much softer tone.

"Difficult to say."

Whipping her face in my direction, she says, "Tell Rufio I'm fine and he can quit pretending he cares about my well-being."

I wince at her outburst. For what she lacks in powers, she compensates for in attitude. I can't imagine what Daisy would do if she were an Idol. Thank the fates she isn't.

24

———

MORPHEUS

"**A**re you sure about what that son of a bitch said?" Rufio whirls around.

"Yes," I answer from the couch, wrapped in the thickest wool blanket I own. The god has departed from my head, but the shadows are still active, which means I'm once again turning into a human Popsicle. I can feel the power of the bracelets diminishing already.

"You also saw her mark," Bryce says from his spot at the window.

"It means nothing. She lied about giving Daisy Silver-voltage," Rufio rebuffs.

"She wasn't lying," I say, staring at no particular object on the coffee table. "The god told me as much. I think...." I shake my head, trying to collect my thoughts. "I think Drusilla has been the one making Fringes take Silver-voltage."

"It fits her MO." Bryce frowns. "He wanted Daisy gone, and we defied his command. Maybe he found a more willing soldier to do his dirty work."

"Well, Phoenix said Ellen scanned Daisy and found no traces of the drug. So what the hell is going on?" Rufio kicks a chair. It topples over, but it never hits the floor, turning to dust beforehand.

"Son a bitch! Will you quit destroying our furniture?" I yell.

"Yeah, and you still owe me a fucking door, asshole." Bryce jumps from the windowsill and heads for his doorless room.

He stops midway when the sound of a key turning catches our attention. I sit up straighter, and Rufio turns toward the door, as tense as ever. Phoenix walks in with a grim expression that only heightens my own pessimistic thoughts.

"Where's Daisy?" Bryce and Rufio ask at the same time.

"In her room." Phoenix looks at Bryce. "She wants her father's diary back, and I think you should give it to her."

"Are you fucking kidding me with this diary shit?" Bryce barks. "And why are you singing a different tune about her now? You were the mastermind of her utter humiliation, after all."

"Why did you take her to meet your folks? Aren't they evil?" I ask.

"Will you stop with the ten thousand questions? I thought you had bad news to give." Phoenix veers toward the kitchen and grabs a cold one from the fridge.

"Drusilla has been marked," I say.

Phoenix moves so fast, he sloshes beer over his button-down shirt. "What do you mean, marked? By whom?"

"Who do you think, idiot? The asshole god from the island of horrors," Rufio replies.

Phoenix's eyebrows meet his hairline. "How? I thought you had to pass his bullshit trials to receive the honor of his fucking mark. Are you saying Dreadzilla got the mark by doing absolutely nothing?"

"I think she received the mark when she agreed to take the hit on Daisy's life," I say.

Phoenix rubs his face, setting his beer down. With his

hands on his hips, he glances at the floor. "Daisy was sure Drusilla had given her Silver-voltage."

"Drusilla shared the same confidence. She believed without a doubt that she had succeeded in her mission," I reply.

"I'm going to have a word with Daisy." Bryce starts for the front door, but Phoenix moves quickly and blocks his way.

"Don't. She's beat, man. Let her rest for tonight. Drusilla gave her something; that much is true. She was high when I bumped into her."

I narrow my eyes, sensing something different about Phoenix's aura. It's less turbulent. I usually don't make it a habit of snooping on other people's energy fields, but the change in his is hard to miss. Something happened today that he's not telling us.

"Why are you Daisy's knight in shining armor all of a sudden? What happened at your parents'?" Bryce crosses his arms in front of his chest.

Phoenix tries to keep his face impartial, but I see the slight twitch of his eyebrows. I'm sure Bryce noticed that too. "Nothing happened. We didn't stay long."

Rufio rips at his hair and begins to pace again. "Fuck. This is maddening. If Drusilla has levelled up, she's going to be a fucking nightmare."

"Do you think she's in the same league as us?" Phoenix asks.

"She evaded my power blast." Bryce steps away from him, but the tension in his frame remains the same, coiled tight. Any little trigger might set him off. It's best if he doesn't see Daisy tonight.

"Like she blocked your blast, or she moved out of the way?" Phoenix watches Bryce closely.

"The latter. Still, she moved way too fast. I don't know if she's a fifteen now, but she's definitely no longer a twelve," I reply, and then a thought occurs to me. "The Knights were interested in Daisy's safety. I wonder if there's a way to contact them."

"Why would we do that? They kidnapped Bryce." Rufio glares at me.

"Exactly. They know a way to neutralize Idol powers. We can't declare open war on Drusilla without serious repercussions. And if she's on our former boss's team, she'll keep gunning for Daisy."

"Our mother." Bryce turns to Rufio. "She also wants Daisy safe. I wouldn't be surprised if she's a Knight herself. I followed her to Unearthly Desires on the same evening they jumped me. She could have tipped them off."

"So what's the game plan? Daisy is safe in her room now, but what happens on Monday? She doesn't share all her classes with us," I point out.

"I'll think of something," Bryce replies with a downcast expression.

"I can't stay here. I need to blow off some steam." Rufio heads for the front door.

"Don't tell me you're going to Unearthly Desires," Phoenix says with a hint of annoyance.

Rufio stops suddenly, shoulders tense. "No," he replies simply before walking out.

Phoenix stares at the closed door for a couple of beats before turning to me.

"Aren't you going to tag along?" I ask.

Phoenix's expression is solemn. There's no mirth in his gaze. "No." He focuses on the blanket wrapped around my shoulders. "Are the shadows bothering you again?"

"Yup. Every time our overlord god comes for a visit, they gain strength. At least he didn't stay long in my head this time or make me wish for death."

Phoenix keeps staring at me as if he wants to say something. "What?" I ask.

He shakes his head and glances at the stove. "I can make you some tea or soup if you're hungry."

My jaw drops of its own accord. Phoenix offering to do something nice for others? That's a first. But he looks like a dog without a bone now, so I'm not going to pick on him.

"Sure, I'll have some tea. Thanks."

Phoenix gets busy in the kitchen, and after a minute I finally decide to offer something in return for his unusual kindness.

"If you have something on your chest that you feel you can't talk to anyone about it, I'm here."

His shoulders tense. "You're not using your freaky gifts on me, are you?"

"I can't read minds, if that's what you're worried about. I'm just offering my ear if you feel like talking, that's all."

Phoenix doesn't speak for several beats before he finally replies. "Thanks, man. I appreciate it."

He's not going to open up now. I can tell as much. Whatever's eating him, I hope it's not something that will destroy him in the end.

25
___

DAISY

I spent at least half an hour staring at myself in the mirror before I finally took a shower and called it a night. I didn't see anything different about my appearance, but I feel strange, almost as if I don't fit in my own skin.

Falling asleep is difficult. I toss and turn in my bed while disturbing thoughts plague my mind: Drusilla's glee after Renata drugged me, the contempt on Phoenix' mother's face, the hatred in his father's eyes.

I'm still in the scene where the man shattered his own windows when suddenly the landscape vanishes. I'm in the woods now, and it's wintertime. I'm dressed for the occasion, wearing snow boots to protect my feet plus a puffy jacket, a woolen hat, and thick gloves.

I don't recognize the place, but it's peaceful. I keep walking the beaten path until a chalet appears at the end of it. Smoke billows from the chimney. I head for the small house without hesitation, almost as if I know who I'll find inside. Giddy anticipation unfurls in the pit of my stomach.

The door is unlocked, so I push it open. "Hello?"

Phoenix comes down the hallway, wearing a thick pullover and dark jeans. His gorgeous face breaks into a thousand-watt smile when he sees me. "Hello, gorgeous."

My heart does a backflip before it starts hammering away as if it wants to leapfrog out of my chest. I break into a run and jump into Phoenix's open arms. He hugs me tightly, kissing the top of my head, while I burrow my face in his chest and take a whiff of his cologne.

"I'm glad you came," he says.

I ease back and raise my face to his. "Were you afraid I wouldn't?"

His smile wilts a fraction. "Yeah, I was."

Rising on my tiptoes, I bring my lips to his. It's a feathery brush first, but it soon turns smoldering hot. With a groan, Phoenix lifts me off the floor. His tongue darts in my mouth while I wrap my legs around his waist, hooking them at the ankles. With expert strokes, he slowly unravels me completely. He tastes like rain and sunshine.

I run my fingers over the short strands of his hair, pulling at the roots a little.

"Daisy, you're going to be the end of me," he mumbles against my lips.

"That sounds ominous." I chuckle.

"You laugh, but I'm serious." He forgets my lips for a moment to worship my neck. With each open kiss he places against my sensitive skin, I melt a little more.

"I think you'll be the death of me," I sigh.

He walks us to the living room. Pulling back to look into my eyes, he asks, "Couch or rug?"

Quickly, I check both options, and then I smile coquettishly. "We can start on the couch."

"A woman after my own heart." He captures my lips again for a toe-curling, panty-dropping kiss.

Slowly, he sets me down without letting go. But I'm in the mood to tease. I flatten my palm against his chest and give him a light shove, stepping back as well. Phoenix stares at my mouth with hooded eyes, which only makes me yearn for him more.

"I'm so terribly hot. I think I should get rid of some layers," I say teasingly.

"Some? How about all of them?"

"Patience, boy."

"I've run out of patience. I've been waiting for this moment for far too long."

"Me too."

I unzip my coat and let it drop at my feet.

"I thought you had nothing underneath that," he says.

"It's cold outside." I pout.

"I'll make you warm in no time, babe." He takes a step forward, but I wag my index finger.

"Not yet."

It's his turn to look like a kid who was denied a lollipop.

Finally, I pull my sweater and T-shirt off in one move and toss them aside. Naturally, Phoenix's heated gaze drops to my breasts.

He licks his lower lip and says roughly, "Daisy, you're a weapon of desire. But you're done torturing me."

With a flick of his wrist, he unhooks my bra and sends it flying out of sight.

"Hey!" I say, but before I can protest any further, Phoenix is on me, mouth and hands everywhere.

We tumble onto the couch, a twist of limbs and urgency. I close my eyes and surrender to the onslaught of the most incendiary sensations running freely through my body.

An annoying noise sounds in the distance, killing the mood. I try to ignore it, but it gets louder with each second. For fuck's sake.

My eyes fly open and Phoenix is gone. I'm in my room, in my bed, tangled in my sheets. But the throbbing between my legs is way too real.

Damn it. He messed with my head again. I didn't think I had to worry about that anymore. I was so fucking naïve. In a huff, I toss the sheets aside and sit up. My eyes travel toward my desk where I left the librarian's book.

I was supposed to have a read-a-thon with Morpheus yesterday, which, thanks to Drusilla, didn't happen. But I already know how to keep Phoenix out of my head. I just don't have a clue how I'm going to make him bleed without my dagger.

Guilt, the last emotion I should be feeling right now, enters my heart. Phoenix was out of his mind with worry when he thought I had taken Silver-voltage. And I'm sure we shared a special moment in the car right before his strange tattoo started to bother him. Does he think that gives him the right to give me erotic dreams?

I'm all fired up and ready to start a fight. Not caring that I'm wearing sleepwear, I veer for the door. The air gets sucked out of my lungs when I find Rosie and Toby standing there.

"Surprise!" Rosie yells.

"Oh my God. What are you doing here?" My eyes drop to her arm, which is no longer in a cast. "When did that happen?"

"Oh, yesterday. Toby took me to the hospital. Now we no longer match." She pouts and looks at his cast.

"And I'm glad about that." He pulls her closer and kisses her on the cheek.

A little pang hits my chest. I've always been responsible for taking care of Rosie, but since I've joined Gifted Academy, I've slacked off.

"How did you get in?" I ask them.

"I still have my credentials, so getting through the gate

wasn't a problem. And I rang some random dude's apartment and he let me into the building," Toby explains.

"Boy, security in this place is tight," I half joke, because my other half is actually concerned about it.

"We came to kidnap you," Rosie continues. "Aren't you going to let us in?"

Stunned, I open the door wider to let them pass. Toby whistles, and Rosie is looking at everything wide-eyed.

"This is way better than my former quarters," he says.

"Oh, Toby. You have to convince your parents to let you come back. The school isn't the same without you." I pout.

"I've tried. If it was only up to my father, I'd still be here. My mother is the problem. And she doesn't know about—" He stops suddenly, probably remembering Rosie doesn't know I was tossed out of a window.

"Know about what?" Rosie asks.

Toby rubs the back of his neck, turning beet red. "Uh, she doesn't know that I faked being a Fringe."

"What's happening today? Where are you kidnapping me to?" I change the subject before Rosie can probe further.

She turns around with a big smile on her face. "Toby's father's employer is throwing his annual barbeque today, and we're invited."

Now it's my turn to make a face. "But doesn't your dad work for an Idol?"

"Yes, but he's not like the assholes in school. He's pretty nice."

I watch my sister closely. "Still, they're Idols, Rosie. Are you okay with that?"

She bobs her head up and down. "Yup. I've already met the guy. You really can't tell he's an Idol. He's super chill. Besides, they have a pool!" she squeaks.

"Okay, okay. Let me get ready, then."

I grab a change of clothes and lock myself in the bathroom.

I hear giggles on the other side, so I feel it's my sisterly duty to yell, "You'd better not be making out in my bed."

"Shut up, Daisy, and hurry up," Rosie replies.

I shake my head while a small smile blossoms on my face. I haven't heard Rosie laugh like that in a very long time. It doesn't matter that my life has been hellish since I came here; as long as Rosie's happy, then all the hardships are worth it.

I glance at the clothes I randomly picked and curse in my head. A pair of faded jeans with several holes that aren't a fashion statement and a T-shirt with a psychotic unicorn on it. *Shit.* I have to change.

Outside the bathroom has become too quiet, so it's no surprise when I walk in on Rosie and Toby in a lip-lock. At least they aren't on my bed. Rosie is sitting on my desk, and Toby is between her legs. Okay, not that much better.

I clear my throat, which prompts Toby to leap back as if Rosie electrified him.

"Are you ready?" Rosie asks, the poster child of innocence. Toby's face, on the other hand, is in flames.

"Almost. I need to change my T-shirt."

"Wait. Is that unicorn saying he's gonna shank some bitches with his horn?" Toby cracks a smile.

"Exactly why I need to change."

"No!" Rosie jumps from the desk. "You have to wear it."

She unzips her hoodie, revealing a tank top with a similar design. Her unicorn is floating lazily in a pool smoking a joint and drinking a beer.

"Rosie! What the hell? Where did you get that?"

"It was a gift from me." Toby looks sheepish. And then he reveals his own inappropriate T-shirt, two popular cartoon characters dressed as pimps.

I raise a brow. "Guys, I thought the party was at the boss's house."

Rosie giggles. "It's a fun T-shirt party, silly. I totally forgot to tell you. But it doesn't matter. Just make sure you keep that covered until the right time."

Wow. There are Idols out there who are fun?

"Okay, now I can't wait to meet the guy."

26
___

DAISY

When Toby takes the exit leading to the mountains instead of the beach, I let out a relieved breath. I haven't had the greatest experience in Saturn's Bay coastal line. The boss is named Gunther Silverstone, and he's an art dealer. Toby's father helps the Idol procure rare pieces for his galleries. This I learned from Rosie. She now knows more about Toby than I do, which makes me feel guilty in a way. He was my friend, yet I never bothered to truly get to know him. No, I was too occupied with four impossibly sexy and hateful Idols. Only now the hateful part isn't so true anymore.

The house—mansion, actually—is an hour away from school. It sits in the Sapphire Mountains on a piece of prime real estate. It has breathtaking views of the wineries all around and also the ocean from the other side, although it's a little far.

Wrought iron gates part when Toby's purple menace approaches the entrance. A man in a polo shirt and khaki pants is waiting in front of the house.

"Is that a valet?" Rosie asks.

"Yep. Welcome to the Idol sweet life."

The valet smirks when Toby hands him the key.

Toby twists his face into a glower. "I know she doesn't look like much, but if I find a scratch on her, you'll have to answer to your boss."

I trade a worried glance with Rosie. I've never heard Toby sound so snobbish before. There's a moment of silence before he and the valet burst out laughing. They then do the bro-hug thing—side hug, tap on the back—and turn to us.

"Rosie, Daisy, this is Stephan Silverstone, the prince of this palace."

My jaw drops. I look closely at him, but I don't sense any Idol vibe coming from him. How is that possible?

"Nice to meet you, ladies." He smiles broadly, showing perfect white teeth.

"You're not an Idol," Rosie blurts out.

Stephan glances quickly at Toby and then his smile turns into a smirk. "Are you sure?"

His power flares up like fireworks in the sky. He didn't become the sun like Bryce, but I sense his power flowing freely now.

"How did you do that?" I ask.

"Hide my Idol nature? It's easy with practice. In theory, all Idols can, but most choose not to."

"Why would you want to hide your powers?" I ask, but then I think about Mr. X, who does it daily so he can pretend to be a Norm.

"I don't enjoy seeing fear in the eyes of Norms, so I do it anytime I know I'll cross paths with them."

"I suppose that's considerate." If not deceiving as hell, but I kept that thought to myself.

Stephan turns to Toby. "It's good to see you, man. You've grown since the last time we hung out."

Toby's cheeks turn bright red. He throws a fleeting glance in

Rosie's direction. "Jeez, thanks, Stephan. Way to make me feel like a little kid."

Stephan catches Toby's reaction. He glances at Rosie, and then it's like a light bulb turns on above his head. "Oh, I see. I didn't mean to embarrass you in front of your girlfriend. Nice job, Toby. She's pretty."

Stephan switches his attention to me. "So, Daisy. Are you single?" He flashes me that bright smile again.

I'll admit, he's easy on the eyes. His straw blond hair is cut in the typical preppy boy style—a little long on top and short on the sides—and he's packing some serious muscles underneath his polo shirt. But I feel nothing, not even a faint fluttering in my chest. I think my heart is at capacity at the moment, filled with four boys already. They each have a hold on me and pull my strings in different ways.

"I'm not interested," I say.

"Ouch." Stephan places a hand over his chest and pretends to be offended. "Tell me how you really feel, why don't you?"

"Don't take it personally, Stephan. My sister would never date an Idol." Rosie looks meaningfully at me. She's obviously thinking about Bryce. Good thing she doesn't know about Rufio.

"It's okay. It was a long shot anyway." The guy laughs.

Man, it would be so much easier if I liked someone like him —that is, if he's being genuine. You never know with Idols. I haven't met one yet who doesn't have a secret agenda.

"We'd better go inside," Toby says.

"Yeah, sure. Dad isn't in yet, but Soren is around."

Stephan climbs into Purple Delight and drives away.

"Is he seriously working as a valet?" I ask.

"Yeah, Stephan and Soren, his younger brother, have to work to earn their money," Toby explains.

Once inside the house, Mr. Silverstone's profession is evident.

There are pieces of art everywhere, ranging in styles but displayed in a harmonic way. We don't linger in the grand foyer though, Toby steering us toward the back of the house where the pool area is.

There are a lot of people there but, oddly, no one our age.

"Uh, Toby?" I say.

"Yeah?"

"Where is the younger crowd?"

"Oh, we're it."

I frown, feeling a little out of place. Not that I was hoping to mingle with Idol assholes my age, but my idea of fun isn't exactly hanging out with adults.

"How old is Stephan?" Rosie asks.

"Twenty. He goes to college in Hawk City."

And just like that, my blood runs cold. What are the odds?

"Toby. You're finally here," a female voice says from behind us.

I turn to see who the newcomer is. Her ginger hair is a dead giveaway. She must be Toby's mother.

"Hey, Mom," he greets her. "I had to make a detour and pick up Daisy."

The woman's eyebrows arch. "Oh, Rosie's sister."

"Yup. That's me." I wave, and the sensation that I'm out of place increases.

A man approaches us. He has a mop of curly brown hair and wears thin wired glasses, which is sharply contrasting with the Snoopy T-shirt he has on.

"Dad, you aren't supposed to show your T-shirt yet," Toby says.

The man crinkles his forehead and then shrugs. "It was getting hot. Hi, I'm Simon Macintosh. Toby's dad."

We shake hands, and then Toby elbows my arm. "Talk to them," he whispers.

"I'm going to show Rosie the pool," he says louder for his parents' benefit, leaving me alone with them.

Great, Toby. Thanks a lot.

I smile tightly at his parents, and my sense of unease grows. I'm not sure why I'm nervous. They're not even Idols, after all.

"How do you like Gifted Academy, Daisy?" Mr. Macintosh asks.

"It's intense, but I'm loving the classes."

"I hope you're not getting into trouble like Toby did. I never liked the idea of him mingling with those Idol kids," the mother says.

"Well, Tori, you can't protect the kid forever," Mr. Macintosh cuts in. "He *will* eventually have to deal with the other kind of Idols."

"It's not so bad," I tell them. "Really. The incident with Renata was blown out of proportion. I don't even think she meant to break Toby's arm. That girl is not the sharpest tool in the shed, if you know what I mean. She probably didn't even realize she was hurting Toby."

Toby's mom scoffs. "Even worse. Those kids arc no better than savages. There's no discipline in that school. It's a jungle, and the students with the highest level of power make the rules."

Damn. Her assessment is spot-on. But I can't give up on Toby.

"Would you feel any better if I told you I'm under the protection of the four most powerful Idols in school?"

I'm such a little liar.

"No, that doesn't comfort me. *You* are protected, not my boy."

"Toby is my friend, and by extension, he's also protected."

"That makes sense," Mr. Macintosh chimes in. "Tori, I really think you should consider letting Toby stay. You know he wants to attend Prism City University. He can't get in if he doesn't graduate from a top institution."

Her expression becomes less tense. I think we're making progress.

"Let me think about it. I'd feel better if Principal Fallon also gave me some reassurance," she hedges.

"Oh, she will," I say. I'll make sure she tells Toby's mother everything she wants to hear. She owes me that much since she couldn't protect me at all.

The front door opens, but Toby's parents are blocking my view, so I don't know who's coming in. It's only when Mr. Macintosh turns to greet the man that I get an eyeful of him. Long blond hair, body built like a mountain, and a pair of intense silver eyes which are now riveted on me. My stomach bottoms out, and my heart skips a beat. I know his face, even if I only caught a glimpse of him for a fleeting moment. He's one of the five Idols who came in and fought with my parents' killers.

I'm shaking as I stand. I don't know if he's a friend or just a different enemy.

"Daisy, this is my boss, Gunther Silverstone," Mr. Macintosh says.

My tongue feels like lead in my mouth, and I can't breathe, much less speak.

"Hello, Daisy," Gunther greets me. "It's nice to finally meet you."

27

DAISY

"Hello," I manage to croak out.

"Are you enjoying the party?" he asks in a friendly way.

If I didn't already know what he's capable of, I wouldn't look his way twice. Like his son, he's also keeping his power contained. But I remember how he came into my childhood home, brandishing a sword made out of fire.

"I-I just got here. I should go look for Toby and Rosie. Excuse me."

I turn on my heels and bolt out of the house. It's not difficult to find them. They're on the other side of the pool, talking to the only other teenager there, a dirty-blond kid with shaggy hair and thick black-framed glasses.

Toby and Rosie glance at me once I join them.

"Daisy, I was just telling Soren about you. He goes to Gifted Academy's sister school in Hawk City," Toby says.

"Hi there. Can I borrow Toby and Rosie for a second?" I grab both of them by their forearms and drag them away without waiting for a reply.

I'm being rude and not exactly subtle, but my nerves are

getting the better of me. Once we're out of earshot, I release their arms.

"What's going on with you? You look as white as a ghost," Rosie says.

"Toby, what do you know about Mr. Silverstone?" I ask.

"Uh, what I already told you. He's an art dealer with galleries all over the country."

"But you never mentioned he was from Hawk City," I hiss.

"Because he's not," Toby replies in the same tone of voice. "What's the matter with you? You're acting weird."

I look over his shoulder and find Mr. Silverstone staring at us. His younger son, Soren, has just joined him at the upper deck. They trade a few words before Soren looks over his shoulder at us and then disappears inside the house.

What was that all about?

"What are you staring at?" Toby begins to turn, but I stop him.

"We need to leave. Now!"

"Why?" Toby's eyebrows meet his hairline.

"Daisy, you're freaking me out. Did Mr. Silverstone say anything that upset you?" Rosie asks.

Shit. They won't leave if I don't tell them something.

"Rosie, you don't remember, but the only reason we were able to escape the attack that killed our parents was due to another group of Idols who came in. Mr. Silverstone was among them."

"What?" Toby squeaks. "Impossible. He wouldn't hurt a fly."

"Well, you don't know your dad's boss as well as you thought you did."

Toby rubs his face, then finally pivots around. Mr. Silverstone is no longer there spying on us, but I'm sure he knows I recognized him.

"He saved you, didn't he?" Toby finally says.

"I suppose he did, but I don't know if he was one of the good guys or just another Idol after us."

"Have you ever stopped to consider that maybe he's—" Toby pauses and makes sure there's no one near us. "—a Knight?" he whispers.

Rosie's eyes become as round as saucers. My heart continues to beat at a rapid pace, but the fear that struck me earlier lessens.

"To be honest, I never dared to believe Knights were real," I say.

Toby looks me straight in the eye. "Me neither, but if there's one Idol that could be part of that rogue group, Mr. Silverstone would be the one."

I nibble on my lower lip while my mind is racing. Knights are supposed to be the protectors of Norms and low-level Fringes, but if they're real, they're criminals in the eyes of the law. Getting embroiled with them, even if by accident, could be lethal to Rosie and me.

It might be too late for that, Daisy. Remember the daggers you were gifted.

"I think we should go," Rosie says, sporting a fearful expression now.

"Okay. If that's what you want." Toby sounds disappointed. He doesn't understand that the memories Rosie and I have of that horrible night seven years ago have scarred us for life.

We head back to the house, finding the host talking with Toby's parents. They stop their conversation when we approach.

"We have to go home. Rosie isn't feeling well," Toby lies.

To his credit, my sister is looking ill. Poor thing. I wish I could erase some of her memories.

"Oh no. That's too bad," Mr. Silverstone says. "I hope it's nothing serious."

"It's probably just a cold," I say.

"Dude, leaving so soon?" Stephan joins us, no longer wearing his valet uniform. He's changed into swim trunks and nothing else. *Whoa, hello abs.*

"Yeah, Rosie is unwell," I reply.

"Too bad. I was hoping to get know you better." He grins like I'm some sort of prize he needs to win. In a way, he reminds me of Phoenix, but he's way less complex than my neighbor, who keeps popping in my head with his erotic visions.

Damn it. Now I'm thinking about the dream.

I snap my fingers with an exaggerated motion of my arm. "Darn it. I guess I shall remain a mystery to you."

His grin widens to a toothy smile as he walks toward me. He leans closer to my ear and whispers, "I don't think so." He continues toward the pool before I can come up with an answer.

My stomach coils tightly. I don't think his remark was merely innocent flirtation.

"Well, we'd better get going," Toby says.

He and Rosie walk to the door first. I say goodbye to his parents and thank Mr. Silverstone for inviting us. But just like his son, the Idol feels the need to leave me with a last comment.

"Say hello to Bryce for me, Daisy."

He walks away as if he hadn't said anything. Meanwhile, I'm frozen to the spot. It's not the fact that he mentioned Bryce but the tone of his voice that implies a hidden message.

"Daisy, are you coming?" Toby asks from the front door.

"Yeah."

***

IT'S BEEN twenty minutes since we left the Silverstone mansion, and no one has said a word. Once again, I'm doubting everything I know. Is it a mere coincidence that the Idol who saved Rosie and me employs the father of my closest friend in school? Or is Principal Fallon in cahoots with him, and she assigned Toby to be my guide because of his connection to Mr. Silverstone?

Fuck, I'm tired of being in the dark. I need answers.

"You're quiet," Toby says.

At first, I think he's talking to me, but I catch his glance at Rosie, who's looking out the window.

"Lots on my mind," she replies halfheartedly.

"I'm sorry about Mr. Silverstone. I had no idea he could be involved in something as dangerous as the Knights' organization."

"We don't know if he is indeed a Knight," I say.

"What else could he be, then?" Toby's worried gaze connects with mine in the rearview mirror.

"Many things," Rosie grits out, almost as if she's angry at Toby.

"Are you mad at me?" he asks her.

So he noticed it too.

"Of course Rosie isn't mad at you," I butt in. I'd hate for them to fight over something that isn't their fault.

"I don't know what I'm feeling. I thought Mr. Silverstone was different than the other Idols. I thought he was... peaceful."

There's another moment of silence, and I'm afraid we're about to go another long stretch of it when Rosie's phone starts to ring, reminding me that I need to buy a new phone too. Shit. I might have to ask Principal Fallon for an advance on my monthly allowance.

"Hello?" Rosie answers.

"Who is it?" I ask.

She lifts her hand in a sign to shush me, and after a moment, she gives me the phone.

"What?"

"It's Luigi looking for you."

With a frown, I take the device from Rosie's hand. Why would the cook of Poppy's Joint call Rosie's cell phone to look for me?

"Hey, Luigi. This is Daisy."

"Thank heavens I was able to track you down, girl. I've been calling your phone for hours."

"What happened?"

"It's Felicity. She was attacked last night."

My heart goes up my throat, only to crash back down like a rock. "What?"

"I don't have the details, girlie. Will you come to the hospital? She's at St. Joseph's."

"Yes, right away. Is she okay?"

"I don't know anything. The doctors won't give me an update because I'm not kin and they're asshole Fringes."

"Does Poppy know?"

I bet he could get information in his true identity as Mr. X.

Luigi sighs. "I haven't been able to reach Poppy either. He hasn't come by the diner in days."

Fuck. That can't be good.

"Hang tight, Luigi. I'll be right there."

I end the call and quickly tell Rosie and Toby the little I know.

"We can be at St. Joseph's in fifteen minutes," Toby says.

"So Luigi knows nothing?" Rosie asks, her face filled with the same fear I'm feeling.

I shake my head, dropping my chin. Tears prick my eyes while a heavy weight settles on my chest. It seems I can't catch a break. Felicity is one of my dearest friends, the sweetest woman I know.

"I can't imagine that someone would try to hurt her," Rosie echoes my thoughts.

"Me neither," I whisper.

28

RUFIO

I went to the treehouse last night because I couldn't handle being in the presence of the guys when my head wasn't right. *Daisy, Daisy, Daisy.* Constant in my head. I can't get rid of her or the feelings she evokes in me. I'm disgusted at myself for caring so much about her, for losing my mind when I fear something awful will happen to her. Years of brainwashing are not easy to erase. Norms are vile, worthless. That's the rhetoric drilled into us since we were babies.

But being in my hiding spot didn't help. No, she managed to crawl in here too. I shouldn't have fucked her when she came. Now every nook of the place is impregnated with her memory. No amount of Silver-voltage could make me relax, and forget sleeping.

I thought for one brief moment about going to Unearthly Desires, but I stomped on the idea almost immediately. I didn't want to see random women strip. I want to see Daisy—with or without her clothes.

The sun is up, and the birds are chirping, but my mood remains in a dark, starless night. I stare at the lightning-glass dagger in my hand. The weapon that can kill Idols. What makes it so special? Is it poisonous once it breaks skin, or is there something else that grants its deadly nature to us?

Guilt settled in my chest. I should never have kept the dagger. If Daisy had the weapon on her when Drusilla showed up, maybe she wouldn't have been drugged.

My sentiment is illogical, of course. If Daisy had struck Drusilla with the dagger, she would have been sentenced to death.

If someone is going to kill Drusilla, that someone will be me.

The thought comes to my mind unbidden. Regardless, it's a truth that can't be denied. I will condemn myself to save Daisy, the Norm who snuck into my cold heart. Once again, I'm reminded of Morpheus's ominous words. Funny enough, even he's willing to sacrifice himself for her now. Why does she have a hold over us like that?

Fury swirls in the pit of my stomach, and as usual the sentiment comes with a surge of my powers. I curl my fingers tighter around the dagger's handle and the dark veins appear, my fingers tingling. The dagger or at least its handle should have disintegrated, but the object remains intact.

Son of a bitch. This is indeed an Idol-killing weapon.

I drop the dagger to the floor as if it could kill me by a mere touch. It's a ridiculous notion since I've been handling it without protection the whole time.

Fuck. I'm truly losing it.

Maybe it's best if I return the dagger to its owner. Even knowing it's dangerous for Daisy to keep it, I can't bear the thought of letting her wander campus unprotected. We can't shadow her 24-7.

And it's all thanks to you, Rufio. You set Drusilla on Daisy, and now you can't control the bitch.

With a roar, I kick the small table in front of me, sending it flying across the room. It breaks through the wall, leaving a gaping hole behind. Great. The guys will love my newest act of destruction.

I'd better get going before I level the entire house to the ground.

Feeling like a complete fool now, I wrap the dagger in a sweatshirt someone left behind. I'm probably being paranoid, but if this shit can't be destroyed by me, then it must be handled with care.

When I return to the apartment, I find Bryce and Morpheus poring over Daisy's father's diary once again.

"Where the hell have you been?" Bryce asks.

"In the treehouse." I set the dagger on the kitchen counter. "Where's Phoenix?"

"He was gone before we were up," Morpheus replies.

"You're looking a little better," I say.

"I don't feel better," he grumbles, then takes a sip of his beverage—hot tea would be my guess.

I stare at the bundle in front of me and debate what to do.

"You know the dagger I found on Daisy?" I start.

"Yeah." Bryce looks up with interest.

"I couldn't destroy it."

I turn to them, and sure as shit, both are staring wide-eyed at me.

"You're joking," Bryce breathes.

"Nope. Not even the handle cracked. This is indeed the ulti-mate weapon against us."

"Do you think the Knights are producing them?" Morpheus asks.

"I'm not sure. If the material is dangerous to us, it's dangerous to them. Wouldn't handling it and molding it into a weapon be unwise?" Bryce poses the question that was on my mind.

"Then they have Norms working for them. Maybe Daisy's

father was one of those Norms," I say, and immediately my brother's posture changes.

"You aren't still holding a grudge against Daisy because of her father, are you?" I ask.

He turns away and doesn't answer my question.

"It's not the diary that's making Bryce act like an asshole to Daisy. It's my vision," Morpheus says.

"Fuck off, Morpheus," Bryce grits out, standing up suddenly.

Bryce and Daisy's infinity band vision. He's upset about that while, when I think about it, all I feel is jealousy. I'm jealous that my brother is destined to form an eternal bond with the girl we shared.

"Maybe you won't form any bond with her," I say.

Morpheus gives me a droll look. "When have my visions never come to pass?"

"Shut up, you two," Bryce growls. "And you're both wrong about why I'm pissed."

"Care to enlighten us?" I raise an eyebrow.

Bryce turns to face us sporting the most pitiful expression I've ever seen on anyone. He looks like a dog without a bone. "I'm angry at myself. I messed things up with Daisy, and I don't know how to fix it."

My jaw slackens, and I catch a similar reaction from Morpheus. He leans forward and grabs the diary from the coffee table. "How about if you return this to her?"

"I was planning to, but I don't think that's going to cut it. I kicked her out while she was ill. She could have died because of me. That's inexcusable."

Hearing the agony in my brother's tone makes one thing excruciatingly clear to me: Bryce is in love with Daisy. Hell, I don't know how I feel about that. It's one thing for us to compete for her attention when it's meaningless fun. But Daisy hasn't been meaningless fun for a while. I'm not sure if she ever was. The strange emotion swirling in my chest, the crushing pain I wish I could eradicate, tells me I might also be in—no! I can't allow myself to even think that. Daisy is an obsession. Nothing more.

I jump off the couch and head for the door. What I need is to find a distraction.

"Where are you going?" Morpheus asks.

"Out."

It seems I have to return to my old habits if I'm to evict Daisy from my mind. Unearthly Desires it is.

29
____

DAISY

With my heart in my throat, I stride across the linoleum floor, ignoring the strong smell of ammonia and other nasty odors I don't want to think about. The nurse behind the desk is on the phone, and she totally pretends she doesn't see me. That would have been fine if the call wasn't personal.

"Excuse me. I need to know where Felicity Thoms is."

With a roll of her eyes, the nurse glowers at me. "Can't you see that I'm busy?"

She returns her attention to whoever's on the other side of the line.

Fucking bitch.

I yank the phone cord and disconnect the handle.

"Hey, what the he—"

I smack my palms flat on the counter and lean forward. "Listen, Nurse Whatever, I don't have time to listen to you gossip about who you think is going to win on a stupid TV reality show. Do your damn job and tell me where Felicity Thoms is. Now!"

The woman, who is a large Fringe who could totally kick

my ass, leans back and widens her eyes in fear. I must be projecting a pretty strong crazy vibe. Crazy people, even Norms, are dangerous.

"She's in room 108, but only kin is—"

"We're her family," I grit out, then head in the direction I believe the rooms are. I just want to get the hell out of the reception area before the nurse wises up and realizes she's dealing with an ordinary puny Norm.

At a crossroads, I immediately veer right.

"Yo, Daisy. I think it's this way." Toby points at the sign with the room numbers.

Ah shit. Rage is making me blind. I turn around and continue down the hallway in the right direction. The only reason I'm not sprinting is because I don't want to draw attention to us.

"That was some serious scary technique you used there," Toby says. "And that nurse was a Fringe."

"I could have taken her," I lie.

We find Felicity's room easily enough. Before I go in, I pull the medical chart from the plastic sleeve mounted on the wall next to her door. Scanning through the documents quickly, my horror increases. Felicity sustained multiple fractures everywhere. Oh my God.

"Daisy?" a masculine voice says from behind me.

"Luigi." I walk over to him, giving him a hug. "Tell me everything you know."

Easing off the embrace, I catch his grim expression. "I don't know much, only what the cops told me after they took her statement. She went out in Emelton, a different bar than the one we celebrated her birthday at. When she was walking back to her car, she was jumped by a motorcycle gang. They were Fringes."

I clamp my jaw shut while I curl my hands into fists, digging my nails into my palms. Fringes. Fucking Fringes. We spend so much time worrying about Idols that sometimes we forget the most dangerous threats to us are the ones lower on the power level.

"I'm going in," I say. "I have to know what happened from her mouth."

"She might be sleeping. I overheard the nurses saying they had given her a sedative."

"I'll wait until she's up, then. But you should go home now, Luigi. You look exhausted."

He runs his hand over his shaved head. "I'm pretty beat. I'll try to catch a few hours of sleep before I come back. I'll keep trying to reach Poppy too. He needs to know what happened to Felicity."

"Yeah, you do that."

Luigi says goodbye and walks away with heavy steps and head hanging low. Rosie and Toby are hanging a little away from me, clutching to each other.

"Are you going in now?" Rosie asks.

"Yeah, I have to."

"We'll wait for you here, then," Toby says, then steers Rosie to the chairs at the end of the corridor.

Facing Felicity's door, I take a steadying breath, and then I enter.

It's dim in the room. The shades are shut, so the only light is from the lamp on the nightstand. But there's still enough illumination for me to see the bruises on Felicity's face, the bandage around her forehead, and her broken arm.

My heart breaks at the sight. *What did those bastards do to you, Fefe?*

With soft steps, I approach her bed. My throat closes up, and a sob escapes my lips before I can contain it. Not only did the bastards beat the shit out of her, they also branded their mark on her chest. I can see the burn scar in the shape of a skull with wings right below her sternum.

Almost immediately, the heartache changes into pure rage. It's a firestorm brewing in the pit of my stomach. The need to obliterate those responsible for Felicity's current state is almost overwhelming. I have murder on my mind, and I don't feel one bit bad about it.

Felicity's eyelids tremble before she slowly peels them open. At first, she doesn't seem to be able to focus on anything until she turns her face to me.

"Daisy?" Her voice is raspy.

I cover her hand with mine. "Yeah, Fefe. It's me. How are you feeling?"

"Like I was hit by an eighteen-wheeler. Everything hurts."

"I thought they gave you painkillers."

"They did, but it's shit."

"What happened?"

Felicity's eyebrows scrunch together as she closes her eyes for a brief second.

"I finally picked the wrong guy," she murmurs.

"What do you mean?"

"I was seeing this biker. I met him online. Last night he invited me to hang out at this bar in Emelton that's popular among motorcycle gangs. I didn't know that until I got there. I'm not that stupid." She laughs humorlessly. "Anyway, I get there and pretty quickly I realize the asshole was planning to share me with his gang members. So I took off. That was when they jumped me and did this."

"What's the name of their gang?" I ask.

She looks pointedly at me. "Why do you want to know, Daisy? I didn't even tell the cops that."

"Why not?"

"You don't understand how those criminals operate. You tell on them, then your life is forfeit, as well as the lives of your friends. They hold grudges like no other."

"They need to pay for what they did to you," I say with enough emphasis that Felicity flinches.

"Just let it go, Daisy. It's for the best." She looks away.

My eyes are brimming with unshed tears, but they're the angry kind. I'm so frustrated I could scream. It's bad enough that we can't do anything to punish Idols when they hurt us. But Fringes too? Hell to the fucking no.

"Tell me at least the name of the bar you went to," I say.

"Who do you take me for, kid? I know you. You're fearless. God, you go to that school filled with Idols without breaking a sweat. I'm not telling you anything."

"But, Fefe—"

"No buts, Daisy. I won't have you risking your life to avenge me. You're not an Idol. You can't fight this battle and win."

I let go of her hand and step back, afraid she'll be able to sense I'm shaking.

"Good morni—oh, I didn't know you had a visitor," a masculine voice says from the door.

"Hi, Dr. Ackerman," Felicity says with a little extra pep to her tone. It's easy to see why. The doctor is cute. Unfortunately, he's a Fringe too.

"I'm Daisy, Felicity's sister. How is she, Doc?" I ask.

The doctor frowns, then peers at Felicity. "I didn't know you had a sister."

"Half sister," Felicity jumps in. "She lives out of town."

"Ah, well. Felicity had a concussion we're keeping an eye on, a broken arm, broken nose, and several lacerations on her face, but luckily no internal bleeding."

"Isn't it nuts how he recites all that as if he's reading a grocery list?" Felicity quips.

"Yeah, nuts," I reply with way less enthusiasm. "When can I take my sister home?"

"Oh, I'd like to keep her for observation for a few more days."

A quick glance at my friend tells me she's not minding that at all. Only Felicity could see the positive in this situation. I wish I could simply brush her attack aside and forget all about it, but I can't. I'm done with the people I love getting killed or hurt.

"Fefe, I'm going to run by your house and grab some clothes and other necessities. I'll be back later." I pat her hand.

"Okay, honey."

I walk out of the room, leaving Felicity alone with her doctor. Toby and Rosie rise when they see me, and we meet halfway in the corridor.

"How is she?" Rosie asks.

"A mess of bruises and a couple breaks, but she's in good spirits."

"Really? And what about the attack? Did she say anything about that?" Toby crosses his arms.

"Not enough. Only that she went to a shady bar in Emelton popular among the MC gang crowd. She didn't give me a name."

"Why would you want the name?" Rosie narrows her eyes.

"No reason." I look away.

"Daisy, please let the police handle this," Rosie pleads.

I don't want Rosie to worry, so I force my face into a neutral expression and say, "Of course. I'm not crazy, Rosie."

But in reality I am. There's no chance in hell I'm going to let those motherfuckers get away with hurting my friend. Fringes or not, they *will* pay.

30

DAISY

There can't be that many bars in Emelton that cater to the criminal underbelly of Saturn's Bay. I'm not too concerned about that. I'm thirsty for revenge, but I know my limitations. There is one person who can help me though. He should be as invested in giving those Fringes the punishment they deserve as me. Felicity has worked at Poppy's Joint for years; she must mean something to Mr. X.

But to speak to Mr. X, I have to wait until Unearthly Desires opens. And I need my own mode of transportation. So when we drop by Felicity's apartment, I convince Toby and Rosie to enjoy the rest of their day. It takes a lot of cajoling on my part to get rid of them. Shit, I practically had to pimp my baby sister to Toby.

Whatever. I'm not going to feel guilty about that. Besides, they're both responsible. Their idea of a hot date probably includes a movie-and-pizza combo. Unlike me, who slept with two different guys in a matter of days. I'm not going to think about that either.

It doesn't take long for me to pack an overnight bag for Felicity and return to the hospital in her car. I'm glad she's asleep when I arrive, because pretending I'm okay with her predicament is fucking hard.

I still have a lot of time to kill, so I drive by Poppy's Joint, but the elusive owner is still MIA. He's never stayed away too long from the diner, and his absence is beginning to worry me. There's nothing left for me to do but drive to Unearthly Desires.

When I arrive, I'm surprised to see the place is already open. I've always assumed strip bars' hours of operation were at nighttime, but I guess perverts need their entertainment at all hours of the day. I circle around the building and park in the back. It's my luck that the same asshole Fringe is manning the back door. Memories of my first time here come to the forefront of my mind. I had been desperate then, and afraid. I'm no longer feeling those weakening emotions, but I'm just as determined to get in.

Taking a deep breath, I exit the car and march toward the mountain of a bully.

He holds up a hand. "Where do you think you're goi—wait a second. I remember you."

"I need to see Mr. X," I say.

"You're the brat who came here a few weeks ago and had an attitude."

"If you remember me, then move out of the way."

His lips turn into a perverted grin. "Oh no, sugar. You're not escaping so easily today. I believe you still owe me payment."

He makes a motion to grab my arm, but quick as a whip, I move out of the way and extend my leg so the big asshole trips and falls on his knees.

"You sneaky little bitch." He begins to rise, his face contorted in rage.

Without stopping to think, I kick his ugly mug. I hear a crunch followed by his bellowing scream. Fuck. I think I broke his nose. How did I do that? I didn't realize I was that strong.

He finally gets up, covering his bloody nose with one hand. I have no idea what kind of gift he possesses, but his beefy fists alone could do serious damage to me. I backpedal until my butt hits the wall. I know I won't have time to slip through the door or run around him.

But then I remember the old pepper spray I have in my bag. It's a safe bet it doesn't work on Idols, so I ended up forgetting I had it. Without breaking eye contact with the Fringe, I shove my hand inside my purse and curl my fingers around the canister.

With a roar, the jackass charges, ready to punch my face. I spray the entire contents of the canister in his eyes. He steps back, rubbing his eyes and yelling like a banshee. I don't waste any time, yanking the door open and entering the dark hallway beyond. Then I lock it and take off into a run toward Mr. X's office, praying he's there. If he isn't, I'm truly fucked. A bolted door won't keep the bouncer out for long, considering he can just walk around the building and use the main entrance.

But my luck has definitely run out. Mr. X is not in his office. Damn it. Without missing a beat, I head for the club. The stage is currently occupied by a girl wearing the same blonde wig I did on my debut night. I only spare her one fleeting glance before my eyes dart around the dark area, searching for Mr. X.

At this hour, the club is relatively empty, so it's easy for me to see he isn't here.

A rough hand curls around my forearm, making my heart leapfrog to my throat. The bouncer found me.

"What the hell are you doing here?" He turns me around, but it's Rufio staring daggers at me. His hair is messy as if he's been ripping at it, and his cheeks are flushed.

"I-I—"

"You! You aren't escaping now, whore!" the bouncer bellows from somewhere behind me.

Rufio looks over my shoulder and, in the blink of an eye, steps in front of me.

"Stop right there, asshole," he commands.

"She's an intruder." The bouncer sneers at me. He's brought reinforcements, another big guy with ill intentions.

"She's with me. Now back off." Rufio takes a menacing step toward them.

The second bouncer's aggressive stance buckles, and he glances warily at his coworker. That's right, the clientele is king in his place. Also, only an idiot would pick a fight with Rufio. I guess I'm one since I've done it several times.

"She broke my nose!" the first bouncer replies indignantly.

"I don't fucking care. Get. Lost," Rufio grits out, lifting his hand in a menacing way. Dark veins have covered his palm, and I sense an ominous energy concentrating there.

That display of power finally deflates the Fringe's bravado. He sends one more death glare in my direction before stalking away.

"Thank—"

Rufio turns to me. "Don't thank me yet. What are you doing here? Missing the stage already?"

His gaze is hard, and there's venom in his tone. All his animosity does is fuel my anger.

"What I'm doing here is none of your business!" I shout, regretting it immediately. Not because I'm afraid of Rufio but because now everyone is staring at us. Curious patrons give me once-over glances, making my skin crawl.

I turn around with every intention to get out of here when Rufio grabs my arm again and steers me toward the back of the club. My instinct is to fight, but I can't give these people more reason to pay attention to us.

Rufio doesn't stop until he takes me to Mr. X's office and closes the door. Finally alone, I yank my arm from his grasp and massage the sore spot.

"What the hell!" I yell.

"Did you seriously break that bouncer's nose?" Rufio ignores my outburst.

"Yes. He wouldn't let me in."

"How?" He stares intently at me.

"With a kick to his face."

His eyebrows arch for a second before they furrow together. With large steps, he approaches, stopping mere inches from me. I tilt my head to keep glaring at him.

"Why did you come here?" he asks again.

"I had business with Mr. X. Why did you?"

As I pose the question, a sliver of jealousy pierces my chest. I shouldn't care about what Rufio does in his spare time, or who he fucks for that matter. So he likes to screw strippers. Not my problem.

"I needed to get you out of my head. You're here all the damn time"—he taps the side of his forehead—"and it's distracting."

I suck in a breath, not expecting that answer.

Watching me with eyes filled with bad intentions—*the best kind*—he runs his hand over my cheek, caressing my lips with his thumb.

"But you're determined to follow me everywhere, so fuck it," he says, a breath away from my face.

He brings his lips to mine, searing my mouth with a passionate kiss that changes the emotion in my chest into a different kind of fury. Violent flames lick my skin, sending my body ablaze. I want to melt into his arms, meld myself to him. It would be easy to succumb to this raw need that's clouding my judgment, but somehow, I'm still in possession of my faculties. With much effort, I break the kiss and push Rufio back.

"We can't do this," I say without a lot of conviction.

"Why not?" He keeps his gaze trained on my mouth.

"Because I have to put my selfish needs aside for once."

He lifts his eyes to mine. "You lost me."

I pull my hair back, staring at Rufio's chest now because it's way less distracting than his face. "My friend Felicity was attacked by a Fringe gang."

The revelation takes more out of me than I expected. I'm not sure if it's because I'm telling Rufio, a cruel boy who couldn't possibly relate to my pain, or if it's something else.

"Is she okay?" he asks after a moment.

Surprised by his question, I look into his eyes. "She's in bad shape, but she'll recover. It doesn't matter though. Those fuckers need to pay for what they did. That's why I came here, to ask for Mr. X's help."

Rufio's eyes flash with a different emotion now. I can't decipher what it means.

"You could have asked me."

"Why would I ask you to avenge my Norm friend? You hate our kind."

"I don't hate *you*."

I open my mouth to call him out on his BS, but he adds, "Anymore."

"Because I slept with you." I hug my middle.

"No. And don't ask me the reason. But I'm here, willing to avenge your friend. So how badly do you want to destroy those motherfuckers?"

"Very badly. I want them gone." I lift my chin higher. I just voiced out loud that I want to kill those men, and I don't feel an ounce of remorse.

The corners of Rufio's lips twist into a cruel smile. "Obliterating things is my specialty. Who are the culprits?"

"All I know is it was a motorcycle gang that has a flying skull symbol." I close my eyes for a brief second. "They branded her chest with it."

When I meet Rufio's gaze again, his blue eyes are electric, and small dark veins have spread through his cheeks. That's the sign of his terrible power. He's destruction, pure and simple.

"Where did the attack happen?" he asks in a tight voice filled with danger.

"Outside a shady bar in Emelton. It's popular among motorcycle gangs."

Rufio squints a fraction, then pulls his phone out.

"Who are you calling?"

"No one. I'm looking online."

I scoff. "You can't possibly find out who those men are by doing a simple search."

Rufio smirks and shows me his phone. "Are you sure about that? Does the symbol you saw on your friend match this one?"

My eyes widen. "Fuck. It does."

Rufio's grin turns into a chilling smile. "All right, then. I have an address. I can drop you off at the diner on my way."

"You're not going there by yourself."

He gives me a droll look. "Daisy, I can handle a few measly Fringes."

"I know you can. But I'm coming with you, and don't give me that look. Felicity is *my* friend. I want to be there when the assholes who hurt her get their dues."

Rufio doesn't say a word for a couple of beats, just stares at me in his intense way.

Finally he says, "You would make an excellent Idol, Daisy."

31

RUFIO

Damn my fucking libido to hell. I've been sporting a boner since I kissed Daisy in Unearthly Desires. I didn't think I could obsess more about her until I discovered her thirst for revenge. She's ruthless, brave, loyal. I meant what I said that she would make an excellent Idol.

But she's only a Norm, so whatever is going on between us won't end well. Idols and Norms aren't fated to last. No wonder Bryce is losing his mind over Morpheus's vision. If Bryce could care that much for Daisy that he'd form an infinity band with her, it means he's going to break hard when she's no longer here.

A heaviness settles in my chest when I imagine a day when Daisy isn't with us. This isn't normal. A fuck, no matter how great it is, shouldn't get me all sentimental and depressed.

Don't think about Daisy dying, Rufio. Think about the destruction and pain you're about to unleash.

The thought manages to cheer me up a little. Only a demented person like me could get happy about the prospect of killing. Well, they're criminals; no loss there.

Shit. I think I grew a conscience too.

I peel my eyes off the road to look at Daisy. Her jaw is set hard, and her brows are furrowed. She's determined to see this through. It's easy to see that she'll walk through fire to protect her loved ones, no matter the consequences to herself. I used to loathe people like her—martyrs, selfless bastards who put the needs of others above their own. The opposite of me. Not anymore. Daisy has changed everything.

The sun is just beginning to set, and the hole-in-the-wall bar is slowly beginning to fill. The bikers come in groups of four or five, all wearing different symbols on their jackets. I know little about the way of life of motorcycle clubs, but one detail I know for sure—they love their precious bikes.

I parked across the street to scope out the place first. I don't have Morpheus's super-enhanced senses, but I can gauge someone's level of power from a distance. And every single person who entered the bar is a low-level Fringe. So they're truly scum.

With a grin, I turn to Daisy. "Should I start by turning their bikes into dust?"

"Can you do that from here?" She rounds her pretty eyes.

"Sure can."

She switches her attention to the building. "Maybe we should take care of Felicity's attackers first. Then you can do whatever you want with those bikes."

"I know you want to see this through yourself, but I want you to wait for me in the car."

"I said I was coming with you," she grits out, ready to fight me on this.

"I know what I can do, Daisy, but that crowd is rough, and they're also carrying guns. Using my gift requires a little bit of concentration. That will leave you unprotected for a moment. I can't take that risk."

Her stubborn gaze doesn't release mine. I'm about to do something I've never done before. Plead.

I cup her face and lean in. "Wait for me here, *please*."

She nibbles on her lower lip and averts her gaze. It takes a paramount effort not to turn her face back to mine so I can savor her lips again.

"Okay," she says in a voice so soft, I almost don't hear it.

I let out a relieved breath. Now that Daisy has made the right choice to stay out of the way, I feel a thousand times better. I wasn't lying about her safety, but I have another reason to not want her around. I'm about to release the monster. Until now, she's only seen glimpses of it, and I want to keep it that way.

Another group of bikers approaches the building and parks right in front of it, a spot that was reserved for the VIPs, I guess. And they're wearing the symbol Daisy saw branded on her friend.

"It's them," she says.

Six of them. All Fringes, but they're more powerful than any of the other vermin who entered the establishment. It doesn't matter. I can handle all of them with my eyes closed.

With my hand on the door handle, I say, "I'll be right back."

I sprint across the street, and as I'm walking between two motorcycles, I can't help gliding my fingers through their bodies. They're nothing but piles of dust by the time I reach the curb. *Oops.*

Once inside the bar, I'm assaulted by the most awful combination of odors: beer, sweat, and BO. The guys sitting closest to the door stop their conversation to glance in my direction. I can immediately sense their tension. *That's right, bitches. You should fear me.* But those assholes are not the ones I'm looking for.

I stride with confidence toward the bar. The bartender stops polishing the counter to watch me with suspicion.

"We don't cater to your kind here," he says.

"Don't worry. I'm not here for you."

"And who are you looking for, heh, preppy boy?" A tall man sporting a Mohawk and ugly-ass nose ring approaches me.

He's one of the gang members who hurt Daisy's friend.

"As a matter of fact, I'm looking for you." I grab the man by the throat and crush his windpipe. I could have easily turned him into nothing, but that wouldn't be that much fun to me.

He clutches my hand, trying to pry free from my hold.

"So you thought it was fun to beat up a puny Norm, huh?" I ask.

The hairs on my neck stand on end, announcing the approach of more enemies. I turn around as I slowly begin to disintegrate the asshole's throat. He's gone by the time I face the crowd, and my stomach coils tightly. The five other members of the gang have formed a wall, blocking the exit. But that's not what's making me fucking anxious now. They have Daisy with them. There's a gash on her forehead, and blood has dripped down.

"Let her go," I grit out while the fury of the gods runs through my body.

"You just killed one of our own. I say we need to get even," the man holding her by the arm says before pressing a knife against her throat.

I lock gazes with Daisy, finding no fear in her eyes. It's almost as if she's telling me to do my worst. I focus on the knife at her throat, willing it to fly out of the Fringe's hand, but it won't budge.

What the hell?

I can't send a destructive wave his way because it'll hit Daisy too. Fuck.

"What's the matter, boy? Can't use your Idol powers on me?" The man cackles.

What happens next has my jaw dropping to the floor. Faster than I can blink, Daisy pulls the dagger away from her throat and bites his wrist. The Fringe lets out a roar before throwing her against the table nearby. She hits the surface hard and slides down to the floor.

My heart constricts painfully in my chest, but I can't run to help Daisy yet. With her out of the way, I unleash my power at the gangster, but instead of turning to dust, he remains standing. No scratch, no nothing. Impossible.

"That's right, fucker. You can't touch me." With a movement of his arm, he sends a gust of wind my way.

It would knock an ordinary man down, but I'm not a Norm. I'm a fucking Idol. I grab the table at my side and hurl it at him with all my strength. He tries to change its course, but he's not strong enough, and the piece of furniture hits him square in the chest. He goes down with a loud bang.

A sense of satisfaction, albeit small, runs through me. But Daisy's scream cuts the emotion like a knife. I whirl around to see that one of the gang members has her by the hair. From the corner of my eye, I catch another attacker coming at me. I stop him midleap, making him explode in a shower of dust.

So only the leader is immune to my gift. Good to know.

I turn two more assholes into dust when a sharp pain in my back sends me down on my knees, howling.

"Rufio!" Daisy yells, but the world around me is spinning out of control, and I can't pinpoint where she's coming from.

Bracing myself on a chair nearby, I get back on my feet.

"Behind you," Daisy warns.

I turn just in time to block another jab at my back. The leader of the gang has something sharp in his hand, a dagger that looks very similar to the one Daisy had. Fuck me. It's a lightning-glass weapon.

My muscles strain as I attempt to keep the pointy end from my eye. This asshole shouldn't be able to best me in a muscle fight, which means the stab served to diminish my power somehow.

Someone howls in pain behind me, but the only important thing is that it wasn't Daisy's scream. In another second, my arms are going to give out, and the Fringe knows it. He smiles victoriously, but then his eyes become rounder and his hold on me slackens. Spewing blood from his mouth, he staggers back and drops his gaze to the rod sticking out of his chest.

He finally drops to the floor into a heap of useless meat, revealing Daisy behind him, breathing hard with a manic glint in her eyes.

But the fight is far from over. Two more criminals are coming for us.

"Duck, Daisy!" I yell.

She drops into a crouch, and I slam the Fringe behind her. He doesn't pulverize on the spot, but he drops like a fly. I'm out of juice, so I had to resort to a good old-fashioned punch to get rid of the last guy standing.

My breathing is coming out in spurts, and my vision is still not a hundred percent. But I can see Daisy as clear as day as she unfurls from her crouch. Her eyes connect with mine for a brief second before she turns her attention to the man she killed. The motherfucker is still holding his damn dagger.

"Go ahead, take it," I say, guessing she's staring at the weapon as well.

Bending forward, she pries the object from his hand, still caked in my blood. She wipes it clean against his leather jacket and then stands up. I amble toward her, trying to ignore the pain in my shoulder.

"You're hurt," she says.

"So are you." I touch the blood smeared on her forehead.

"Just a scratch. We need to get you help." She hooks her arm with mine and guides me toward the exit.

I never thought I would be in a situation where I'd lean on a Norm, but here I am. The front of the bar cleared out. There are only a few bikes left, probably the ones belonging to the gang Daisy and I slew. But when we cross the street, I begin to get a picture of what happened to Daisy. The passenger window is smashed, and the door is ajar.

"They came out of nowhere," she says, guessing where my thoughts are. "I'm sorry."

"Why are you apologizing?"

"You're hurt because of me." She opens the back door, but I dig my foot into the ground.

"I can drive."

"No you can't. He got you good with that dagger, and we don't know the extent of your wound."

I peer into her eyes, and the electric spark in them turns me to flames. Forgetting for a moment where we are, as well as the burning pain on my shoulder, I pull her to me and crush my lips against hers. My tongue invades her mouth savagely, without mercy. Daisy grabs the front of my T-shirt, curling her fingers around the soft fabric.

There's so much urgency and need in this kiss that I wish I could teletransport us to a different place.

She eases off and breathlessly whispers, "Get in the car."

32

DAISY

I'm still riding on adrenaline, but there's also something else making my body tremble. The kiss Rufio just stole from me. I wasn't expecting it, but I sure as hell regret ending it so soon. My heart is beating a staccato rhythm, and my knuckles are white from gripping the steering wheel too tight.

"Where should I go?" I ask.

"Just take me back home," Rufio groans, his voice laced with pain.

"No way. You need medical attention. Which hospital caters to Idols?"

We're on the highway, at least half an hour from school. It's late, so the nurse is probably gone already. I wish I remembered the way to her house.

"Daisy, you need to pull over," Rufio says.

"Why? Are you going to be sick?"

"Just pull over, please."

There he goes again using that word. I don't think he's ever said it before, at least not to a Norm.

I turn on the blinker and park the car on the side of the

highway. The road is completely dark in this area; the only faint glow is coming from streetlights that are too far apart to do any good. To make sure we're not rear-ended, I turn on the emergency lights.

When Rufio doesn't make a motion to get out, I unbuckle my seat belt and make my way to his side.

"Talk to m—"

He cups my face and kisses me again with just as much ardor as before. His tongue against mine works like a spark, starting the fire in the pit of my stomach. There's still adrenaline coursing through my veins, and it mixes with the sudden desire in an explosive way.

"What are you doing? You're hurt," I whisper between feverish kisses.

"It's nothing. Just a flesh wound."

I don't know if I should believe him, but I can't stop what's happening now. The raw yearning takes over my senses, and before I know it, I'm unzipping Rufio's pants and straddling him. He brings his hands to my ass and squeezes it.

"Fuck, why are you wearing jeans today?" he says against my mouth.

"I didn't think I'd need to grant anyone easy access to my panties."

His lips abandon mine to leave a scorching trail down my neck.

"Shit. You're wearing way too many clothes," he murmurs.

"You should be thankful for them. It protected me from the glass when they broke your window."

Rufio tenses suddenly, then grabs a fistful of my hair, pulling me back and staring hard at me. "Don't remind me of what those assholes did to you. I wish I could have obliterated them all."

"But you did."

"No, not the main guy, but...." Rufio pauses, sweeping his

tongue into my mouth for a glorious, hot kiss. "Seeing you kicking ass was hot as hell."

His hand finds its way inside my T-shirt, and I can tell he's a moment way from ripping it in two.

"Wait," I say.

I take my sweatshirt off, and Rufio's gaze immediately zeroes in on the T-shirt's design. "You're wearing a unicorn T-shirt."

"A savage-as-fuck unicorn."

He gives me a crooked smile. "I love how filthy your mouth is." He kisses me again, then helps me out of my top and bra. When he captures my nipple with his mouth, I think I'm going to combust on the spot. I accidently touch his wound, and Rufio hisses. *Crap!*

"We shouldn't be doing this. You're hurt," I remind him.

"And you're the only medicine I need."

Common sense is telling me this is a terrible idea, but hell, we almost died. I'm craving this connection. I need his touch like I need air to breathe.

While Rufio is busy playing with my boobs, I slip my hand inside his boxers, curling my fingers around his cock. He's so hard already that I think I could send him over the edge without much effort. Using my thumb, I spread precum over the head, which only makes Rufio suck my nipple harder.

I gasp out loud, and in retribution, I run my hand up and down his shaft.

With a groan, Rufio curls his fingers tighter around my hair and yanks hard until it causes a little pain.

"I can't... I need more," I whisper.

He pivots me around, laying me flat on the seat. With eager hands, he peels off my jeans and underwear, then spreads my legs as far as the tight space allows.

"You're so beautiful." He slides his hands up my legs. "And strong." His fingers caress the insides of my thighs. "And fearless." He swipes his thumb over my clit, making my hips buckle. "Easy, darling."

He keeps playing, first applying pressure to my bundle of nerves, then sliding a finger inside of me.

"Are you happy now?" he asks as he inserts another finger.

"About... what?" I close my eyes and let out a moan.

"Killing those motherfuckers."

My eyes fly open and I lock gazes with him. "Yes." My voice is hard now, and it somehow ignites a spark in Rufio's gaze.

He pulls his hand away and retrieves a condom from his pocket. Wrapped tight, he positions himself between my legs, bracing his forearms on the leather seat so as not to crush me. But I catch the flinch. His shoulder is bothering him more than he wants to let me know.

"Rufio, you're not okay."

"I will be in a moment." He lowers his mouth to mine, cutting off my next argument, and at the same time, he slides inside of me.

Then I get lost in the moment, in the feel of him. I'm aware of every tiny sensation he provokes with his tongue, with his thrusts. I slide my hands underneath his shirt, flattening my palms against his lower back. Then I grab his ass and silently urge him to go faster. This is not the time for words. Not telling, only showing. And I try to show him with my caresses how glad I am that he allowed me to exact my revenge without judgment, without hesitation.

The orgasm hits me in the precise moment the memory of me skewering that Fringe comes to the forefront of my mind. I yell Rufio's name out loud and try not to think how twisted it was for me to climax with murder on my mind.

Rufio's release follows soon after. He grunts and trembles, then kisses me long and hard as he rides the last tendrils of his orgasm. He tries not to collapse completely on top of me and ends up falling through the crack between the front and back seats.

"Damn. Talk about a graceful finale," he says, making me chuckle. "Oh, you're amused now."

"I'm sorry, but that statement coming from you was pretty funny."

I sit up so Rufio can do the same. He gets rid of the condom while I search for my clothes, but in the darkness, it's pretty hard. Suddenly, the bright glow of a flashlight and a loud knock on the window earns a yell from me and a curse from Rufio.

"Daisy? Is that you?" a familiar voice asks.

"Who's out there?" Rufio moves so he's protecting me from prying eyes.

"Mr. X. Put your clothes back on and get out of the car."

With my heart still thundering inside my chest, I search for my clothes blindly. My mind is going at a hundred miles an hour. *What the hell is Mr. X doing here?*

33

BRYCE

The only sound in the dining room is of silver spoons hitting china. If I thought dinner at my folks' was a depressing affair, Morpheus's parents take the first prize. Morpheus and I came over for supper in the hopes of cornering his father later. We still don't know anything about Daisy's lineage, and Morpheus's father is the closest expert in history we have.

But the man is as cold as a winter storm. He barely spared his own son a couple of words. I don't understand where his animosity comes from. He should treat Morpheus like a king. There aren't many Fringe families who produce an Idol heir.

"How are things at school?" Mrs. Malek asks. She, at least, seems to care about her only child.

"Good." Morpheus doesn't meet her gaze.

She stares at him for a couple more beats before she turns to me. "How about you, Bryce? This is your senior year, isn't it?"

"Yes, ma'am."

"Do you know which school you're going to after you graduate?"

"I haven't given it much thought," I shrug. "Prism City University has excellent programs."

"How can you not know what field you want to specialize in?" Mr. Malek speaks suddenly, watching me with a disapproving glare.

Boy, he and my father should hang out.

"Maybe because I'm a Gemini and I can't make up my mind," I joke, which flies right over the man's head. I realize being a smartass is not going to win me any brownie points, so I decide to change my approach. "Truth is, I asked to tag along tonight because I wanted to ask you a few questions."

I look quickly in Morpheus's direction. He sets his spoon down and watches me with a frown.

"Oh? Are you interested in becoming a historian?" Mr. Malek asks, clearly less antagonizing now.

"History is my favorite subject in school, but honestly, I have no idea what kind of work I could do after I get a degree in it."

Mr. Malek cleans his mouth with his napkin and then folds his hands together. "Well, there's always teaching."

"Do you enjoy being a teacher?" I ask.

He nods. "I do, but what I really like is doing research for publication."

"Tarek has written several scholarly books," Mrs. Malek says with pride.

I catch Morpheus's wince, then him shrinking in his chair. It's no secret to us that he feels lacking when it comes to his performance at school. I've tried to tell him it's all in his head. None of us are geniuses, and our GPAs are definitely average. But his issues are obviously related to his father, a well-respected professor in his field.

"Really? Do you only write about Idol history, or do you also dabble with Fringe and Norm history as well?"

"Well, a good historian can't focus solely on one race. That wouldn't give an accurate account of the truth, would it?" he replies.

"It makes sense. Sadly, most of the history events covered at school revolve around Idols."

Mr. Malek nods. "That's usually the case. It's no surprise when Idols are the dominant race. They get to dictate the narrative."

We're talking in circles now. I have to get straight to the point.

"Even so, I stumbled upon an article about this Norm family that accomplished quite a few things."

Mr. Malek arches his eyebrows in curiosity. "Oh? What family?"

"The Rodales," Morpheus replies before I can, eliciting a frown from his father.

Shit. I want to kick him under the table. Things were going smooth with his old man. I hope he didn't ruin the progress I made.

"I can't think of a famous Rodale in history," he replies.

"Are you sure? I could swear that was the family's name," I say.

Mr. Malek pushes his chair back and stands up. "There was a very infamous Norm family in the 1700s, the only one I'm aware of. Their last name started with an R. Come with me. I believe I acquired a book that talks briefly about them."

I trade a quick glance with Morpheus, and we both stand up to follow his father.

"But you haven't had dessert yet," Mrs. Malek complains.

Ah damn. She had to bring up dessert. Considering food at dinner was amazing, I'm betting the sweet treat will be out of this world.

"Come on, Bryce. You can get your sugar fix later." Morpheus snaps me out of my paralysis.

Mrs. Malek smiles. "Don't worry. Dessert isn't going anywhere."

I grin and then follow Morpheus down the corridor. His father is already in his study, pulling books from the shelves.

"I know I've read a passage about this Norm family somewhere," he says over his shoulder.

"If you could remember their name, I could maybe help locate it," I offer.

Mr. Malek looks over his shoulder. "You can do that?"

I remember the time I found the information Daisy was looking for in the book she borrowed from the library. The memory brings a pang to my chest, but I'm still torn about what I should do about her.

Realizing Mr. Malek is still waiting for my answer, I reply, "Yes, sir."

He sets a few more old books on his desk and begins to organize them in different piles. He doesn't look up, keeping his brows scrunched together, until finally, after several minutes have passed, he picks a particular one from the collection.

"Aha! Here it is. The family was called the Rinnegati. They were Italian. Here, see if you can locate the article about them." Mr. Malek hands me the tome.

Focusing on the name, I let my hand hover above the book. The pages begin to flick rapidly until they stop. The name Rinnegati is written in bold letters at the top. I'd read the entire passage myself, but I sense Mr. Malek staring at the book eagerly.

"Found it." I hand it to him.

He reads a few lines, then says, "Yes, now it's coming back to me. Rinnegati literally means renegades."

"What did they do that granted them space in one of your history books?" Morpheus moves closer to the tome in question, looking down at the open page.

"They didn't do anything grand, per se. They were famous because of the legend associated with their name."

"What legend?" Morpheus and I ask at the same time.

"The legend of the Idol who reneged on her powers."

"I don't follow," I say.

"It's said that many millennia ago, there was a very powerful Idol who had such a terrible gift, she asked Gaia to take the power back."

"Gaia? As in the mother of the universe?"

"Yes. Seeing how this Idol's gift burdened her, Gaia granted the wish and changed the Idol into a Norm."

"And the Rinnegati relate to that legend how?" Morpheus asks.

"They were her descendants."

Shit, as interesting as this information sounds, it does nothing to decipher the mystery surrounding Morpheus's vision.

"But of course, this is the watered-down version dispersed by Idols in power," Mr. Malek continues. "Another intriguing theory, and much more dangerous, is that the Idol didn't give up her power. It was taken from her."

"Why?" I ask.

"Because she was disgusted with the way Idols treated Fringes and Norms. She believed the sacred duty of Idols was to protect the weak. If they refused the call, they shouldn't keep their powers."

Holy shit. That's exactly what Daisy's father believed. There must be a connection there.

"Is there any chance the Rinnegati family changed their name or is related in any way to the Rodales of Hawk City?" Morpheus asks.

Understanding finally dawns on his father's face. "You're referring to Paul Rodale, aren't you?"

"What if I am?" Morpheus raises his chin stubbornly.

His father closes the book with a loud thud. He looks pissed.

"Then you'd better drop the subject at once. Paul Rodale was a fool who liked to antagonize very powerful people in Hawk City, and he was killed for it."

"He was a Norm and easy prey," Morpheus retorts.

"Do you think those people care what race you are? Besides, you're the only one in this family who was *blessed* with Idol powers."

I don't miss the venom lacing Mr. Malek's words, and neither does Morpheus. He takes a step back, looking like a dog that's been kicked to the curb.

"I didn't ask for it," he grits out.

"It doesn't change the outcome, does it?" His father turns his back on him and begins to put the books back in their places. "I think it's best if you return to campus at once."

"You don't need to say it twice." Morpheus storms out of the study, leaving behind a trail of dark miasma. Shit. He's not doing anything to rein in his gift.

I run after him, finding him already out the door. Mrs. Malek joins me in the entry foyer carrying a large plastic container.

"What happened?" she asks.

"Morpheus and your husband had a disagreement. We're off to campus."

Mrs. Malek lets out a sad sigh. "This is all my fault."

I don't understand what she's implying, but I don't get the chance to ask.

"Yo, Bryce. Are you coming or not?" Morpheus yells from inside his car.

"Yeah, I'm coming." I turn to his mother. "I'm sorry we have to dine and dash. Thanks for dinner, Mrs. Malek."

"Oh, don't worry about it. Here. I packed dessert for you. I know you have a sweet tooth."

My stomach grumbles, despite everything. "Thanks, Mrs. Malek."

Morpheus presses on the horn, and I curse in my head. The ride back to school is going to be hella fun.

I barely have the chance to close the passenger door when Morpheus peels out.

"Damn it, Morpheus. Relax." I clutch the container tighter, trying to prevent it from toppling over and spilling everything out.

"I knew he was going to say something to piss me off," Morpheus grumbles under his breath.

"He didn't say anything awful." I open the container, unable to wait another second. "Yes! Baklava." I take one of the sticky treats out and shove it in my mouth.

Morpheus doesn't reply, but from the corner of my eye, I see the shadows are agitated again. Licking my fingers, I say, "He did get pretty antsy when he realized we were asking about Paul Rodale."

"No, he didn't become nervous because I was asking about Daisy's father. He actually got angry because I said I wasn't afraid to poke around."

"I noticed that too. What was that all about?"

Morpheus rubs his face. "I don't want to talk about it."

"Fine." I eat a couple more treats as silence reigns supreme for a few minutes.

The amount of sugar coursing through my veins should have put me in a better mood, but the fact that the renegade Idol and Paul Rodale shared the same ideals is sitting heavily on my mind. There's gotta be a relationship between the two.

"Do you think the Rinnegati and the Rodales are related?" Morpheus breaks the silence, echoing exactly what I'm thinking.

"Honestly, I don't know. But if the Rodales and the Rinnegati are family, and the Rinnegati are indeed related to an

Idol who gave her powers back, then that means Daisy could possibly have demigod blood."

"It would explain why you could bond to her with an infinity band in my vision."

I clench my jaw and don't say a word. My brain is too occupied trying to connect all the dots. Daisy could have an extremely weak link to an Idol, but why does that make her important to my mother and the Knights?

It seems the more we uncover, the further in the dark we plummet.

34

DAISY

We're forced to abandon Rufio's car and return to Unearthly Desires in Mr. X's vehicle. He's so angry that he doesn't say a word to us during the entire ride there. It's a miracle Rufio didn't rebel against the idea of being bossed around by the guy. Then again, he doesn't know Mr. X is a Fringe and not the Idol he projects to be.

As for me, I'm too embarrassed to say anything. Poppy, Mr. X's alter ego, was my former boss and, in a way, a father figure. There's also the old picture of him with my father that's adding more confusion to my head. I want to ask point-blank what Mr. X's relationship with my father was, but I don't want to do so in front of Rufio. Sleeping with the Idol twice doesn't mean I trust him.

We enter the club through the back door, and I notice the absence of the brute who tried to prevent me from entering by force. Hope that he got fired makes me less apprehensive, but inside the club is too quiet, which means it's already closed. So the asshole bouncer probably didn't get sacked. His shift is simply over.

Mr. X doesn't say a word until Rufio and I are in his office.

The Fringe doesn't bother sitting behind his desk, just whirls on us as soon as the door is closed.

"What the fuck!" he yells, making me wince.

"Why are you yelling at us?" I ask.

"Do you really have to ask that?"

"Daisy and I are adults. We can do whatever the hell we want," Rufio grits out, maybe believing Mr. X is pissed because of how he found us.

"Do you think I give a rat's ass about your sex life? I'm pissed because Daisy came into my establishment, broke my bouncer's nose, and then decided to pick a fight with the Skull's Angels gang. I really expected more from you, girl."

"Let me get a couple of things straight. Your bouncer's nose is broken because he's a pervert and an asshole. And I didn't simply 'decide to pick a fight' with those criminals on a whim. They attacked Felicity. They deserved retribution. It was the reason I came here in the first place, to ask for your help."

Mr. X narrows his eyes. "I knew about Felicity, Daisy. You should have never gotten involved."

"Why not? The waitress is Daisy's friend. She had every right to seek revenge," Rufio defends me.

Mr. X turns his wrath on Rufio. "Oh yeah? And how did that work out for you two? I can smell your blood from here, boy. That gang member got you good, didn't he?"

"He got lucky," Rufio seethes.

"Luck ain't got nothing to do with it. Aren't you wondering why you couldn't turn him into dust just like you did the others?"

Mr. X's question gives me pause. How did he know Rufio's power didn't work on the man?

"I'm guessing by the smug grin on your face that you know why. So cut the crap and spill it already," Rufio retorts.

"It was his jacket. More precisely, the thread used in the emblem embroidered on the back."

"What about it?" Rufio asks.

"The thread contained microscopic pieces of a material that neutralizes Idol power."

"Son of a bitch."

"Is the material lightning glass?" I ask.

Mr. X doesn't seem surprised that I know about it. "Yes."

"The Knights used a similar thing on my brother," Rufio mutters, almost to himself.

"The Knights? What have they done to Bryce?" My voice rises to a shrill.

Rufio turns to me, his eyes flashing electric blue. "They kidnapped my brother. Held him hostage for two days."

A sinking feeling hits me, making my chest unbearably heavy with worry. There's no mistaking the hatred in Rufio's eyes now. If he was standing in front of a Knight in this moment, he would strike him dead.

Swallowing the lump in my throat, I turn to Mr. X. "How did a gang member get a hold of such material?"

He shakes his head. "I don't know, Daisy. The Knights discovered lighting glass and made weapons and power suppressants with it. How those tools ended up on the black market is a mystery to me."

"Maybe the Knights distributed them on purpose," Rufio replies.

Mr. X cuts him a glare. "The Knights exist to protect the weak. They wouldn't arm criminals."

"How do you know so much about them?" Rufio eyes Mr. X with suspicion now.

"I'm a businessman working in a dangerous industry. I make it a priority to stay informed."

"Right. But you knew about the gang member I couldn't gank, and you also knew where to find us."

With a sigh, Mr. X puts his hands on his hips and glances at the floor. "I went to that bar to set things straight." He lifts his eyes to meet mine. "You couldn't imagine my surprise when I found the bar trashed and Dick Bravo skewered like a shish kebab."

"You went after that gang alone?" I ask.

"No, not alone. I knew what I was dealing with."

"Fine. But how did you find us?" Rufio insists.

"By chance. But you should be glad I did. You got stabbed by a lightning-glass dagger."

"I'm fine."

Mr. X laughs without humor. "Ah, the usual Idol arrogance. Boy, you know nothing. Take off your T-shirt, and let's hope it's not too late."

"What do you mean?" I ask, catching the warning in Mr. X's tone.

With a grunt, Rufio peels off his T-shirt and turns around.

I can't hold back my gasp.

"What? How bad is it?" Rufio tries to see the wound in his shoulder.

"Ah fuck." Mr. X heads for his desk and retrieves a few glass vials from a drawer.

"Daisy, say something." Rufio looks at me.

"The skin around the wound is turning black," I reply.

"What? Why? How come I don't feel anything?"

"Because that's how lightning glass works. It's not only able to pierce Idol skin, but it also leaves poison behind. If you don't die from the blow, you die from the poison."

No. Rufio can't die like that.

"What should we do? Is there an antidote or something?" I ask.

Mr. X doesn't answer; instead, he dumps the contents of one of the glass vials over Rufio's discarded shirt. "Here, take a hit."

"Is that Silver-voltage? Why are you giving him Silver-voltage?" My voice is loud and shrill, making me sound like a damsel in distress.

"To help with the pain."

"What about the poison?" Rufio asks.

"Lay on your belly. I'm going to pour the rest of my Silver-voltage stash over it."

"Is that going to work?" He eyes Mr. X with incredulity.

"Hopefully yes."

"*Hopefully*?" Rufio's eyes brighten and the dark veins make an appearance, but they're not as sharp as usual. The poison is probably what dulled his powers.

"It's the best I can do. Now stop with the questions and let me help you, jackass."

Rufio flares his nostrils and squints. He wants to kick Mr. X's ass.

I touch his arm. "Please, let him do his thing."

His facial features relax a bit as he looks into my eyes. I hope he knows I had no idea lightning glass could do that to him.

"Time is not on your side, boy," Mr. X presses.

Rufio brings his drenched T-shirt to his nose and takes a big whiff. He then lies on Mr. X's couch and faces the backrest. Crouching next to him, Mr. X uncaps four glass vials and dumps it all over the small gash on Rufio's shoulder. Rufio grunts, and the muscles on his back become tense. A hissing sound fills the air when the liquid hits his skin.

"Is it working?" I ask.

"Give it some time."

"How long?"

Mr. X looks at me, annoyed. "I don't know, Daisy. I've never done this before."

Blisters form over the blackened skin, and the distressed noises coming from Rufio grow louder.

"What's happening?" I step closer.

"The drug is burning away the poison."

My stomach twists into knots as guilt consumes me. I can

only guess how painful the experience must be for Rufio. He's an Idol, and if he can't hide his agony from us, it must be off the charts.

The blisters pop, revealing raw skin underneath, but at least it's no longer black. However, the entire process takes at least half an hour. Thirty minutes of torture. When it's finally over, Rufio doesn't move. He's also not making any more sounds.

"Rufio? Are you okay?" I ask meekly.

"I think he passed out five minutes ago, Daisy. Too bad it wasn't sooner."

Mr. X heads for his desk again and grabs a box of tissues. I don't understand why he's offering it to me until I touch my cheeks and find them wet. I didn't even realize I cried.

"Do you think he's going to be all right?" I glance at Rufio. The black is gone, thank heavens.

"I think so. When did this happen?"

"I told you—"

"I'm not talking about your unfortunate experience. I'm referring to when you started caring for him."

I avoid Mr. X's probing stare. "I don't know."

"Daisy, you know how stupid that is, right?"

I whip my face to his again. "You're lecturing me?"

"Yes, I guess I am."

"Why? You're nothing to me."

Mr. X winces, and now it's his turn to look away. "I'm sorry you feel that way."

With Rufio passed out, I blurt out the question that's been burning inside my brain since I saw that old picture of Dad.

"What was my father to you?"

His eyes turn rounder. "Where's that question coming from? I've never met your father."

"You can stop lying to me now. I found an old picture of you, Dad, Principal Fallon, and another man I didn't recognize. So I'm asking again, how did you know my father?"

Mr. X can only maintain my stare for a few seconds before he turns around and leans against his desk. "I was only trying to protect you, Daisy."

"Protect me from what?"

He turns back to me, his eyes filled with unshed tears. "From the monsters who took our family away from us."

"*Us*? I don't understand."

"Your father was my brother."

35

DAISY

"That's not possible. You're a Fringe."

"Your grandparents adopted me when I was five. They didn't know then that I was a Fringe, but even when I couldn't hide my powers, they didn't care."

"How come Dad never talked about you?" I ask, getting choked up.

Mr. X sits at the edge of his desk. "The other man in the picture was our older brother, William. He was killed when he was eighteen by Idols."

Just like Dad. The knot in my throat becomes bigger.

"We were afraid the men who killed him would hurt us too, so we split up. Your grandparents moved to Prism City and, mercifully, died of natural causes."

They were already gone when I was born; at least that's what Dad told me. I'm not sure now if that was true.

"All this time you pretended to be a stranger. You could have told me you were my uncle." The first angry tears roll down my cheeks.

"I wanted to so many times, but I couldn't risk people

making the connection. I didn't know how else to keep you safe."

"You let me strip for your customers!"

"I didn't want to, but you begged me for the job, Daisy. If I simply gave you the money, it would look too suspicious."

"To whom? I would have never guessed you were giving me money because we were related."

"Many people, allies and foes alike. I'm constantly being watched. Just the fact that I helped you tonight will be problematic."

"I'm sorry to be such a burden." I wipe the tears from my face. "You haven't explained one detail though. What was Principal Fallon doing in that picture?"

"She was William's girlfriend and the reason he was killed."

I curl my hand into a fist and press it against my forehead. All this information at once is hard to reconcile with the lies I've been told all my life.

"I need to get out of here."

"I can take you and Rufio back to the academy." Mr. X stands up.

"No. I don't want to go anywhere with you." I turn to Rufio and fish his cell phone from his jeans pocket.

It's password protected, but all I have to do is press his index finger to the screen to unlock the device. Scrolling through his contacts, the first name that pops up is Bryce's. My finger hovers over the Call button, but considering Bryce thinks I'm a two-faced bitch, I forgo the idea quickly. Instead, I call Morpheus. The phone rings and rings until finally, probably just before the call goes to voice mail, he answers.

"Rufio, where have you been? We've been trying to reach you for hours," Morpheus says, clearly irritated.

"Morpheus, it's Daisy."

"Daisy? Why are you calling from Rufio's cell? What happened?"

"I can't explain it over the phone. Could you please come get us? We're at Unearthly Desires."

"Why can't Rufio drive back?"

I pinch the bridge of my nose. "He just can't, Morpheus. Please, I'm begging you. Come get us, and don't tell Bryce."

Morpheus curses. "You're scaring me, Daisy. But okay. I'll be there as soon as I can."

"Thank you. Oh, and use the back door."

I end the call and glance at Mr. X. I can't believe he's my fucking uncle and I don't even know his real name.

"What does the X stand for?" I ask.

"Xavier. That's my name."

"Do you work for the Knights?"

Fear flashes in his gaze. "I assist... *sometimes*."

"Was it you who sent me a lightning-glass dagger inside a cake?"

"No. I wouldn't risk that. If anyone who knows what those weapons can do caught you in possession of one, your life would be forfeit."

"I was sent two daggers. The first one appeared in my dorm room in my first week at school."

Xavier becomes tenser in an instant. "Son of a bitch. I can't believe she did that."

"Are you talking about Principal Fallon?"

"She's the only one who would have access to your room, and she doesn't care as much about your safety as I do."

I suspected as much. She didn't even bother telling me that Bryce and Rufio were her sons.

"Do you know what she wants with me?" I ask.

"No. She tried to tell me that she wanted to help the niece of the man she loved, but Jodie isn't selfless like that. Don't trust a word she says."

"I don't, but I also don't trust you." I cross my arms.

"Fair enough." Xavier keeps staring at me as if he wants to read my mind. "Why didn't you call Rufio's brother? I thought you were close."

I pinch my lips, reluctant now to give Uncle Dearest an answer. "We had a falling-out."

He narrows his eyes, looking at me intensely. "Why?"

He's not going to drop the subject. I look at my shoes, nibbling my lower lip. I don't want to talk about Bryce, because it hurt so much when he turned his back on me. But Xavier is probably the only person I can actually tell the truth to.

"He found out I'm Paul Rodale's daughter, and he knows why my father was killed. He thinks I'm out to destroy them all."

"Who else knows besides him?" There's a hint of alarm in his tone now.

"Rufio, Phoenix, and Morpheus."

He rubs his face and begins to pace. "You need to leave immediately. I can make some calls and find someplace safe for you and Rosie."

"Whoa. Hold the cavalry." I lift my hand. "I'm not going anywhere."

"Are you crazy? I've spent the past seven years trying to protect you from the Idols who killed your parents, and now you're cozying up with their offspring!"

"What do you mean, their offspring?" I take a step back while my heart hammers inside of my chest.

"Oh, my God, Daisy. How can you be so naïve after all these years on the run? The Idol behind William's murder, and probably your parents' too, is Jonathan Kent, Rufio and Bryce's father."

～

MORPHEUS

Daisy couldn't possibly have known that Bryce was standing next to me when I took her call. And now he's alternating between cursing me for not getting more information from her and cursing Rufio for whatever problem he got into.

"What the hell are they doing at Unearthly Desires together?" He hits the door, putting a dent in the plastic.

"Calm the fuck down, Bryce. And please do not destroy my car."

"How can you be so calm? What could be the reason that Rufio is unable to drive or even call?"

"We're going to find out soon enough. We're a couple of minutes out."

"I can't believe she asked you not to tell me." He balls his hands into fists, and sparks of electricity cover them.

"I swear, Bryce, if you fry my car, I'm going to kick your ass."

His reply is a grunt. While I'm busy trying to pacify the guy, I can't ignore the sense of doom hanging over my head. I don't think it's a premonition, but I know shit is about to get way more complicated once we find out what's going on.

Finally I turn on the street where the strip joint is located. Per Daisy's instructions, I park in the back. Bryce is out of my car before I turn the engine off. Never mind that he finds the door to the place locked; he yanks it off its hinges with a hard pull, setting off the security alarm, which he kills in the next second.

"Was that necessary?" I ask, but he's not listening to me.

He strides down the corridor until he meets Mr. X, who just came out of his office to investigate the commotion.

"What the hell did you do to my door?" Mr. X demands.

"Where are Daisy and my brother?" Bryce cuts to the chase.

Knowing Bryce is about to blow, I step in front of him, blocking his way. "Where are they?"

"In my office." Mr. X points behind him.

I enter first. Daisy is sitting behind the desk with her eyes glazed. And Rufio is lying on the couch, unconscious with a big gash on his shoulder.

My jaw drops. "Son of a bitch. What happened to him?"

Bryce follows me, and who knows what's running through his head now.

Daisy lifts her gaze to mine. "What is *he* doing here?"

"He was with me when you called."

I glance at Bryce, who is glowering at Daisy. She doesn't flinch or cower under his furious stare.

"Are you going to tell me what you did to Rufio, or do I have to force it out of you?" Bryce asks.

Daisy stands up, her eyes flashing with anger. "I didn't do anything to him. A Fringe attacked him, and Mr. X saved his life."

"How could a Fringe injure Rufio?" I ask.

"He had a lightning-glass dagger on him," Mr. X answers as he moves closer to Daisy.

Bryce crouches next to his brother and shakes his arm. "Rufio, wake up."

"You better let him sleep. His body needs time to recover."

Noticing the raw skin surrounding the gash, I ask, "Why does it look like he was burned alive?"

"The lightning glass can not only cut through Idol skin, but it's also poisonous," Mr. X supplies.

I switch my attention to Daisy, but she's back to sporting that haunted look from before. I'm not an idiot. I know they're only giving us the watered-down version of the events, but considering Bryce's state of mind, it's best if I don't try to get the whole truth now. We'll get it from Rufio when he wakes up.

Bryce lifts his brother from the couch and heads out the office without saying another word. But the tension on his frame is there, coiled tight.

"Daisy, are you ready?" I ask.

She blinks a couple of times before she walks around the desk. "Yeah."

Mr. X can't keep his eyes off her, and I don't know what I should be feeling here. I'm annoyed, I'm not going to deny that. He's double her age; he shouldn't be looking at her in that intense manner.

"Stop gawking at her like that," I say. "She's not a piece of meat."

The man seems puzzled by my outburst, but his whiskey-colored eyes darken in the next second. "Instead of worrying about me, you should keep your friend away from Daisy. If he touches one hair on her head, he's dead."

Mr. X's threat feeds the darkness that's always brewing in my core. The shadows gain power, turning my wrists into ice. I'm tempted to give the son of a bitch a taste of fear, but Daisy is already gone, and I shouldn't leave her alone with Bryce. I slip out of the office before I fall into temptation, then pick up my pace until I'm walking side by side with her.

"Are you okay?" I ask quietly.

"No."

"I get that you don't feel like talking right now, but you won't be able to keep the details of what happened a secret from us. Bryce wi—"

"I don't fucking care about what Bryce will do!" she snaps.

"You should care. He can kill you, Daisy."

She doesn't reply, but I catch the impact of my words on her expression. Despite the tough act, Daisy is hurting because of Bryce. I don't think he's wrong for reacting the way he did, but at the same time, I'm pissed that he's making Daisy suffer. I'm a ball of contradictory emotions, and it sucks.

Bryce is already in the back seat with Rufio, which leaves the shotgun spot wide open for Daisy. She doesn't head for it though. Instead, she veers toward an old red Mustang parked two spots to the right. Before she enters the car, she looks straight at me.

"All of you can kill me, and there's not a damn thing I can do about it."

36

RUFIO

The first thing I sense when I come to is the tenderness in my shoulder. I'm in my bed, and it's morning already. Slowly, the memories of last night return. I was stabbed and poisoned by lightning glass, and Mr. X saved my life.

"Good, you're up," Bryce says from behind me.

I turn and find him sitting in the chair in the corner. He looks like he's been through the ringer. His clothes are wrinkled, and his hair is a mess.

"How did I get home?" I ask hoarsely.

"Daisy called."

"How is she?" I try to sit up, but the pain is too acute still.

"Don't worry about her. She's probably sleeping like an angel in her bed. I want to know what the hell happened last night, and don't give me some bullshit answer. I've heard plenty of nothing from her and Mr. X."

Great. Bryce is pissed. Exactly what I want to be dealing with after a close brush with death.

"I went to Unearthly Desires to unwind and bumped into Daisy there."

Bryce squints while a muscle in his jaw twitches.

"She wasn't there to strip, if that's what you were thinking."

"Don't presume to know what's on my mind," he responds through clenched teeth.

Yeah, whatever, bro. I know you.

"She wanted help to avenge her waitress friend. You know, the older blonde chick," I explain.

"Felicity? What happened to her?"

"She was attacked by a motorcycle gang, and Daisy wanted them to pay. She was hoping Mr. X would help."

Bryce leans back and glances away. "Son of a bitch. Why didn't she come to us?"

"Really? After you kicked her out, did you seriously think she would come to us for help?"

He turns to me and gives me a death glare.

"Stop eyeballing me. You know what you did," I say. "Mr. X wasn't around, so I stepped in."

"Were those men Idols?"

"No. All Fringes. But the leader was wearing a jacket that gave him immunity to my powers. Lightning glass can also be used in threads and ropes, and it nullifies Idol gifts." I stare at him, letting my words sink in.

In a split second, understanding shines in Bryce's eyes. "That's what those motherfucking Knights used on me. But how come those Fringe lowlifes had access to lightning glass stuff?"

"Mr. X claims he doesn't know. And he doesn't believe the Knights willingly distributed that shit. But who knows if that's true or not."

"Fuck!" Bryce shoots out of his seat. "What are we going to do? We can't simply sit on this information and do nothing."

"I think it's time we go looking for the man who kidnapped you, bro."

Bryce turns to me, his face a mixture of emotions. "I don't disagree, but what are we going to do about Daisy?"

"Do you still believe she's behind some crazy conspiracy to end us all?"

He looks at the window, crossing his arms. "I don't know."

"She saved me yesterday."

Bryce looks over his shoulder. "How?"

"After I got stabbed, I lost most of my juice. And the gang leader was immune to my power anyway. Daisy killed him."

Bryce keeps staring at me in his intense manner for several beats before he looks away again. "I don't hate her, Rufio. Actually, my feelings are on the opposite side of the spectrum. You have no idea how torn up I am about this whole thing."

I can't believe he's confessing to me. He's never opened up like this before.

"I hear ya, brother. I'm just as confused as you are. I'm only certain of one thing: I can't let anything happen to Daisy."

Bryce lowers his chin, sighing loudly. "Me neither."

***

Phoenix

MY EYES ARE GLUED SHUT, thanks to the swelling. I knew pissing off my father would have consequences, but I didn't realize how deep his hatred for Norms ran. He summoned me on Friday, right after school. No surprise when I found the house deserted. No mother or servants to witness my humiliation. And my father did enjoy doling out my punishment. I'm bleeding everywhere, and I don't need a mirror to see that my face must be all shades of purple.

He brought me to his dungeon of pain, a room in the basement designed for sex and torture. I haven't left since I got here. My wrists are numb from being tied to the chains hanging from the ceiling for too long. My back is on fire thanks to the countless whiplashes I've received.

I hear the door at the top of the stairs open, and my body tenses up. It must be Sunday, so it means I have another day of brutalization to endure. The only thing that's helped me through this ordeal is imagining the thousand ways I can kill the monster who spawned me. And now that Daisy and her Idol-killing weapon have come into my life, ending my father is no longer just a fantasy.

He approaches slowly, wearing another pristine black suit. It hides the blood.

"Good morning, son. Did you have pleasant dreams?" He smiles wickedly.

He wouldn't even give me that reprieve. He forced me to send him the most disgusting visions the entire night.

"Go to hell!"

"That Norm whore must be rubbing her beliefs off on you. There's no hell for Idols, son. You must know that."

He stops in front of me and then grabs my hair, pulling my head up. "Now, I don't think that last vision of yours did the trick. But nothing beats the real thing."

His dark eyes flash with malice right before he shoves me to the floor. I hear the sound of a zipper opening and immediately rebel. But it's useless. The tattoo on my wrist begins to burn, rendering me completely at his mercy. All I can do is shut my eyes and try not to scream.

37

DAISY

My alarm blares, and I wake with a start. An immediate headache follows, the result of two nights in a row of barely a few hours of sleep. I haven't been able to rest at all after the ordeal on Saturday. How could I? First I discover I have an uncle who's been in my life for the past two years pretending to be a stranger, and then I find out the boys I care about are the sons of the Idol who is most likely responsible for my parents' death. It's all too much for one person to deal with in such a short period of time.

I spent all of Sunday with Felicity. She's recovering, which is the only positive note from the weekend. I was tempted to tell her that her attackers are dead, but I was afraid the news would only upset her, so I let it be. I'll tell her when she's back on her feet so she doesn't keep looking over her shoulder in fear.

In a strange twist to the story, I don't hate Bryce and Rufio despite their possible connection to my family's destruction. They bring forth a lot of emotions from me: lust, fear, obsession, and maybe even love, but definitely not hate. That sentiment is now reserved for one person, the catalyst of it all. Principal Fallon.

I blame her solely for everything horrible that has happened to my family. She's from a prominent Idol family. What did she think would happen when she presented a Norm as her boyfriend to her folks?

And now she's brought me here under false pretenses. She allowed her son and others to bully me, despite her promises I'd be safe. The woman is as shady as they come. But I can't leave now. I'm in too deep, and I have to figure out what she wants from me.

Determined to see this day through with chin held high, I get ready early and head for class. I conveniently forget the book I'm supposed to return to the librarian in my room. Fuck it. If she wants it badly enough, then she can come get it herself. I'm not going to make it any easier for her. As far as I'm concerned, she's in cahoots with Principal Fallon, which means she can kiss my ass.

In the entry hallway, I stop by the vending machine to get a snack for later. But the sound of the door to the garage banging against the wall makes me jump in fright. With my hand pressed against my chest, I turn around. Who could possibly be making all that racket?

The person hasn't come around the corner yet, but the grunt and loud thud that follows propel me to investigate. Maybe it's another Fringe overdosing on Silver-voltage.

I gasp when I find Phoenix on his hands and knees, trying to get up.

"What happened?" I crouch in front of him and wince when I see the state of his face. It's swollen beyond recognition with several lacerations on his forehead and cheeks. "Oh my God, Phoenix. Who did this to you?"

"Please, no... questions. Can you just... help me?"

I throw his arm around my shoulder and help him get vertical again. He winces with the movement, which means he has other wounds in area I can't see.

Slowly, we progress toward the elevator.

"No... the stairs," he protests.

"You can barely walk. The elevator will be faster."

"I don't want anyone to see me like this."

"No one is up yet. Trust me."

Finally, he allows me to steer him toward the metal box. We don't speak while we ride the three floors up, but when we reach our corridor, Phoenix freezes.

"The guys... I can't."

I know what he's trying to say. He doesn't want his roommates to see him in this state either.

"Let's go to my room," I say.

"Thank you, Daisy."

Once inside, I veer toward my bed. Phoenix simply collapses on it, but he doesn't lie down.

"I have a first aid kit in my bathroom. I'll be right back."

"I don't think there's anything in that kit of yours that can help me."

I ignore him and get the box anyway. Phoenix has his eyes closed when I sit next to him. His current condition reminds me of Felicity in the hospital. The rage I felt then returns. My hands are shaking as I grab a piece of gauze and dab it in rubbing alcohol. This usually helps clean wounds in Norms and avoid infection, but maybe it doesn't affect Phoenix at all.

He hisses when I press the cloth against a gash above his eyebrow.

"Relax, I'm just cleaning it."

"With what? Fire?"

"Rubbing alcohol. Don't be such a baby."

A long stretch of silence follows. Phoenix doesn't complain anymore and lets me clean the dried blood from his face. I see patches of it staining his polo shirt and jeans as well. I'm afraid to know the extent of his injuries, but I have to see.

"Can you take off your clothes for me?"

He opens his eyes and stares at me with a crooked grin. His lips are busted, yet he still finds a way to be amused.

"So that's what it takes for you to finally succumb to my charms?"

"Don't be an idiot. I want to check your other wounds."

The easygoing smile wilts to nothing. "Better not."

Suspicious that he's more messed up than I thought, I circle around the bed and stop behind him.

"Daisy, I mean it." He begins to turn, then stops suddenly as if the movement is too painful.

I pull the sleeves of his hoodie down before he can stop me, but I freeze when I see how badly stained the back of his shirt is.

"Phoenix—" My voice breaks.

"It's nothing, Daisy."

Nothing, my ass. With trembling fingers, I grab the edge of his shirt and slowly peel the fabric up. Phoenix's entire back-side is lacerated. I can't help the gasp that escapes my lips.

"Who did this to you?" I ask, but I already have an idea.

"Doesn't matter. I'll be okay, Daisy. I just need to rest."

"You need medical attention. I'll go get Nurse Ellen." I take a step back, but Phoenix twists around and reaches for my hand.

"Don't. She'll ask too many questions I can't answer."

The pleading in his eyes breaks my heart, but I can't just not do anything.

"I can't help you get better, Phoenix. I wouldn't know where to begin."

"You don't need to do anything. I heal faster than Norms. By tomorrow, all my cuts will be closed, and the swelling will be gone."

I nibble on my lower lip, not knowing what to do.

"I'm begging you, Daisy." His eyes are pleading. "Don't tell anyone I'm here."

"Okay. But can I get you anything? Food, soda?"

"No, sweetheart. All I need right now is to borrow your bed."

My eyes widen, an involuntary reaction.

"To sleep, nothing else," Phoenix amends. "You don't need to stay with me and miss class on my account. I'll be okay. Promise."

"If you're sure," I say, already agreeing with this crazy idea.

"Thank you. Now go. Don't let me keep you from whatever you were planning to do this early in the morning."

I head toward the door. I can't believe I'm agreeing to let Phoenix stay in my room for the entire day. But considering Bryce already found my father's diary, there's not much left for Phoenix to unearth besides my father's old picture. There's nothing to do now besides hope Phoenix doesn't plan on doing some snooping around while I'm gone.

My head is not in the present moment as I make my way to the main building. It's early enough that the hallways are still relatively empty. I'm still reeling from the gruesome image of Phoenix's back and the bruises on his face. I'm almost certain his father did that to him. But why couldn't Phoenix fight back? Why did he take the beating?

I see the sign for the girls' restroom and make a beeline for it. I need a splash of cold water on my face to calm down. But it seems today is the day I'll bump into every broken Idol. This time, it's Drusilla who I find on the floor, writhing in pain. Her usual luscious red hair is in tangles and matted. When she lifts her sweaty face, she reveals her bleeding nose. Shit, it almost looks like she's suffering from a Silver-voltage OD. But that's impossible. She's a high-level Idol.

"What's going on?" I run to her and try to lift her up. She bats my hand away.

"Go away, Norm. I don't need your help."

From the corner of my eye, I see a discarded glass vial. Drusilla follows my line of sight and hisses.

"You're not going to tell anyone about what you saw here."

My eyes go rounder. She's using her special voice, which means she's compelling me.

"You need to see the nurse," I tell her.

"Get out, you stupid bitch!" she yells, twisting her face into a scowl.

I'm shaking as I try to fight her command, but all the effort does is make me sick. I stop offering resistance and the nausea passes. Fine. She doesn't want my help. She can suck it. If she dies, it's one less Idol to worry about.

I walk out of the bathroom, seeing nothing. I'm so done with all the assholes around me.

"Daisy? Are you okay?" Morpheus, of all people, is right outside the restroom.

"I'm fine."

"You don't look fine. You're as pale as a ghost."

"I said I'm fine." I begin to walk toward the classroom.

Morpheus grabs my arm and turns me around. "And I know you're lying. Are you in trouble? Was it Drusilla?" He narrows his gaze.

His question brings back the nausea from before. Maybe it's because he guessed right. I shake my head, afraid that if I speak, I'll end up barfing all over his uniform. A group of students rounds the corner, and naturally their gazes immediately turn to us. With the way I'm super close to Morpheus, I know what it must look like. Great. By second period, I'll be the school slut. I kissed Bryce, orgasmed in class thanks to Phoenix, and now it looks like I'm about to make out with Morpheus.

He ignores the other students and continues. "It was her, wasn't it?"

"No," I croak.

In that precise moment, Drusilla steps out of the restroom.

Morpheus lets go of my arm and strides in her direction without a second thought. Shit. He grabs her arm in a vise grip, shaking her as he asks, "What did you do to Daisy?"

"Let me go, asshole." Drusilla tries to break free, but she's clearly still not recovered.

"Shit, look at his hand." Someone to my right points at Morpheus's shadows, which have broken away from his bracelet and are now writhing all over his hand.

With a chilling smile, he shoves Drusilla away from him. She staggers back until she hits the wall. Morpheus widens his stance and curls his hands into fists by his side.

"Morpheus! Don't do anything," I plead. There are too many witnesses, and he'll get in trouble if he attacks Drusilla, especially since it was unprovoked.

"Son of a bitch," a familiar masculine voice says from behind me. Bryce.

I don't glance in his direction; instead, I step toward Morpheus with every intention to stop what he's doing. But Bryce grabs my arm and stops me.

"Don't. It's not safe."

"Let me go and stop him." I pull my arm free from Bryce's hold.

But Bryce doesn't move fast enough. A black miasma forms around Morpheus, and even though the power isn't aimed at me, I gasp nonetheless.

"Stay away from Daisy. No matter how powerful you think you are now, you can't escape from your own nightmares."

Drusilla collapses on the floor in a heap. She leans on her elbows and lifts her tear-streaked face to him. "You will pay for this, Fringe spawn."

Morpheus's lips twist into a cruel smile while his eyes flash brightly as if his irises are made out of lightning. "Oh, but I'm not a Fringe's spawn."

He throws his arm forward and the shadows circling there

detach, forming a whip. It hits the wall above Drusilla's head, missing her by less than an inch. She stares wide-eyed at the large crack that could have been in her skull.

"Remove yourself from my sight, or I won't miss your head next time," Morpheus grits out.

Drusilla gets back to her feet, seething with rage. She eyes the crowd that's formed around the perimeter, and then she glances at me and Bryce for a fleeting moment before bolting down the corridor.

I look back to Morpheus. His breathing is coming out in bursts, and the shadows have spread so much that I can see them peeking from underneath the collar and seams of his shirt. Pretty soon he'll be completely consumed by them. That can't be good.

On a crazy impulse, I run toward him and touch the center of his chest.

"No!" Bryce yells.

The shadows writhe and coil around my palm, but they don't attack me like they did before. Instead, they slither away, recoiling toward Morpheus's bracelets. His eyes return to normal as he stares at me. I can read the surprise in them just before he drops to the floor, out cold.

38

DAISY

"You're fucking crazy, you know?" Bryce yells at me as he carries an unconscious Morpheus to Nurse Ellen's office.

"At least I tried to help him. You just stood there and did nothing."

He throws open the door to the infirmary using telekinesis, and it bangs loudly against the wall.

Ellen jumps from her chair with a look of fright. "What the he—oh shit. What happened to Morpheus?"

"We don't know," Bryce tells her. "He used his powers, and the shadows almost took him over completely."

"Has that ever happened before?" Ellen opens the curtain to the examination room and motions for Bryce to lay Morpheus on the bed.

"Not this bad."

She pulls the sleeves of Morpheus's jacket up and finds nothing but his bracelets. No sign of the shadows. "They're gone."

"I touched him while the shadows were all over him," I say. "Did I do something wrong?"

"Yes!" Bryce whirls on me. "You could have died."

"But I didn't! And why do you care anyway?" I curl my hands into fists and step in his direction.

"Okay, I need you both to get out of my office now. I can't do my job while you two are at each other's throats. Take your lovers' quarrel someplace else."

She pushes us out of the room and shuts the curtain. But I'm still too fired up to keep quiet, so I walk into the hallway. Classes are already in session, so there's no one around. Bryce follows me out, and it's clear he still has a lot on his mind.

"Why did Morpheus lash out at Drusilla like that? What did she do to you?" he questions.

I open my mouth to reply, but my tongue won't move. Nausea rolls over me again, increasing in strength the longer I fight it.

"She compelled you not to say anything, didn't she?" he continues when I don't answer.

I nod.

"I'm going to kill her." Bryce hits the wall, breaking through bricks and plaster.

Destruction. It's all they know.

"Don't," I say. "It's bad enough that Morpheus attacked her in front of witnesses. She didn't try to hurt me, so don't worry your pretty head." I can't help the sarcasm in my tone.

Bryce wanted to kill me last night. I could read the desire in his stormy eyes. *Like father, like son.* The thought enters my head unbidden.

He turns to me then, so furious that I step back until I have nowhere else to go. He invades my space, pressing his palms against the wall on each side of my head.

"I will never stop worrying about you, and that's the fucking problem. You're all I think about. You're under my skin. Worse, you're in my heart." He hits his chest with a closed fist.

His confession is like a dagger through me. I'm so angry and frustrated that fat tears run down my cheeks. His family is the reason mine is broken forever.

"What am I supposed to do with that? I believed you were different, but you betrayed me when I needed you the most."

"I know, and yet I can't say I'm sorry. I don't trust you. I still believe you're going to stab me in the back. But I can't stop wanting to be near you, to protect you."

He cups my face and wipes the tears with this thumb. I suck in a breath, but I don't move away. I don't break eye contact with him. When Bryce kisses me, I kiss him back. It seems we're both gluttons for punishment. We're two people standing on opposite sides, destined to hate one another but unable to stay away.

A throat clearing behind Bryce cuts our mistake short. That's the only thing I can call succumbing to my stupid feelings for him. Nurse Ellen is standing there, sporting a knowing smirk. My face becomes hot in an instant.

"He's up," she tells us. "I thought you would want to talk to him."

Bryce pushes his long bangs back and steps away from me. "Right."

He glances at me with an undecipherable glint in his eyes, and I feel the walls around my heart crack. Quickly, I break the connection and follow Ellen back into the infirmary. Inside the cubicle, Morpheus is already sitting up.

"How are you feeling?" I ask.

"A bit tired," he admits. "How did you do that? The shadows should have hurt you."

"I don't know."

"Touching my shadows like that could have done irreparable damage to you."

"I'm fine."

"Maybe when I healed Daisy, I gave her immunity to certain things," Bryce suggests.

"Do you really think so?" I ask, then wonder if his healing also made me almost die in the woods.

"It's a guess." He shrugs.

"Fuck! We're going to miss the math quiz if we don't hurry up." Morpheus jumps from the bed and sways on the spot. Bryce and I reach for him at the same time, going for his arms.

"Whoa. You're not going anywhere, mister," Ellen says from the desk in the corner. "You're going back to bed."

"I can't miss that quiz," he insists.

"It's too late, Morpheus. The class already started."

"I can speak with your teacher and explain what happened. I'm sure he'll let you take the quiz at another date," Ellen says.

"That means we can study more." I offer him a smile. Then, sensing Bryce's stare, I turn to meet his gaze. "What? Do you have a problem with that too?"

"Nope. Not at all. You can let go of him now. I'll walk him back to the apartment."

Catching the cold tone in his voice, I release Morpheus and step back, but only because I don't want to involve him in my fight with his roommate.

"Do you think I can get a second chance from Mr. Atkins too?" I ask the nurse.

"I'll see what I can do." She winks at me.

I wait until Bryce and Morpheus are gone to have a private word with her.

"Have you heard of a case of an Idol overdosing on Silver-voltage?"

She raises an eyebrow and leans back in her chair. "No. Why do you ask?"

The answer is on the tip of my tongue, but because of Drusilla's compulsion, I can't say anything. "No reason. I was just curious."

Ellen watches me closely. I don't think she bought my vague answer.

I hitch a thumb behind me. "I'm going to head to the library and kill time until my next lecture. Thanks for helping Morpheus."

"No need to thank me. It's my job. Take care, Daisy."

My heart is heavy and my steps drag. I have no intention of going to the library. Since I don't want to return the book yet, I'll be avoiding the place for as long as I can. Instead, I head for my next class, biology, which I hate. And it's going to be even more dreadful without Toby around.

I park my butt on the stairs opposite the classroom and pull my book out. I might as well do some reading ahead. Heaven knows I haven't had much time to study these past few days. But I can't concentrate on the subject to save my life. I keep reading the same line over and over again because my brain is too busy replaying the events from the weekend and today. It's not until I sense a presence hovering in front of me that I return to the here and now.

"Toby? What are you doing here?" I jump to my feet and give him a once-over. He's back in his Gifted Academy uniform.

"Whatever you told my parents worked. Mom finally agreed to let me come back." He's grinning from ear to ear.

I hug him, so glad that at least something good happened for once. "That's wonderful news, Toby."

I ease off the embrace with a big smile on my face.

"What are you doing waiting here? Aren't you supposed to be in math class?" he asks.

Not wanting to kill Toby's good mood with bad news, I wave my hand dismissively. "It's a long story. But how come you aren't in class yourself?"

"I skipped first period because it was a quiz, and Principal Fallon arranged for me to take it at a later date since I missed a week of classes."

"I'm glad she was able to accommodate you." My reply is bitter, and Toby notices.

With a frown, he asks, "What's up? Did she do something to you?"

"It's more like what she didn't do for us. But I don't want to talk about that now."

Toby watches me without a reply for a couple of beats, then continues. "Rosie told me you spent the day with Felicity yesterday."

"Yeah, I did. She was in good spirits."

"That's good to know." Toby looks left and right before he moves closer in a cagey manner. "About the little discovery you made last Saturday, I have news on that front."

Apprehension licks the base of my spine. I tense as I wait for Toby to elaborate, but just then, the bell rings, announcing the end of first period. The hallway fills with students, making it impossible to have any secretive conversation. Damn it. Waiting for it will be a bitch. There goes the slim chance I get to pay any attention in class.

39

DAISY

Only after the school day is over do I get to have a moment alone with Toby. We're walking back to the senior dorm building when I deem it safe enough to bring the subject up.

"So, what is it that you wanted to tell me about you know who?" I ask, conscious that we could be overheard, even though there's no one nearby.

"I questioned my father, but he knows nothing about Mr. Silverstone's other business."

"You didn't ask point-blank, did you?"

"Of course not, Daisy. I don't want to worry my dad. If he suspects his employer could potentially be, you know, *that*, then he'll most likely resign. I can't do that to him. He loves his job."

"What's the news you wanted to tell me, then?"

"I got an internship with Mr. Silverstone. I'll be working at his gallery downtown."

"Toby, that could be dangerous. Besides, it'll eat time away from your studies."

"I just have to work on Saturdays. But I couldn't pass up the chance. You want to know if he's indeed who we think he is, right?"

I frown. "You don't think he suspects you'll be snooping around? I wasn't very subtle at his house. He knows I recognized him."

He also asked me to say hello to Bryce, and Rufio told me his brother was kidnapped by Knights. *Shit!* I can't believe I didn't make the connection until now. I'm almost certain Mr. Silverstone is behind Bryce's kidnapping. What am I going to do with that information now? I can't tell Bryce, at least not until I know what Mr. Silverstone's game plan is.

"I'll be careful. Don't worry. Besides, I really don't think Mr. Silverstone is the bad guy here. He saved you and Rosie. He's a hero in my book."

"There are no heroes when Idols are involved, Toby. Remember that."

We arrive at my building, and Toby seems inclined to accompany me all the way to my room. But Phoenix is there, and it'll be strange when I don't invite Toby in.

I fake a yawn. "Boy, I'm beaten. I think I'm going to take a nap before I tackle homework."

"Oh, I was hoping we could talk more, you know, catch up."

"Can we get a rain check? Last weekend wrecked me." I smile, hoping Toby doesn't insist.

"Sure. I suppose I should bury my face in books too. It's surreal how much I missed in one week."

"All right, then. I'll see you tomorrow in class."

Toby turns around and heads for his building. I wait a couple of seconds before I head in. The entry hall is buzzing with students milling about. Some glance in my direction, but mercifully, none of those stares linger. In any case, I take the stairs.

I only open the door a sliver, just enough for me to slip in. Can't risk the security cameras catching Phoenix inside by chance. He's still in bed, curled up in a fetal position. Moving closer, I find him deep asleep.

A myriad of emotions hits me all at once. I'm gutted that Phoenix has to endure such abuse from his own father. Living on the streets when I was younger, I learned to spot the signs. This wasn't the first time Phoenix suffered under his father's steely fists. And who knows what other despicable things that bastard has been doing to him.

I feel guilty that I was somehow the cause for his harsh punishment. But mostly I'm enraged that the monster has been doing this to Phoenix for a long time and no one has intervened. Phoenix has gone out of his way to keep his friends from knowing, but what about his mother? She must know.

Phoenix turns, lying on his back now. His face is scrunched up, and he begins to moan, then beg for mercy. *Fuck! Is he dreaming about his torment?*

I sit next to him to shake his shoulder. "Phoenix. Wake up."

"No, no, Dad. Leave me alone!" He trashes, shaking his head from side to side.

I grab both his shoulders and shake him harder. "Phoenix!"

His eyes open at the same time as he sends me flying backward. I let out a yelp, but I never connect with the wall. I stop midair and remain floating for a couple of beats. Phoenix sits up with wide eyes and erratic breathing.

"Daisy...."

In an instant, I drop to the floor with a loud thud. "Ouch."

Phoenix jumps out of bed and runs to me. "Are you okay? I'm so sorry. I didn't mean to do that."

"It's okay. At least you stopped me before I crashed."

Phoenix stares at me with eyes that still show surprise. He blinks a couple of times before he replies, "I don't think I stopped."

"You must have. How else do you explain me floating on air like that? I didn't suddenly become a fairy who can fly."

"I don't know. Maybe I did stop without realizing." He offers me his hand and lifts me from the floor.

"Your face. It looks so much better already." I lift my hand to touch his cheek, but I stop before I do so.

Without breaking eye contact, Phoenix captures my hand and flattens my palm against his cheek. "It's okay. You can touch me."

Heat spreads up my arm, and I become all too aware of his presence. The last erotic dream he sent me comes to the forefront of my mind, not helping me one bit.

"You were having a nightmare," I say.

He frowns, dropping my hand in the process. His Adam's apple bobbles up and down as he swallows hard. "Did I... say anything?"

"Yes."

"What?" A glimmer of fear flashes in his eyes, breaking my heart.

"Enough."

Phoenix takes a step back, facing the window. He rubs his chin and glances down. "It's pretty obvious, isn't it?"

"You never told anyone?"

"No. I can't. His mark prevents me from ever disclosing the truth."

"You mean that strange tattoo on your wrist?" I ask.

He looks at me, not hiding the tears that have escaped his tormented eyes. "Yes. It keeps my mouth shut and stops me from defending myself."

"How long has it been going on?"

"Long enough." Phoenix looks away, drying his face with the back of his forearm. "You can't tell anyone."

"Why not? Your father can't keep doing that to you without retribution. He needs to be stopped."

"Yes, he does. But I'm the one who's going to make him pay."

"How? You just said you can't because—"

"I know what I said!" he snaps, making me wince. His face is contorted in rage, but it changes to remorse when he sees me through his fury.

He crosses the distance between us and holds me by the shoulders. "I'm sorry. I didn't mean to lash out at you."

Tears are prickling my eyes now, and my nose is burning. I'm moments away from crying my eyes out. I want to help Phoenix, but I don't know how. If I weren't a powerless Norm, I'd make his ruthless father suffer, despite Phoenix's desire to get revenge himself.

"I know. I'm sorry too. I wish I could help."

"You're helping."

The intensity of Phoenix's gaze changes, going from utterly broken to smoldering in a few seconds. The atmosphere changes with it too, and my heart responds in kind.

Phoenix caresses my face with the tip of his fingers, sending tingles down my spine.

"I don't know why I feel this way when I'm around you," he murmurs. "I wanted to hate you so badly when you started here."

"I think you did."

He shakes his head. "No, I didn't. Not you, per se. I hated that you could see right through my bullshit."

"It didn't stop you from torturing me with your visions."

Phoenix's eyebrows twitch. "I was a jackass. And you were right about those. They were my wet dreams, my deepest desires."

He runs his fingers down my neck to the middle of my chest, leaving a trail of goose bumps in their wake even through my clothes. My breathing is already coming out in bursts, and heat has pooled between my legs.

"What was the last vision you sent me? Why that cabin?" I ask.

He frowns. "Cabin? What are you talking about?"

"Cabin in the woods, wintertime, fireplace?"

His eyebrows arch suddenly, and his mouth makes a perfect O. "Daisy, that wasn't a vision. That was a dream. *My* dream."

"Are you saying you didn't send it to me on purpose?"

"No."

There's no mirth in his gaze, no shade of lie. He's telling the truth, which makes me even more confused.

"We shared a dream?" I ask. "What does it mean?"

Phoenix captures my face between his large hands. "It means we're more connected than we thought. Tell me you feel it too, Daisy. This link between us."

I remember the immense sense of peace I felt in the dream. I was happy and safe in Phoenix's arms. And when I was high and my reservations were gone, I felt the same way. My eyes drop to his lips. The split from before has healed, leaving only a faint scar. Before I can stop myself, I rise on my tiptoes and kiss him, softly at first, but Phoenix is not inclined to take things slow, it seems. His tongue darts inside my mouth, twisting with mine in a delicious dance. I step into his space, and he releases my face to lift me off the floor. Just like in the dream, I wrap my legs around his hips, clinging to him like a monkey.

Phoenix begins to move, and then we're back to my bed. Still lip-locked, he removes my jacket and unbuttons my shirt. He cups my breast over my cotton bra, squeezing gently.

"So soft," he mumbles against my mouth.

In retaliation, I run my fingers over his washboard abs. His skin is hot and taut, but I take a great sense of satisfaction when I feel goose bumps form where I touch him.

"Daisy, you're playing with fire."

I ease off the kiss to peer into his eyes. I know where we're going, and despite our history, I don't want to stop. I want to see if the feelings in our shared dream are real.

"I know."

Phoenix stares at me with hooded eyes. "I don't want you to do anything you'll regret later."

His words are laced with emotion and pain, and it makes me even more sure of what I want. The physical attraction between us is off the charts and undeniable, but I also have this burning need to make Phoenix forget about his horrible ordeal.

"I want you," I say simply.

"Thank fuck." He captures my lips again, pushing me gently back until I'm lying on the bed.

Despite my statement, Phoenix doesn't lower his body to mine. He keeps the distance, bracing on his forearms as he devours my mouth. I reach for his jeans, brushing my fingers over the bulge there.

Phoenix trembles and moves out of my reach. His mouth goes south, leaving wet kisses down my neck and chest. Cupping one of my breasts, he licks the exposed swell, making me arch my back with a sigh. Then he pushes the fabric out of the way and traces lazy circles with his tongue around my nipple. I'm squirming now while a delicious ache blossoms between my legs. Sensing my need, Phoenix cups my sex, bringing forth a loud moan from me.

"That's it, Daisy. Show me how much you want this."

He pushes my panties aside and flicks my clit with his finger.

"I need more."

Misunderstanding what I mean, he inserts a finger inside of me. The sensation is delicious, but what I really want right now is a taste of him. I press my hand against his chest and push him back.

"What?" he asks.

"Take off your clothes."

Phoenix's lips curl into a lopsided grin. "Bossy. I love this side of you."

He stands up and slowly removes his jeans and boxers. His

hard cock springs free, making my mouth water. Sitting on the edge of the bed now, I reach for him, curling my fingers around his shaft. Phoenix closes his eyes and lets out a hiss. Precum pools on his head as I glide my hand up and down.

"Fuck, Daisy. You're killing me here."

He dips his chin, locking his gaze with mine as I lick his base. Slowly, I draw my tongue up his length. When I cover the head with my mouth, Phoenix grabs a chunk of my hair and yanks a little. He wants to take control, and I let him have it, instinctively knowing that's what he needs. I let him fuck my mouth as I dig my fingers into his ass. I take everything he wants to give me and more. His cock gets harder in my mouth, his grunts louder. He's close to the edge.

But then he steps away suddenly, breathing hard.

"What?"

"No, I don't want our first time to be this way, savage and manic. I want to come inside your pussy, Daisy. Nice and slow."

With a flick of his fingers, he removes the rest of my clothes. Exposed, I lose a bit of my bravado.

"You're nervous," he says.

"A little."

"Do you want to stop?"

"No."

Relief washes over his face. He takes a step closer, dropping to his knees and placing his hands over my thighs. "Can I taste you, Daisy?"

The image of a sex god kneeling before me and asking if he can taste me makes me tongue-tied. I nod, earning another smile from him. He parts my legs and moves his mouth to my core. One flick of his tongue and I'm a goner. I collapse back on the mattress and lose all grip on reality. With each stroke, Phoenix pushes me further and further to a land where everything is bliss. But it's not until he sucks my clit into his mouth that I shatter into a billion particles and cry out his name.

Seconds or minutes might have gone by when I sense Phoenix stand again.

"Please tell me you have a condom," he says gruffly.

With my eyes still closed, I say, "In the bathroom, under the sink."

I hear the hinges of a door opening, then the sound of a wrapper being torn. But I only open my eyes when Phoenix covers my body with his and the head of his cock is at my entrance.

"I promised you nice and slow, but I confess, I'm about to explode."

"Explode then, but inside."

He slides in, almost sending me over the edge again. To give him credit, he does try to pace himself, but his thrusts soon become harder and faster, and in no time, he reaches his climax. I can't complain, because he takes me with him, and it's just as good as the first time.

40

DAISY

The sun has set, and Phoenix is sound asleep. He might have lost control during the first time, but he made good on his promise during the second round. Who knew I could have so many orgasms in such a short period of time? My clit is still tingling from it.

But now that I've satiated my hunger for him, the grim reality comes back to haunt me. I stare at the tattoo on his wrist, and the fury from before returns with a vengeance. I have to find a way to free Phoenix from his father's hold.

An idea strikes me. I get out of bed and grab a piece of paper and a pencil. Then I return to Phoenix and sketch the tattoo's design to the best of my ability. Maybe the rare book still in my possession has details about it and how I can remove it.

Tiptoeing so as to not wake Phoenix up, I get dressed and walk out. I'm not sure what time it is, but it can't be too late to bother my neighbors. Bryce was able to find the solution to Phoenix's mind invasion with his powers. I'm hoping he can help me again. It shows how desperate I am to help Phoenix that I'm willing to put my pride aside and ask for Bryce's help.

But it's not Bryce who answers the door. Morpheus does. "Daisy? Is something the matter?"

"Can I come in for a second?"

"Sure." He lets me through, and when the door closes, he asks. "What's on your mind?"

"Is Bryce around?"

"No. He and Rufio went out to grab something to eat. Why?"

"I was hoping he could help my find some particular information here." I show Morpheus the book.

His eyebrows almost hit his hairline. "You haven't returned that yet?"

"No, and I don't plan to."

A grin unfurls on Morpheus's face. "I like your rebel side, Daisy. So, what is it you're looking for?"

"Have you ever seen this design before?" I show him my sketch.

He takes the piece of paper from me and frowns. "Is this Phoenix's tattoo?"

"Yes."

Morpheus looks straight into my eyes. "What do you want to know about it?"

I nibble on my lower lip. Phoenix is adamant that his friends don't find out about his torment, and I can't betray his trust. Revealing his secret would be a violation. "I want to know what it means."

"Riiight. Well, I don't know how Bryce helped you before."

"He let his hand hover over the book until the pages flipped to the information I was looking for."

Rubbing his neck, Morpheus pinches his lips. "I don't think I can help you with that. But... can I have the book?"

He takes it to the couch, placing it on the coffee table before taking a seat.

"What are you going to do?" I ask.

"I can't use the same method Bryce did, but like most Idols,

I'm pretty fast." He then proceeds to flip the pages manually so fast that they become a blur.

"You're going to rip them," I say.

"No, I'm not."

It takes him only a minute to find what I'm looking for.

"Here it is, the mark of Ogmios." Morpheus points at a design fairly similar to the one I sketched.

"Ogmios? What's that?" I peer closer.

"Not a what, a who. He was an ancient binding god who had the ability to bind people to himself and control their actions. Nasty piece of shit. Why would Phoenix want to tattoo Ogmios's mark on himself?"

Crap. I can't let Morpheus ponder too hard about it. He might suspect something.

"Come on. Isn't that kind of what Phoenix does with his visions? In a way, he's controlling other people's actions. I'm pretty sure he admires this god."

Morpheus drops his gaze to the book again. "Maybe."

I pull the book from his grasp, folding the corner of the page before I close it. "Okay, thanks for your help. I guess I'll see you tomorrow."

"Probably not."

"Why not?" I ask.

"Didn't you hear it? I got a week's suspension for attacking Drusilla."

"What? That's bullshit. She was— " Words fail me, and I suddenly feel sick.

"I can't believe you still can't tell me what she did to you. Son of a bitch."

His remark makes me so fucking angry that I push through the nausea. The room begins to spin as I fight to break free from her compulsion.

"I... caught her.... Ugh." I take a seat opposite Morpheus and dip my head between my shoulders.

"Don't force it, Daisy. You can get seriously ill."

"No… I have to. Fuck!"

I imagine the compulsion as bindings around my tongue. One by one, I picture them snapping until my tongue is free. "She took some new drug… and it looked like… she was OD'ing."

As the last word finally rolls out, the nausea passes. I broke Drusilla's compulsion.

"A new drug?"

I lift my gaze to his. "I thought it was Silver-voltage at first, but I asked Nurse Ellen, and she's never heard of an Idol overdosing on Silver-voltage before."

Morpheus seems troubled. "Or maybe Drusilla got a bad batch of it. It serves her right. I'm convinced she was the one distributing Silver-voltage to Fringes, or worse, forcing them to take it against their will. Of course, I can't prove anything."

"And it wouldn't matter either. It seems nothing she does earns a punishment here at school."

Morpheus's gaze becomes darker. "That's why I don't mind the suspension. She felt my power at full blast, and it lingers. She won't bother anyone for a while."

"It's still not fair that you were suspended. Maybe I can speak to Principal Fallon on your behalf."

"Yeah, I don't think that's going to help much. Drusilla's parents asked for my expulsion. Principal Fallon negotiated for a week's suspension. I should be glad I'm still here."

I stand up, knowing Bryce and Rufio might return at any minute. "I'll bring you notes from math class. I hope Mr. Atkins will allow you to take the quiz at another time."

"Thanks, Daisy."

I'm at the door with my hand on the knob when Morpheus speaks again. "Say hello to Phoenix for me."

I turn around with wide eyes. "What?"

Morpheus smiles, but it doesn't reach his eyes. "I can smell him all over you. Don't worry. I'm not judging."

Mortified, I can't find the words to reply. I simply walk out with my face in flames. But the worst of this exchange is that I feel guilty. Over what, I don't know.

When I return to my room, Phoenix is sitting on my bed, holding something in his hand. The light on the nightstand is on, casting a soft orange hue over his golden frame. He lifts his head to meet my eyes when I enter.

"Where did you go?"

"I went to ask Morpheus something." I clutch the book against my chest. Phoenix is giving me seriously weird vibes right now. "What do you have there?"

He looks down again and laughs without humor. "Honestly, I have no idea. Maybe you could explain to me why you have an old picture of Principal Fallon and Mr. X."

41

PHOENIX

With deer-caught-in-headlights eyes, Daisy takes a step back. Her face pales, and she hugs the book she's carrying tighter against her chest. I have a wild guess of who one of the other men in the picture is based on her reaction. I confess I felt sucker punched when I found the photo by accident. But the time I spent staring at it before Daisy came in helped me calm down and not jump to conclusions.

"Daisy?" I prompt.

"It's not what you think."

"You don't know what I'm thinking."

"I swear I didn't know Principal Fallon's and Mr. X's connection until very recently."

"And what *is* their connection?"

She drops her gaze to the floor. "I don't think you're going to like my answer."

Her body is shaking. She's terrified of me, of my reaction. Shit. I don't want her to ever feel that in my presence again. I'm not sure when I completely flipped, but I'm firmly on her side now, no matter what her agenda is.

I stand up and approach her slowly. "Hey, whatever it is, you can tell me. I'm not going to hurt you."

She lifts her chin, and I notice her hazel eyes are brighter than before. "Mr. X is my uncle."

"What? How is that—"

"Adopted uncle," she adds quickly. "I only found out a couple of days ago."

"Son of a bitch. And this picture?"

"It came from an anonymous sender last week."

"Shit. So Principal Fallon and Mr. X knew each other since they were our age? I can't believe it. Do Bryce and Rufio know?"

"Of course not. And you can't tell them." She takes a step in my direction.

"Why not?"

She looks away, nibbling on her lower lip, something she does when she's nervous.

"The other two men in the picture are my father and his older brother, William. He and Principal Fallon were involved."

Holy shit. Everything is beginning to make sense now. "That's why she fought so hard to get you here."

"So it seems." Daisy still won't meet my gaze.

"Hey." I move closer and touch her shoulder. "You don't have to worry about me. I won't tell anyone about this."

"I know I asked you not to, but why would you keep quiet? I'm nothing to you."

Fuck. She truly believes that.

I touch her face, caressing her soft skin. I could tell her she's the opposite of nothing, but I can't say that without sounding like an idiot. "You're keeping my secret, and it's only fair that I keep yours."

She stares into my eyes without blinking, maybe trying to guess whether I'm lying or not. Finally she says, "Thank you."

The close proximity to her is reawakening certain urges. My dick twitches in my boxer shorts. I'm a second away from kissing

Daisy when she steps away. "Morpheus is alone in the apartment, and he guessed you and I… well, he figured we hooked up."

There's a sudden tightness in my chest. "And are you bothered by it?"

"No."

"Daisy, don't lie to me."

She lets out a sigh. "Okay, if you must know, I was embarrassed."

"Why?"

"Why?" Her voice rises to a shrill. "Maybe because in less than a month, I slept with you, Bryce, and Rufio."

"So what?" I shrug. "You have needs. I get that."

"That's your answer? I have needs? Aren't you even a little jealous?"

I hold back a grin. "Do you want me to be jealous?"

She doesn't answer right away. I wish I had the power to read minds.

"I don't know." She pulls her hair back. "I'm so confused."

"Then let's simplify things." I head for the door, not caring that I'm only wearing underwear. The whip marks on my back have healed; I checked in the mirror earlier.

"Where are you going?" she asks.

"Not where *I'm* going. Where *we're* going." I grab her hand and steer her into the hallway. When she sees where I'm headed, she digs her heels into the floor.

"Please let me go. This is nuts."

"No, this is the smartest thing to do." I open the door, and like I sensed, I find Bryce and Rufio in the kitchen, pulling take-out food from their plastic bags. They freeze when they see me with Daisy.

"Oh crap," Morpheus mutters from the couch.

"What's the meaning of this?" Bryce walks around the kitchen counter, tense as hell.

"This is an impromptu meeting to clarify a few things," I reply.

Bryce turns his attention to Daisy and frowns. "What things?"

"Oh, fucking great. You finally got what you wanted, huh?" Rufio pouts like a child.

Understanding finally seems to hit Bryce. "You slept with him," he addresses Daisy.

She pulls her arm free and glares at me first before turning her ire on Bryce. "Yeah, I did. So what?"

Bryce doesn't answer, but he's clenching his jaw so tight that a muscle twitches.

"Yo, before you blow a fuse, let's all calm down. I like Daisy, and I want to keep seeing her," I say.

"Really?" Bryce asks. "Since when? Not too long ago, you wanted to get rid of her at all costs."

Man, he has me there. But I'm not going to let him create a chasm between Daisy and me by reminding her of my mistakes.

"Bryce, don't you know there's a fine line between hate and passion?"

"Oh my God. He's spewing clichés now." Morpheus shakes his head. "We're fucked."

"Bite me, asshole."

"The question is, does Daisy want to keep seeing *you*?" Rufio raises an eyebrow.

Heat surges through my cheeks. I didn't stop to consider that she might not want anything to do with me. *Shit.* I'm an idiot. I watch her closely, afraid she'll laugh in my face for having such crazy notions.

"All of you, stop staring!" she yells, totally pissed off.

Rufio walks over to her. "Why would she settle for you when she can have *me*?"

Bryce curses under his breath and moves across the living room.

"I'm right here," she retorts. "Stop talking like I'm a blow-up doll you picked up at a sex shop."

The cocky grin wilts from Rufio's face. "I'm sorry. I didn't mean—"

"To sound like an ass? Well, you did." She turns to the food on the counter. "What do have there? I'm hungry."

She moves toward it without waiting for Rufio's reply and opens one of the boxes. "Pepper steak, my favorite." She nabs a set of chopsticks and, with box in hand, walks to the door.

"Where are you going?" I ask.

"Back to my room. And for the record, I'm not choosing."

She slams the door shut, leaving me speechless. I turn to Bryce and Morpheus, who are equally flabbergasted.

"I'm not giving her up," Rufio announces.

"Me neither, douche," I say.

We both look at Bryce, who's still watching the front door.

"I think Daisy broke your brother," I tell Rufio.

He finally unfreezes and glares at me. "She didn't break me, but she almost cost Rufio his life."

"No, she *saved* my life," Rufio insists. "She never asked me to go fight those gang members. I offered, and I'd do it again."

"What's your problem with her?" I ask. "Yeah, her father hated our kind, but he was a Norm. They all do."

"Daisy doesn't," Morpheus pipes in.

"How can you be so sure?" Bryce asks.

"I know she doesn't, and if you pulled your head out of your ass, you'd agree with me."

Bryce drops his chin and stares at the ground. "Well, she fucking hates me now."

"Have you tried apologizing?" Rufio raises an eyebrow, smirking.

"You want me to mend things with Daisy? Why?" he asks.

"Because I'm not stupid. I know she has feelings for you."

"She's linked to all of us," Morpheus adds. "And I think it's in our best interest to see where this connection leads instead of fighting it. Remember what we discovered at my father's," he says to Bryce.

"Which was?" I ask.

"There's a possibility Daisy has demigod blood."

I quirk a brow. "Whoa, back up. If she had demigod blood, wouldn't she be an Idol or at least a Fringe?"

"Not if she's related to the Idol who reneged on her power and gave it back to the gods."

"You think she's related to Magia?" I ask.

"Who?" all three ask at the same time.

"I can't believe you've never heard of Magia, the anathema of our society."

Seeing their blank stares, it seems the story my horrid father used to tell me is not as well-known as I thought.

"All I know is there was this Idol named Magia who gave back her powers many millennia ago."

"Any chance you know Magia's last name?" Morpheus asks.

"Nope. I always thought the story was stupid. Never bothered to ask more details." Mostly because of who was telling the story.

"Okay, I guess I'll have to work with only her first name," Morpheus says.

"Why is this important anyway?"

Bryce stands up. "Because there are too many powerful players interested in Daisy. If she's not working for them, then she's a pawn and therefore not safe."

42

———

DAISY

A WEEK LATER

After the embarrassing meeting Phoenix forced me to participate in, I avoided all those assholes when I could. In the few classes I had with them, I purposely ignored the group. I still shared the notes from math class with Morpheus, but I refused to step foot in their apartment. I guess he'll just have to handle math on his own until I can figure out what to do with my life and all the secrets I'm keeping.

Morpheus was right about one thing though. Drusilla, and consequently her friend Renata, left me alone the whole week. But I should have known my peace wouldn't last a very long time. And Bryce is the one determined to wreck it.

When I walk out of biology, he's there waiting for me. I tense up on the spot. Rufio, Phoenix, and Morpheus have been nothing but nice to me, but Bryce is still giving me a hard time. And when I say hard time, I mean his silent treatment.

Something is different about him today though, and my heart is already going crazy, beating out of sync as I drink the guy in. The yearning hits me hard, as it always does when I'm near him. Today is especially off the charts. I hate that I crave his touch when I know he doesn't deserve it.

He had to show up looking like this on the day I don't have my partner in crime. Toby has the flu and missed class.

As much as I want to appear strong, Bryce hurt me more by shunning me than if he'd hit me with a physical blow.

"Bryce? What are you doing here?" Rufio asks, stopping next to me.

"I came to talk to Daisy, *alone.*"

I sense a shift in the air, a darkness, and I can guess who's projecting that energy. Morpheus. Today was his first day back from suspension. I don't want them to fight in the middle of the hallway. If Morpheus is involved in an altercation again, he might not get another chance.

"All right, let's get this over with." I veer to my right without waiting for Bryce's reply. He catches up though and walks next to me.

My throat is dry and choked up. I thought I was fine being estranged from him, but it turns out I was in Denial Land. I'm so nervous now, it's not even funny. I haven't forgotten that his father killed the uncle I never knew or that he could have ordered my parents' murder. But is it right to blame Bryce and Rufio for the sins of their father? I know Bryce doesn't share the man's views, and truth be told, Rufio doesn't either.

My nervousness goes away when a couple of girls to my right attempt to get his attention with giggles and hair tossing.

"Hi, Bryce. Looking good this morning," one of them says, stepping closer to him.

Her friend turns to me with glee in her eyes, almost as if she's daring me to do something. My blood is boiling now, and I want to gouge their eyes out with my bare hands, but I'm not on Drusilla's level of crazy.

I quicken my steps, leaving Bryce behind to deal with his

fan club. A second later, he's next to me again, walking at the same rapid pace as me.

"Why are you mad now?" he asks.

"Who said I'm mad?"

"I can tell. I just don't know if it's because I asked to spend time with you alone or those girls back there set you off."

"The former, obviously. I don't give a rat's ass about...." I can't bring myself to finish the sentence. Of course I care about other girls coming on to him. But I'm not going to admit it.

"About what? My love life?" Bryce continues.

"Whatever. You wanted to talk to me alone, so talk."

"We aren't alone. Even the walls have ears in this place. Let's have lunch off campus."

There's a lurch in my chest. I'm not sure I'm ready to be alone with Bryce again. My heart is pounding, and my ears are buzzing. But I let Bryce steer me toward the exit. Instead of heading to the garage, we go to the front of the school building where his shiny SUV is already parked by the curb.

"Where are we going?" I ask when we're both inside his car.

Bryce turns on the engine, and without looking at me, he replies, "I discovered my mother's connection to Mr. X. I followed her to Unearthly Desires one day."

My stomach bottoms out. *Fuck, fuck, fuck.* Did Phoenix tell him? No, he wouldn't do that, would he? I look out the window, regretting agreeing to come out with him alone.

"It was where your mother recruited me," I say, hoping Bryce doesn't know about the picture.

"Wait, what? She was there on the same evening we were?" Bryce's tone is agitated now.

Okay, maybe he doesn't know about my father's connection to Mr. X and his mother.

"Why are you getting all worked up about it? Mr. X said they were friends."

"They're in cahoots about something, Daisy. My mother doesn't do anything without purpose. She has plans for you."

I close my eyes for a brief second. Bryce is getting too close to the truth.

"What kind of plans?"

"I don't know. It might not be to your liking. She gave Rufio carte blanche to bully you on your first week."

If he had told me that a month ago, I would have been surprised, but not anymore. Xavier warned me not to trust her.

"Why would she do that?" I ask.

"I still haven't been able to get a straight answer from her. She keeps talking about how we all have a role to play in the board game of the gods."

I rub my forehead, trying to ward off the headache that's brewing.

"I'm such a fool," I murmur. "I should have listened to my instincts and never come here."

"Please don't say that." Bryce glances at me.

"Why not? Nothing good has happened to me since I joined Gifted Academy."

A few good things have happened, but I'm feeling wretched and in the mood to whine.

"Nothing good, huh?" He quirks a brow.

My cheeks become warmer, and I avert my gaze. "Sex doesn't count."

Lies. It does, especially when I got it from three incredibly sexy guys.

Bryce doesn't speak for another minute. He takes the nearest exit and stops at the first junk food restaurant that pops up.

Staring straight ahead, he asks, "How did your parents die, Daisy?"

The question feels like a steely knife perforating my chest. I curl my fingers around the fabric of my skirt without meeting his gaze.

"I told you already."

"You told me a lie. I want the truth now."

Tears prick my eyes, clouding my vision. Shit, he's going to make me cry. The last thing I want is to talk about that terrible night, especially now knowing what his father might have done. But I'm trapped in his car with nowhere to go.

"It happened in the middle of the night. I couldn't sleep well, so I was eavesdropping on my parents' conversation when Idols blew our door open and attacked. They killed my mother first, then my father."

"How many?" Bryce's voice is low and tight, which prompts me to lift my gaze to his.

"Three."

His eyes, which in the past week have been cold and hard, are swimming with emotion now.

"How did you and Rosie escape?"

"Some other Idols came in, and they fought our attackers off. Rosie and I slipped out and went down the fire escape ladder."

"It never occurred to you that those Idols might have been Knights?"

Another guess too close to the truth. I know they were Knights, and I met the guy. But again, not something I can tell Bryce. He was kidnapped by them, and as far as he's concerned, the Knights are the enemy. It doesn't help that they're manufacturing Idol-killing weapons and neutralizers that somehow made it to the criminal underbelly of Saturn's Bay.

"No. I didn't dare to believe there were Idols who cared about Norms. It was easier for me to hate all of you."

"And do you still feel that way?" He inches closer and wipes off the rogue tear that rolled down my cheek.

"Sometimes I wish I did."

Bryce's touch is electrifying against my skin; it makes me tingle all over and crave more than just his fingers on my face. My lips part when I guess what his intention is.

"I don't want you to hate me, Daisy, even though you have every right to do so. I shouldn't have lashed out at you the way I did. Or blamed you for Rufio's attack."

"No, you shouldn't have."

"You make me feel things I've never felt before. It's like you reanimated my dead heart. I was afraid I'd given a piece of me to someone who despised me, someone who wanted me dead."

He's too close. Too damn close.

"Bryce, I don't despise you. How can I hate someone who brought me back from the brink of death? How could I wish you were gone?" My voice gets choked up at the end.

"I know it's hard to believe, but I'd run through hellfire to save you, Daisy. You're like fireworks in a starless night, and I'm done being afraid of what this feeling means."

My mind is racing, and my heart is not far behind. I don't know what to make of Bryce's confession. *Is it true or only a heartfelt lie?* He cups my cheek and breaches the final distance between us, obliterating any coherent thought in my head. All I can feel now is Bryce's lips against mine and the taste of his tongue. This is not our first kiss, but it's the one that's going to leave a mark.

I run my fingers through his soft hair and then pull him closer to me. An electric current is exchanged between us, and even with my eyes closed, I notice the brightness all around us. The same thing happened when Bryce healed me. The only thing in need of mending today is my broken heart.

Bryce breaks the kiss to lean his forehead against mine. "Thank you," he says.

"For what?"

"For letting me do this. I know I don't deserve your forgiveness, not after what I put you through, but I'm hoping you'll let me in again one day."

I pull away from him to stare into his eyes. I see no trace of deceit in them, but he's right in assuming I haven't forgiven him yet. My body might be quick to succumb to the undeniable connection between us, but my mind can't let go that easily.

"I want to trust you, Bryce. I really do. But...." I look away. I don't want him to read in my gaze that I'm also being deceitful. But I can't share what I know if I don't trust him. Too many lives might be destroyed if Bryce isn't the guy I want to believe he is.

"All I'm asking for is another chance." He pinches my chin between his forefinger and thumb and turns my face to his again. "Please, Daisy."

"What does that mean?"

"For starters, let us protect you."

I frown, ready to offer a retort.

"Yes, *us*," he continues. "I know you have a connection with the others, and I don't begrudge you that."

"Are you saying you don't care that I slept with Rufio or Phoenix?"

Bryce returns to his side of the car and laughs sarcastically. "Of course I care. I'm flawed and selfish. I don't want to share you with anybody, not even my brother. But if that's what you want, if it's what you *need*, then I'm game." He looks at me again.

"And also, I've been meaning to return this to you." He pulls my father's diary from the storage compartment between our seats. "I'm sorry I've kept it for so long."

I clutch my most precious possession against my chest as I stare at Bryce, speechless. But thankfully, I don't have to come up with a reply right away, as his phone pings, announcing an income message.

He looks at it, then back up at me. "It's Morpheus asking where we are."

"Shit. We totally lost track of time. We have to get back or I'll be late for class."

"Don't worry. We're not too far from campus. So, are we good?" he asks.

My heart wants me to say yes, but my head hesitates. The gleam of hope dims in his eyes, making me feel guilty as hell.

"I get it. Don't worry, Daisy. I'll earn your trust again."

43

MORPHEUS

First come the shivers down my spine, and then my hands and arms become numb from the cold. The shadows are restless again but somehow still contained by the bracelets. I stumble out of the cafeteria with my phone already out, not waiting for Rufio and Phoenix to join me. I want to call Bryce, but the hallway is packed with students, and I don't want to be overheard. No sooner do I finish texting him than someone bumps into my shoulder.

"What the fuck!" I yell, but the culprit, Pietro, doesn't even look at me. He's pushing people out of the way as he sprints toward the school's exit.

What the hell is wrong with him?

"Any word from Bryce yet?" Rufio asks as he and Phoenix join me.

"No."

"Who are you glowering at?" Phoenix follows my line of sight.

"Pietro Armani. The idiot bumped into me like he's walking blind."

"He's a moron," Phoenix replies. "He was playing Formula

One in the garage the other day."

White-hot pain flares up on my forehead, making me hiss. I press the heel of my hand against it and close my eyes for a second.

"Oh shit. Is the god in your head again?" Phoenix asks.

"No," I grit out. "I think I'm about to have another vision."

Rufio and Phoenix grab each of my forearms and help me walk to an empty classroom. It's humiliating how my gift can turn me into a useless mess. I take a seat and lean my elbows on the desk, holding my head in my hands. The bracelets are ice cold, and they burn against my skin.

"I'm calling Bryce," Rufio announces.

Nausea has my stomach rolling, forcing me to clamp my jaw tight. A groan escapes my lips.

"Dude, what can we do to help?" Phoenix asks.

I lift my chin to look at him. "I think I'm going to be sick."

"Fuck. Hold on." He runs to the corner of the classroom and grabs the garbage can.

"Bryce won't answer the phone now. Son a bitch." Rufio glares at the device in his hand. Tiny dark veins appear on his cheeks, and his eyes flash brighter.

"Whoa. Don't you dare go crazy now. I can only handle one of you at a time." Phoenix sets the garbage can in front of me and steps away.

"Bite me, asshole." Rufio stares daggers at him.

I open my mouth to tell them to chill the fuck out when another round of white-hot pain slams into my head. I involuntarily close my eyes, and then the vision comes. Bryce's SUV on the highway, followed by Pietro's flashy sports car cutting him off, and then an explosion.

My eyes fly open. "Daisy!"

"Daisy what?" Rufio is in front of me. "What did you see?"

I jump out of the chair, ignoring the throbbing pain in my head. "A collision. We need to get on the road immediately."

BRYCE

It's hard to keep my eyes on the road when all I want to do is stare at Daisy. I wish I could read minds. There have been occasions when I thought she heard me in her head, but I don't have any solid proof of that.

But the tension inside the car can't be denied. Does she regret kissing me? She didn't hesitate or pull away, but now her body is tense as she's staring out the window.

"Do you want to listen to some music?" I ask.

"Sure." She shrugs.

I turn on the radio and tune in to her favorite station, The Freaks. I don't know what song is playing, but the background noise does little to ease the heaviness in my chest.

"A penny for your thoughts," I say.

"I'm not thinking about anything worth sharing. I'm just trying to process everything."

"I never asked you, who gave you that dagger?"

She lets out a heavy sigh. "Strangers. I was on a bus coming back from Saturn's Bay when it broke down. I wasn't far from school, so I decided to walk the rest of the way. Then this old couple offered me a ride."

"You accepted a ride from strangers?" I can't help the alarm in my voice.

"No, at least not at first. But eventually I did. In hindsight, I think they could have been Knights in disguise. It's possible they compelled me to hop into their car."

A strangled noise escapes me. "They could have been working for the ones who are trying to kill you."

"Don't you think I know that?" she snaps. "It's not like I can protect myself from compulsion."

"I'm sorry. I'm not mad at you. I'm fucking pissed that I can't protect you at all times."

"Nobody can, Bryce. It's an impossible task."

My phone stars to ring. I see Rufio's name flashing on the screen, but I'm not in the mood to deal with him right now.

"It shouldn't be impossible to me."

"Because you're a level seventeen?" Daisy scoffs. "Don't let your ego go to your head."

"It's not my e—" A red sports car zooms past me on the highway. "What the hell!"

A second later, it swerves sharply to the right, completely cutting me off. I press on the brake, but I know I won't avoid a collision.

"Fuck!"

Daisy yells and everything seems to happen in slow motion. My tires screech while I unbuckle my seat belt with my mind and throw myself in front of Daisy. She reaches for her own seat belt, unbuckling it too.

What the hell? Is she crazy?

She then opens her door and grabs me by the lapel of my jacket, yanking me while she jumps out of the moving car. We both hit the ground hard, but not as hard as we should have with the way my car was speeding. We roll together in a tangle of limbs, ending up on the grassy part of the side of the highway.

It's then that I realize we *were* actually moving at a snail's pace, and suddenly, normal speed returns. My SUV slams into the sports car, and both cars explode in a shower of twisted metal and fire. I throw my body over Daisy's while projecting my power outward. Bright light envelopes us, shielding us from the blast. But the protective dome can't deflect the deafening sound of the explosion. The noise seems to go on forever, or maybe it's just the ringing in my ears.

After a moment, I rein in my power, and the brightness

fades. The soil surrounding us is charred, and there are still a few pieces of metal that are bright red. Dark smoke is quickly blown in our direction, which can be just as deadly.

"Come on." I get to my feet, dragging Daisy with me.

She's staring at everything wide-eyed and with mouth agape. I curl my arm around her shoulder, bringing her flush against my body. She's shaking, damn it.

Together, we amble away from the crash, but it's impossible to stop staring at it.

Finally, when we're at a safe distance, Daisy speaks. "Do you think the other driver was able to get out?"

"Not likely. I don't know how we did."

Daisy looks at me, stunned. "You mean you didn't slow time to a crawl?"

I stare at her for a moment, at a loss for words. "No, Daisy. I can't bend time."

"Are you sure? You didn't know you could heal either."

I shake my head. "But I knew what I was doing as I healed you. I could feel the power coming from my core. I felt nothing while everything was happening in slow motion. It wasn't me."

"What does the power feel like?"

"I... it's hard to explain."

The sound of a vehicle approaching grabs my attention. Rufio's car stops on the other side of the crash. He, Phoenix, and Morpheus jump out, and at first, they don't see us. Rufio lets out a roar and runs toward the burning mess, ripping at his hair.

"We're okay," I yell and wave.

I finally get their attention, and in another second the three of them are standing in front of us. Rufio yanks Daisy from my hold and crushes her into a tight hug.

"Fuck. I thought you were gone," he whispers.

"I'm okay." She hugs him back, but after a moment, she eases off.

Rufio gives her a once-over, and then he looks at me. "How did you get out of the car before it exploded?"

"I don't know."

"Are you okay?" Morpheus asks Daisy.

"Yeah. A bit sore from the jump, but no broken bones or anything."

"Shit, girl. You're a disaster magnet." Phoenix pulls her into his arms now and kisses the top of her head.

"I don't mean to be," she replies in a small voice. After a moment, she steps away from him and glances at the wreckage.

I wrap my arm around her waist, needing to offer her comfort as much as I need her to comfort me. I can't deny that I'm still shaken.

Phoenix turns his attention to the crash site. Then he moves closer to it.

"Where are you going? There could be another explosion," Morpheus says.

"Do you know who was driving that car?" Daisy asks.

"Yes. Pietro Armani. I had a vision about it," Morpheus looks at me.

"Shit. Why would he do such a thing?" I ask.

"I don't know. He left school in a hurry, almost as if he was *compelled* to go somewhere."

I don't miss Morpheus's insinuation.

"Do you think Drusilla forced him to commit suicide and take us out in the process?" Daisy asks.

Rufio's gaze darkens, and then it flashes brighter as his dark veins appear. "It has to be her. Who else wants Daisy dead and can use compulsion?"

"Don't jump to conclusions and do something stupid, Rufio," I say, dead serious. "You know what the consequence is for Idol-on-Idol murder."

"What is the consequence?" Daisy asks fearfully.

Rufio stares into her eyes. "Death."

44

RUFIO

There's absolutely no fucking way I'm going to let Drusilla get away this time. I don't need proof that she sent Pietro on a suicide mission. Whether she's guilty of that is irrelevant. She's tried to kill Daisy twice now, and that's enough reason for me to end her pitiful existence.

By the time Bryce and Daisy gave their statement to the police and we returned to campus, class was already over for the day. It doesn't matter. I'll get Drusilla alone eventually.

But the day is far from over for me. Naturally, my mother wants to have a word with Bryce and me. The moment the office door closes behind us, she begins the interrogation.

"What the hell happened today?"

"I already told you. Pietro decided to play kamikaze," Bryce replies.

"I do not appreciate your tone, young man. I spent my entire afternoon on the phone with board members trying to explain how three of my students were involved in a fatal car accident. Never mind the other incident that I had to sweep under the rug."

"What other incident? Drusilla's murder attempt on Daisy?" I ask.

Mom narrows her eyes, clamping her jaw shut. "No, Morpheus going psychopathic on Drusilla."

"The only reason Morpheus used his gift on her was to protect Daisy. You asked me to keep her safe. Is that no longer your priority?" Bryce takes a menacing step toward our mother's desk.

"Of course it's my priority, but Morpheus isn't even a full-blooded Idol. His parents are Fringes, so it was much harder for me to convince the board to not expel him."

"If Morpheus goes, then I'll go," I say.

"Me too," Bryce adds.

"Oh please. Your childish threats are ridiculous." Mom waves her hand dismissively.

"They aren't threats. Maybe I'll join the Knights," Bryce grits out.

Finally we get something from our mother other than contempt. Her face blanches. "You don't know what you're talking about."

"I beg to differ. I did spend an entire weekend with them, after all."

"What do you mean, you spent an entire weekend with the Knights?" Mom rises from her chair.

"Exactly what I said."

"Bryce, don't even say that as a joke. The Knights are a radical group, and most are wanted dead. They're dangerous."

"Really? I was under the impression you were buddies." Bryce raises an eyebrow.

Mom's eyes widen. "Don't ever repeat such blasphemy. The Knights are traitors to our kind."

"Aren't you a traitor as well?" I ask. "Didn't you have a Norm lover when you were younger?"

"Where did you hear that?"

I shake my head. "It doesn't matter. It's high time you share with us what you want with Daisy and why you played us like fools."

Mom rubs her face and sits back down, swiveling her chair to face the window.

"It's true that I fell in love with a Norm once. His name was William, and he was the most wonderful man I've ever met. But of course, your grandfather would have never allowed his only daughter to marry a lowly Norm." Mom turns to us, her mouth twisted into an ugly grin. "I don't need to tell you the grim details of how that story ended."

"Our father killed him," Bryce says.

Mom's eyebrows twitch. "You were eavesdropping on my argument with your father, weren't you?"

"Yes. What I don't get is why you had to call Mr. X right afterward," Bryce continues.

"Xavier was William's adopted brother. And you wanted to know where Daisy fits in all this, right? William's last name was Rodale. He was Daisy's uncle."

And just like that, Mom dropped a bomb on us. I'm stunned, and by the look on Bryce's face, so is he.

"Does Daisy know?" Bryce asks.

"No. Xavier is adamant that she never finds out."

"Why? He's her only living relative besides her sister," I say.

"He's afraid if people find out, it'll put Daisy and Rosie in danger."

"That's bullshit. If he was so concerned about Daisy's safety, he would have pulled her out of here after the first attempt on her life. Or better yet, he would off Drusilla himself," I say.

"Rufio, I'm only going to say this once. Stop your obsession with Drusilla. She wasn't the one who tried to drown Daisy, and she wasn't in school today either."

"What? Bullshit."

"I'm not lying. She went home this weekend and was absent

today. So if Pietro was compelled to cause the accident, it wasn't her doing."

"You don't think he truly committed suicide, do you?"

"I can't rule out any possibility."

"No, no way. Pietro was a narcissistic junkie. He wouldn't simply kill himself," I say.

"You don't know what goes on in the head of anyone, son. But now that you know all the facts, I hope you forget your need for revenge. I can't deal with any more scandals in this school, especially with the Founder's Ball coming up."

"It's that time of the year again? It seems you just forced us to attend the idiotic event," Bryce grumbles.

"Yes, it's that time again, and you'd better make sure it goes smoothly."

Bryce and I trade glances. He's grimacing, and I'm sure I share a similar expression. He dealt with his obligation in previous years by being his weird, antisocial self. Phoenix, Morpheus, and I got high and drunk out of our minds. It was during last year's Founder's Ball that I made the mistake of hooking up with Drusilla. Yeah, happy memories. I'm so not looking forward to this year's bullshit.

MORPHEUS

I wait until Phoenix goes to the gym before I check on Daisy. I'm sure he stopped by her room first on his way out, but I don't sense his presence anymore. I grab the plastic container sitting on top of the counter and head out.

My heart is beating a little faster than usual as I wait outside her room. I'm not sure why I'm nervous. I knock before I lose my nerve. When Daisy opens the door, the feeling that I'm way out of my depth increases.

"Hey," I say like an idiot.

"Hi. Did you come to check on me too? I'm fine."

"Yeah, I can see you're fine. I brought treats." I offer her the box.

She peers through the plastic lid. "Cake?"

"My mother sends me baked goods sometimes. The only reason I have some left is because Bryce didn't see it."

My mention of Bryce makes Daisy frown. Shit. I forgot they're still at odds.

"Do you wanna come in?" She opens the door wider.

"Yeah."

"I saw Mr. Atkins asked to talk to you after class. Did he set a date yet for the quiz you missed?"

"Next week." I glance at Daisy's bed, and for whatever reason, heat rushes to my face. I quickly look to her desk.

"I'm sorry I canceled our lessons. I needed time away from you guys." She sets the box down and peers at me.

"I understand. You've been through a lot." Not knowing what to do with my hands, I shove them in my pockets.

"Morpheus, can I ask you something?"

"Sure?"

"What does it feel like when you use your powers?"

Of all the things I thought Daisy could ask me, that wasn't it. "I'm the last person you should be asking that."

"Why?"

"Because my power is different."

"Different how?" She braces her hands against her desk and leans against it.

"Most Idols feel a warm sensation in the center of their chests when they use their powers. It's natural, pleasing. All I feel is pain when I use mine. That's why I have to wear these bracelets." I raise my hands to show her.

"Do you think you react like that because your parents are Fringes?"

Her simple question creates all sorts of havoc in my mind. I'm angry, sad, torn. Suddenly, I feel like telling her the truth about my birth, but I stomp on the impulse. She's my tutor, not my friend. Although, I wish she would be more than both.

"Maybe," I say. "But why do you want to know how it feels when Idols use their powers?"

She sucks her lower lip in, crossing her arms and dropping her chin. "Some strange things have been happening to me since Bryce healed me."

"What kind of things?"

"On the night I went missing, I never left campus. I couldn't walk far, so I hid underneath a tree to wait until the storm passed. Throughout most of the night, I was plagued with the most excruciating pain imaginable. It felt like I was burning alive."

"But you looked like a million bucks the next day."

"I know. And I felt great. Invincible."

I remember how she confronted Drusilla without fear, how she avoided the punch by moving out of the way faster than I thought possible.

"What other strange things have you experienced?" I ask.

"Phoenix and I shared a dream, and he swears it wasn't one of his visions. And there was one time where he sent me flying by accident and I stopped midair."

"And it wasn't him?"

"He didn't think it was, but it had to be him, right?"

I glance away while my mind is racing. If Daisy has diluted demigod blood, could she somehow become a Fringe?

"What are you thinking?" she asks.

"I don't know yet. I'm curious about one thing. How did you and Bryce get out of the car before it crashed against Pietro's?"

Daisy stands up straighter, becoming visibly tense. "I don't know. Everything happened so fast, it was almost a blur."

"I had a vision about the accident before it happened.

There was no way you guys would've had enough time to get out of the SUV before it crashed."

"I thought that maybe Bryce slowed down time."

"He can't do that, can he?"

"He doesn't think it was him. If not him, who did it, then?"

"Do you think *you* bent time?" I move closer.

Her eyes are wide with fear, and I hope it's not because of me.

"That would be impossible," she whispers. "I'm a Norm. I don't have powers."

I stop in front of her and, needing to touch her, unfold her arms and lace our hands together. She drops her gaze to them, sucking in a breath before she lifts her chin.

"What if I said you might the descendant of an Idol?"

"What?" She tries to pull her hands away, but I don't let her.

"I suspect your family is linked to an Idol who gave up her powers many years ago."

"But even if that were true, when she gave her powers away, she severed her link to the gods. Why would they return to me?"

"I don't know, Daisy."

"I'm scared, Morpheus."

I know too well what it's like to be afraid of what's inside of you. I've lived with the fear most of my life. Kind of ironic for a fearmancer to be afraid of his own ability.

"Don't be. I'm here for you," I assure her.

"Why would you want to help me?"

I step even closer, about to do a very foolish thing, when I sense Bryce and Rufio nearing her door. I release her hands at once, moving away.

"Bryce and Rufio are coming home. I'd better go," I say.

"Okay. Thanks for the cake and the talk."

"Any time. And don't worry, I won't tell the guys what you

told me, not until we can figure out what's happening. Promise."

"Thanks, I really appreciate it."

I nod, already wondering why I said that. I should at least confide in Bryce about my suspicions. But I know the reason I made the vow. It was the fear in Daisy's gaze about the possibility that she might be turning into something more than a Norm. It gutted me.

45

DAISY

"You must have a very powerful guardian angel watching over your shoulder, Daisy. I've seen the pictures of the crash online. I can't believe you survived that," Toby says, watching me closely.

His scrutiny makes me super uncomfortable. He's my best friend at school, and he knows most of my secrets, but I can't tell him that I think I might be turning into a Fringe. Mainly because it's nuts, but also, after he pretended to be one for so long, I don't know how he'd take it if my suspicions were true.

"Not a guardian angel, just a level seventeen Idol with a guilty conscience." I drop my gaze to my fries, but speaking about what happened yesterday has made me lose my appetite.

"So you still haven't patched things up with Bryce, huh?"

"It's complicated," I say.

"Well, I can always set you up with Stephan." Toby smiles in a cheeky way.

I roll my eyes. "Right, because things with him would be sooo much simpler."

He shakes his head. "I know. Bad joke."

We're having lunch outside, and there isn't anyone near us,

so I ask, "How are things going at the gallery? Did you learn anything?"

"No." Toby's shoulders sag. "It's been pretty boring, actually. Mr. Silverstone is overseas on a business trip."

I push my tray away. I'm definitely not going to eat anything. "That's too bad."

Toby's gaze zeroes in on my fries. "You're not going to eat that?"

"No. Go ahead. You can have them."

He switches his tray with mine and digs into my uneaten lunch. After a couple bites of fries, he speaks again. "So, I've been meaning to ask you something."

"What is it?"

"There's a social event this weekend at school. You've probably seen the posters splattered all over the walls."

"Honestly, I haven't given those posters a second glance."

"It's the Founder's Ball. It's a big deal, bigger than the prom. I was wondering if it would be okay for me to bring Rosie as my date."

I freeze. The idea of Rosie mingling with the awful students in this school makes my blood run cold. "I don't know, Toby. I don't think Rosie would feel comfortable hanging with our lovely peers."

"Actually, I kind of already told her about it, and she's excited."

My heart sinks. I'm not even surprised. Rosie loves to dress up. Of course she would be excited to attend a fancy ball. I want to be angry at Toby for telling her without asking me first if it was all right, but I can't bring myself to do it.

"If she wants to come, then it's fine with me."

I feel a little better when I see the happiness in Toby's gaze.

Things haven't been easy for him either, and he deserves a little joy.

"Thank you, Daisy. I promise I'll keep Rosie away from all the assholes."

"Hard task." I laugh. "Shit. That means I need to go shopping for dresses."

"I can take you girls to the mall sometime this week."

My stomach twists. I'm embarrassed to tell Toby that we never buy clothes at the mall. It's secondhand stores and thrift shops for us. As I'm still wrestling with the idea, Toby drops another bomb.

"Who are you going to the ball with?"

"What? Do I need a date to attend this thing?" My voice rises to a shrill.

"Well, it's not obligatory, but it's a ball, Daisy."

I dip my chin, resting my head in my hands. "Great. Just fucking great."

"What's fucking great?" Phoenix slides next to me on my bench, throwing his arm around my shoulders.

Where the hell did he come from?

I lift my face and catch Toby's blanched expression. He doesn't know about my hookups, so I expected more from him.

"Daisy is stressing about the ball," the traitor replies.

Why would he tell Phoenix that? I'm going to kill him later.

"What's to stress about?" Phoenix asks.

"She doesn't have a date." Toby shoves a fry in this mouth.

"Toby! Shut up," I snap.

"Who says you don't have a date, silly girl? You're coming with me, naturally." He kisses me on the cheek, making my already hot face burst into flames. We haven't hooked up since that first time. I put all the guys in relationship limbo because I can't deal with the complication of my love life on top of finding out about my family's past. It's just too much.

But knowing what his father did to him after he brought me home for dinner makes me less inclined to accept his offer.

"Phoenix, can I talk to you for a second?" I begin to stand.

"Sure."

I steer him away from the building until we reach a large tree. Partially hidden from view, I turn to him. "I can't go with you to the ball."

"Why not?" He frowns. "Are you still mad about that group meeting?"

"Yes. But that's not the only reason. I don't think it's wise for us to be seen anywhere together."

"Is this because of Bryce and Rufio?"

"No, it's because of your father."

All amusement leaves his face. His crestfallen expression twists my heart, hurting like a mother.

"I don't care about that asshole," Phoenix grits out.

"I care about what he can do to you. I can't bear it if he hurts you again because of me."

Phoenix's stormy expression softens. He cups my cheek tenderly, and damn, it feels good. "You have no idea how much what you just said means to me." He leans in and steals a kiss.

We're out in public and anyone can see us, but the moment his lips connect with mine, all common sense leaves my brain. I'm clutching the lapels of his jacket now, completely into him. Surprisingly, it's Phoenix who eases off, ending the kiss too soon.

"As much as I'd love to keep savoring your sweet lips, I have to control myself."

"Why?" The question leaves my mouth automatically, making me sound like a desperate nympho.

He chuckles. "Oh, Daisy. You don't know the effect you have on me, do you?"

The school bell rings and the moment is broken. Phoenix

walks backward, still grinning like a fool at me. "The ball is this Saturday. I'll pick you up at seven."

I head back to the picnic table. Toby has both our trays in his hand and is waiting for me.

"So, you and Phoenix, huh?"

I narrow my eyes to slits. "Why did you throw me under the bus like that?"

Toby widens his eyes in a show of innocence. "I didn't do that."

"You told Phoenix I was freaking out that I didn't have a date to this stupid ball."

Guilt flashes in Toby's eyes. He drops his gaze to the tray. "I have a confession to make."

"Fuck, Toby. What did you do?" I place my hands on my hips.

"I know you and Phoenix hooked up."

"What? How?"

Toby meets my eyes again. "He told me. But since you've been giving him the cold shoulder lately, he asked me to help him out."

"And you believed him?"

"Are you saying you didn't hook up?"

I sigh, pinching the bridge of my nose. "Ugh. I did, and it's a mess."

"Do you—"

"No! I don't want to talk about it. Let's go. We'll be late for class."

46

PHOENIX

"Will you quit looking so smug, asshole?" Rufio grumbles from the couch as he dabs Silvervoltage on a piece of cloth.

"Only if you stop acting like a jealous little bitch." I laugh and then finish my beer.

Bryce enters the living room, ready to play his part of the dutiful son. He glances at me for a moment before glaring at his brother. "You're not ready yet?"

Rufio brings the cloth to his nose and takes a deep breath. Then he relaxes against the couch and stares calmly at his brother. "I'll be done in a minute. You can't expect me to attend this stupid party sober."

Morpheus is the last one to join us. His long hair is secured back in a man bun, and his tux is sharp and wrinkle free.

"You clean up nice, bro. Trying to impress the ladies?" I ask.

He grumbles and then pulls the sleeves of his jacket down to hide his bracelets.

"All good there, Morpheus?" Bryce asks.

"Yup. No headaches, and the shadows are quiet. It's possible tonight will go down without a hitch."

"Mom will be happy." Rufio stands up and heads for his room.

I throw the beer bottle in the trash can and pop a mint in my mouth. "How do I look?" I pull on my tux jacket, puffing my chest.

"Like a glorified penguin," Rufio mutters before he disappears through the door.

"Don't be a hater because you didn't have the balls to ask Daisy to be your date," I yell.

"Just keep her safe, man. There will be a lot of people at this party who want her dead." Bryce looks pointedly at me.

He doesn't need to say it twice. My father, if he decides to make an appearance, is one of them. I'm risking another weekend in his dungeon if he catches me with Daisy, but I didn't hesitate asking her to be my date to the ball. Fuck him. He took too much from me already. He won't dictate who I care about too.

I glance at my watch. It's seven o'clock sharp. I grab the corsage from the fridge and head for Daisy's room. In the hallway, I bump into other seniors dressed to the nines as well. Some girls give me appreciative once-overs despite the fact that their dates are present. When they see me stop in front of Daisy's door, they widen their eyes and gossip in hushed tones. That's just the beginning. We'll be turning heads the whole evening.

I only need to knock on the door once before she opens it. My jaw drops to floor and my tongue rolls out, cartoon style. Daisy is wearing a deep red, snug mermaid dress with a plunging neckline that has my cock hard in an instant.

"Hi," I say roughly.

"Hey." Her eyes drop to my shoes before she slowly brings them up to meet mine again. "You look nice."

"Forget about me. You look incredible."

She looks at her own dress and then attempts to make the neckline less revealing.

"It's a little too snug for my liking," she says.

"It's perfect."

She watches me from under her eyelashes, and by heavens, I want to forget about the ball and spend the entire night worshipping her body. I've never craved anyone this badly before.

"Would you like to come in? I still have to put my shoes on."

"Yeah, sure."

She shouldn't have done that. The moment the door closes, I turn her around, push her against the wall, and kiss her. She only has the chance to let out a little squeak before I cut the sound off with my tongue.

My cock is straining against my pants, begging to come out and play. It's hard to ignore the desire, but when Daisy grabs my ass and pulls me closer, I fucking lose it. I'm grinding against her like a sex-deprived pervert.

"I miss you, girl," I say between kisses.

"We should be heading out."

"I know."

Neither of us is willing to stop though. I'm a second away from removing Daisy's dress when a knock on the door interrupts our moment.

I pull back and glance at it. "Are you expecting anyone?"

"Daisy, are you still there?" a female voice asks.

With a gasp, Daisy pushes me off her and attempts to smooth the wrinkles on her dress. "Yes, I'm here. Hold on, Rosie."

Rosie? Ah, her sister.

Daisy runs to the bathroom and curses softly. I must have ruined her makeup. Curious to meet her younger sister, I take it upon myself to open the door. I not only find the girl but also Toby standing in the hallway.

"Hi. Daisy will be out in a second."

Her sister's jaw slackens as she stares at me. My lips curl into a smug grin.

"Rosie, this is Phoenix. Daisy's date," Toby introduces us.

"I thought Daisy was going to the ball with Bryce."

And just like that, my good mood deflates.

"Bryce had other plans," I reply dryly.

"Uh, can we come in?" Toby asks.

Daisy pushes me out of the way. "Don't just stand there, let them in."

Rosie keeps staring at me as she walks inside, and when her gaze connects with Daisy's, I read the question there. An awkward silence follows.

"Well, are you two ready?" Toby asks finally.

"Yeah, Phoenix just got here," Daisy tells them.

I then remember the corsage in my hand. I can't believe I didn't drop it when I was dry humping Daisy.

"Here, I got this for you." I take the flower out.

"Oh, thanks."

I wrap the corsage around her wrist and then offer her my arm. "Shall we?"

DAISY

I don't know what possessed me to almost fuck Phoenix before the stupid ball. I've been so good at avoiding him and the others for the past two weeks, but damn, the boy looks fine in his tux. Thank heavens for Rosie and Toby's interruption.

I can sense her staring at us the whole way toward the gymnasium where the party will take place. In hindsight, I should have told her about Phoenix, but I honestly didn't want her to grill me about him or why I wasn't going with Bryce.

What would Rosie think if she knew I'm involved with three guys at the same time? Would she think I've lost my mind? Sometimes I do.

The path toward the gym is illuminated by twinkling lights that have been placed on the trees skirting the edges. It's kind of romantic, and it makes me feel giddy. Or maybe it's the sexy-as-hell guy next to me who's awakened the butterflies in my stomach. I never thought I'd feel anything for Phoenix besides hatred, but somehow I fell for his charms, and I don't even know when it happened. Maybe I'm just attracted to broken things, and there's no denying the boy is broken. God, I have to help him somehow.

When we enter the gym, my jaw drops as I gawk at everything. I can't believe they managed to convert a sweat-smelling, boring gym into a high-class ballroom. It has a chandelier and everything.

"This is so pretty," Rosie says.

"Indeed," I reply.

"Do you guys want anything to drink?" Phoenix points at the refreshments table, which seems kind of desolate.

"No one is drinking the punch," I say.

"No one has spiked it yet. That's why." He winks.

"What's the point of spiking anything?" Rosie asks. "You guys are immune to alcohol."

"That's not really true," Phoenix replies.

"It isn't?" I arch my eyebrows. "I was always under the assumption that Idols were immune to almost everything."

"Don't look so shocked, sweetheart. Your spirits don't affect us. We have our own special brew. So, going once, going twice...."

"Yeah, okay, I'll have a drink," I say.

"Me too," Rosie adds.

Phoenix turns to Toby. "Wanna help, buddy?"

"Sure." He looks nervously at Rosie.

"Relax, dude. No one will touch them while I'm around," Phoenix says.

"Go. We'll be okay." I shoo him away.

No sooner are we alone than Rosie grabs my arm and pulls me closer. "I thought you liked Bryce. What are you doing with that blond? Wasn't he an ass to you?"

"To be fair, they all were in the beginning. But Phoenix is not who I thought he was." I glance at him, so tall, handsome, and strong, but also so vulnerable.

"Oh my God. You're falling in love with him!" Rosie says loud enough that she draws other people's attention.

"Shhh. I'm not."

I better not be falling for him, because then it means I'm also falling for the other three. Even Morpheus, who so far I've kept a platonic relationship with, has carved out a place in my heart.

She puts her hands on her hips. "I know that look."

"Oh yeah. Why? Is that what you see in the mirror every day?" I cross my arms in front of my chest.

Blush tinges her cheeks. She looks in Toby's direction and sighs. "I think so. Toby is so cute and attentive and nice. It sucks that I only get to see him on the weekends."

"Good grief. You just turned into a ball of goo. Do we need to have the talk again?"

Rosie whips around to face me with round eyes and lips parted. "Hell no. I don't need Sex Ed lectures from you."

Someone whistles next to me. Phoenix. I didn't even sense his approach. Toby isn't far behind, looking redder than a tomato.

"Oh my God. Kill me now." Rosie drops her chin, resting her forehead in her hand.

"I happen to know Daisy could be an exc—"

I elbow Phoenix's stomach, which is akin to hitting a brick

wall. His abs are made of solid steel. But at least I got him to stop talking.

"I cannot believe this," a cruel masculine voice says from behind us, making the hairs on the back of my neck stand on end.

Immediately, Phoenix wraps his arm around my shoulder and brings me closer to him.

"Hello, Father."

The cruel Idol glowers at us with so much hatred that I feel it in my bones.

"I thought I was clear the last time we spoke."

He means the last time he tortured Phoenix. Motherfucker. Fury unfurls from the pit of my stomach, leaving me shaking.

Phoenix hisses, hunching forward a little.

"Mr. Westbrook. I didn't realize you were coming tonight." Principal Fallon joins us, staring hard at the man. Bryce and Rufio are next to her. By their closed-off expressions, they must sense the tension in the air too.

"Since when do generous alumni need to RSVP to stupid school events?"

Her nostrils flare, and her gaze narrows. "I don't care how much money you donated to the school. You won't cause trouble under my watch."

He chuckles. "So feisty. I see Jonathan wasn't able to tame you at all. Don't worry, I've seen enough."

He walks away, but not before he spares one more hateful glance at Phoenix. A look with the promise of retribution.

As soon as the man's gone, Phoenix steps aside and loosens the tie around his neck.

Principal Fallon turns to her sons. "Remember what I said. No shenanigans." She strides across the dance floor, disappearing from view soon after.

The band begins to play a lively tune, and Toby, bless his heart, invites Rosie to dance. When they're gone, I check on

Phoenix, who's looking quite pale now. On a hunch, I drop my eyes to his wrist. His tattoo isn't glowing, but that doesn't mean his father isn't hurting him another way.

"Dude, are you all right?" Bryce asks.

"I need some fresh air."

He staggers forward, walking like he's drunk.

"Did he take anything?" Rufio watches him go.

"Don't just stand there," I demand. "Can't you see he's in agony?"

I follow Phoenix out of the gym, pushing people out of my way roughly. He's already in the hallway when I catch up with him, leaning against the wall with his eyes closed. His face is twisted into a grimace.

I touch his face. "Phoenix. Talk to me."

He opens his eyes and glances down. "Fuck. I hate that man."

He grunts and closes his eyes again while a faint glow comes from his wrist.

Son of a bitch. His father is torturing him again.

47

MORPHEUS

I feel it when I'm halfway to the gym building. I was the last to leave the apartment, and when the first telltale signs that I'm about to have a vision manifest, I realize I forgot my cell at home. Fuck.

Grunting, I focus on putting one foot in front of the other. It's not only the headache that's bothering me; the shadows decided to have a party too. With each passing moment, the pain increases to the point that it turns my vision blurry.

It takes me double the time to walk to the gym, and when I finally enter the building, I'm about to throw up. Ambling forward and clutching my stomach, I hope to get to an empty room where I can lie down.

The band has already started to play, but there are still students milling about in the hallway. I catch a few glances in my direction, but no one tries to help me. I wouldn't either. I round a corner and bump into someone who was running in the opposite direction. The impact almost knocks me down. I brace against the wall and glare at the culprit.

She glances at me for a fleeting moment, but I recognize her nonetheless. Cherise, Drusilla's minion. What the hell is she doing here? Expelled students aren't allowed on campus grounds. She disappears down the hallway, but it's not like I can follow her.

White-hot pain splits my skull in two, and a roar comes from deep in my throat. I clutch my head while I slide down to the floor. Then the vision comes. The ballroom, Toby and Daisy's sister dancing, a giant chandelier, then shards of crystal all covered in blood.

My eyes fly open. *Fuck. I need to warn them.* My world is still spinning. I'm also cold, so very cold, but I attempt to get up anyway. I don't have much time. Laughter sounds in my head. *His* odious laughter.

"You're too late. There's nothing you can do," the god says.

I hear a loud crash in the distance. The music suddenly stops playing and is replaced by a bloodcurdling scream.

DAISY

Phoenix is still panting in pain when a crashing sound comes from the ballroom. The music stops suddenly, and then the screams take its place.

"Rosie!"

I'm running before anyone can stop me. Once inside, I push through the throng of people who have already formed a circle around something. When I finally manage to get to the front, I find Toby in Rosie's lap, staring at the ceiling. A random crimson stain slowly spreads through his white tuxedo shirt. *No.* There's a piece of broken glass sticking out from his abdomen. Shards of glass surround them. It takes me a moment to understand they're pieces of the chandelier that was hanging from the ceiling.

Rosie lifts her tearstained gaze to mine. "Daisy...."

"Someone call an ambulance!" I yell through the lump in my throat, then crouch next to them.

Toby begins to spit out blood, and I know he doesn't have much time left.

"Out of the way, Daisy. Let me help." Bryce crouches next to me.

I clutch his arm and beg, "He doesn't have much time. You have to heal him. Please."

With round eyes, Bryce nods. He didn't know he could heal before, and I'm not sure if he can summon his healing powers at will, but I'm hoping he can. He's Toby's only hope.

Bryce touches Toby's chest and closes his eyes. At first nothing happens. A great sense of doom takes hold of me. I'm sobbing, crying my eyes out.

Strong arms circle my shoulders, pulling me into a hug. I recognize Rufio's cologne immediately.

"It's going to be okay, Daisy," he whispers in my ear.

Finally, light pours from Bryce's hand and spreads over Toby's body. Rosie lets out a gasp, but she vanishes from view when the brightness spreads to encompass all of us. A minute or less goes by before the light begins to fade. I blink several times to adjust my eyesight.

Bryce is sitting on the balls of his feet now, his shoulders sagging forward and his chin dipped low. He looks spent.

"Toby, talk to me." Rosie touches his face.

He turns to her and then sits up slowly. The piece of broken glass sticking out from his belly is gone, but the bloodstain on his shirt remains.

"I'm okay."

She reaches for his torn shirt and spreads the fabric apart. There's no gash where one should have been. "You're healed."

Toby touches the area gingerly, almost as if he can't believe it's gone. He turns to Bryce and says, "You healed me. I can't believe it."

"You're welcome." Bryce sways on the spot and then topples sideways.

I gasp, but he doesn't fall onto the broken glass. Phoenix is standing just outside the circle with his hand raised. The grimace of pain hasn't left his expression, but he was strong enough to come to his friend's rescue.

We lock gazes, and there are so many emotions exchanged in that connection that I can't begin to put it in words.

Mayhem ensues soon after when the adults finally join us. Principal Fallon blanches when she sees Bryce passed out and starts issuing orders. Other teachers soon join us and begin to clear the room out.

I'm still reeling from the experience when Rufio urges me to stand up. Bryce is now being carried out of the room by Phoenix, and my impulse is to follow, but I have to make sure Rosie and Toby are okay first.

"What happened?" I ask.

"The chandelier fell on us. Toby pushed me out of the way, and the rest you saw." She's clutching her boyfriend for dear life, and who can blame her? She almost witnessed him bleed to death.

Nurse Ellen materializes out of nowhere. "There you are. Toby, you need to come with me."

"What about Bryce?" I ask.

"I'll check on him too. Phoenix is taking him to the infirmary as we speak."

"Come on, Daisy. Let's go," Rufio says.

We begin to follow the nurse out, and it's then that I realize I haven't seen Morpheus anywhere.

"We need to let Morpheus know about what happened," I say.

"He should be here already." Rufio pauses and glances at the destruction in the middle of the room.

I don't like how his jaw becomes tense. "Do you think something happened to him?"

He looks me in the eyes and says, "A chandelier doesn't simply drop from the ceiling, Daisy. So yeah, I'm worried something happened to him."

As if I couldn't get more worried than I already am.

Toby and Rosie stop when they notice we've fallen behind. "Daisy? Is something the matter?"

I'm torn. I want to stay with Rosie and make sure she's okay, but at the same time, I can't ignore the apprehension I saw in Rufio's eyes.

"I don't know yet. Stick with Ellen. She'll make sure you're safe. Rufio and I have to find Morpheus."

Rosie watches me without blinking for a few seconds before turning away. But it was enough for me to read the hurt in her eyes. I just put an Idol before her. Guilt stabs through my chest, making me want to cry again.

"Daisy, are you okay?" Rufio asks.

"No." My answer comes out as choke. "Everything is wrong."

"Everything will be fine. You'll see." He smiles at me, a vain attempt to infuse me with positivity. But I can see right through his bullshit. I'll give him points for trying though.

"Let's find Morpheus."

We don't find him. He actually finds us as we're coming out of the room, agitated as hell.

"Please tell me he was lying. Please tell me I didn't fail," he says.

"Whoa. Slow down." Rufio holds his friend by the shoulders.

"What's going on?" I ask.

"I had a vision of the chandelier falling on top of Toby and your sister. I tried to come warn you, but I was too late."

"Everything is fine now, Morpheus. Bryce healed Toby, and they've all gone to the infirmary."

Despite the good news, Morpheus doesn't seem relieved.

"Is there more you're not saying?" I ask.

"Yes. Cherise was here tonight."

Rufio and I trade glances. I can imagine what he's thinking because I'm doing the same. She shows up on school grounds on the same evening someone tries to kill Toby and my sister. That can't be a coincidence.

48

DAISY

When we get to the infirmary, Ellen has finished checking on Toby. Bryce, however, is lying on the examination table with his arm over his eyes. When he healed me, it was almost like his batteries got completely depleted. It seems the same happened again. But I can't go check on him before speaking with Rosie first.

"How are you?" I ask her.

"How do you think?" She glares. "My boyfriend almost died tonight."

"But I didn't." Toby pulls her toward him and kisses her cheek. She melts into his embrace, only it does nothing to erase the angry expression aimed at me.

"Are you coming home?" she asks.

I blink several times without answering. I wasn't planning on doing that, but it's kind of obvious that she would assume I would. Tomorrow is Sunday, and she was almost killed along with Toby. She must be feeling pretty shaken after everything.

"Oh my God. You aren't?" she shrieks.

"I didn't say that. It's been a long evening. Why don't you just stay here with me?"

Any other day, I'd go with her without a second thought. So why am I hesitant to leave school grounds tonight? It's almost like a strange premonition is telling me I'll be needed here.

"Hell to the no. I refuse to sleep under the same roof as these ruthless Idols. I want nothing to do with them." She sneers.

I wince because I sense her outburst is also a criticism of my dating choices. A couple of months ago, I'd be completely on her side. Now, I'm just a mess of contradictory emotions.

"You should go with your sister, Daisy," Bryce says from the examination room.

He's attempting to sit up with Rufio's help. Ellen orders him to lie back down.

"I'm fine, Ellen," he counters. "I just need to sleep this off in my own bed."

"Let me scan you one more time, at least," she insists.

"You already did and found nothing out of the ordinary."

"Toby, can you drive? I want to go home." Rosie starts to walk out of the room.

"Rosie, wait." I grab her arm. "I'll come with you."

She pulls herself free. "Don't bother. I'd rather spend time with someone who truly cares about me."

"That's not fair."

"Hey, hey, girls. Please don't fight." Ellen moves in between us. "It's been a stressful evening, and you're all still reeling from it."

Rosie turns to Toby. "Can you sleep over?"

"He can't stay with you, Rosie. Are you crazy?" I raise my arm in a pleading gesture.

"You're not my mother!"

It's not the first time she's told me that, but tonight, the punch to the gut is much harder.

"Stop it! Seriously. Daisy, I know where you're coming from, but maybe it's best if Toby spends the night with Rosie. I'm sure nothing besides sleeping will happen." Ellen looks pointedly at Toby.

With wide eyes and a blush on his cheeks, he says, "Oh my God. Of course we're not going to do anything besides sleep. I swear it, Daisy."

"Fine. If that's what Rosie wants." I cross my arms, feeling completely dejected and powerless.

"It *is* what I want. Come on, Toby." Rosie walks out.

Toby throws me an apologetic glance and follows her.

"Do you think it's safe for them to be driving alone at this hour?" I ask Ellen.

She puts her hands on her hips and then curses. "Shit. You're right." She glances at Bryce, who's already on his feet and attached to Rufio's side as if he were drunk. His head is hanging low. "You really won't let me scan you again, huh?"

"Nope. You can follow Toby and Rosie home," he says without glancing up.

With a sigh, she nods. "Fine. I will. But if you feel like you're getting worse, call me or just head to the hospital."

"Yes, ma'am."

No sooner is she gone than Rufio says, "If you think Toby will keep his promise, you're seriously mistaken."

"Can you please not put disturbing images in my head? You sound just like Phoenix."

"Where is Phoenix anyway?" Morpheus, who until now had kept quiet, asks.

"He dropped me off here and then said he had to make a call, but he never came back," Bryce replies.

I freeze. His father was furious after seeing Phoenix with me and had already started to use the tattoo to punish him.

"Did Phoenix make any strange sounds, like he was in pain or something?"

Bryce tilts his head to the side. "As a matter of fact, he did grunt a few times when he carried me here."

"It couldn't have been from the physical exertion," Morpheus points out.

"It wasn't. Guys, Phoenix is in big trouble," I tell them.

"What kind of trouble?" Rufio asks.

I'm about to break Phoenix's trust, but I can't let him face his father again and not do anything about it. So I tell his friends how I found him all messed up coming from his parents' house, and also about his tattoo.

"That's why you were asking about that symbol you drew," Morpheus says.

"Yes. I wanted to find out if there was a way to neutralize its powers."

"Remember those odd bruises Phoenix would show up with sometimes when he was younger?" Rufio turns to Bryce. "He never had a good explanation for them."

"Son of a bitch. I can't believe we were that blind." Bryce presses a fist against his forehead. "Let's go. We're getting Phoenix out of that house."

I can tell Rufio and Morpheus want to run at breakneck speed, but with Bryce still recovering and the slower-than-molasses Norm here, they have to contend with long strides. During the walk to the garage, Rufio tries reaching Phoenix via his cell phone countless times, but on his latest attempt, it goes straight to voice mail.

"Damn everything to hell. He must already be there," he curses.

Once in the garage, Rufio turns Bryce over to Morpheus and zaps toward his car. I know the guys are superfast, but I've never actually seen him run like that. His car is the same SUV model Bryce used to have, only it's black. I don't know when he got it back from the side of the road or got the window fixed, but it looks brand new again.

He backs out of the parking spot before we even reach him, and as soon as we hop inside, he takes off, burning rubber.

"Jeez, take it easy. We're still in the garage," Bryce complains next to me.

"How are you feeling. Still tired?" I ask.

He turns and watches me with eyes that are beginning to close. "Nah."

"You're such a bad liar."

He slides his hand across the leather seat and covers mine. "I'm glad my healing powers weren't a fluke."

I picture Toby lying in that bed of broken glass while his life ebbed way in a crimson river and get choked up all over again. "Me too. Thank you for trying."

"I'd do it for anyone, not only because it was Toby."

His statement makes my heart expand and finally let go of the resentment I hadn't been able to until now. He didn't know what healing again would do to him. His first experience left him almost completely useless. But I believe he wouldn't let an innocent person die while he watched if there was a slim chance he could save that person.

I scooch closer and kiss him softly on the lips. He sighs into me, resting his forehead against mine. Then he simply collapses on top of me.

"Shit. Bryce, wake up."

Morpheus turns around in the front seat. "What happened? Is he breathing?"

"Yeah, I think he just passed out from exhaustion."

I shift in my seat, trying to make Bryce lay his head on my lap.

"How long did he stay out the last time?" Rufio looks at me through the rearview mirror.

"I don't know. I found him out cold in the shower, but I don't know how long he'd been sitting there."

"As long as his problem is only tiredness, then it's fine. We can handle Mr. Westbrook ourselves. He's only a level fourteen Idol."

"What about his staff? That place was more like a fortress than a house. He must have security there," I say.

"Don't worry, Daisy. We'll handle them too."

I don't want to poop all over Rufio's confidence parade, but he also said he could handle those gangbangers and he almost died doing so. And they were Fringes.

"I wish I had my lightning-glass dagger with me." I look out the window. I kept the dagger the gang member used on Rufio, but after what Xavier told me, I didn't want to carry it around.

"Morpheus, look inside the glove compartment," Rufio says.

"Son of a bitch," Morpheus exclaims. "What are you doing carrying this around?"

I lean forward to see what Morpheus is holding now. "Is that the dagger I left at the treehouse?"

"Yeah. Since you kept the one used on me, I decided it wouldn't hurt having a surprise weapon as well, just in case."

Morpheus holds the dagger with care as he hands it over to me. "A bit nuts on your part, but at least Daisy isn't defenseless anymore."

Five minutes later, we're inside the gated community where Phoenix's parents live. But when his house looms at the end of the street, Rufio lets out a string of curses.

"What is it?" I ask.

"The walls and the gate are protected. I can sense the invisible energy coming from them."

"Yeah, I can too. It's fucking strong," Morpheus adds.

"What does it mean? You can't breach it?" I say with a hint of alarm.

"Oh, we'll breach it." Rufio steps out of the vehicle, and Morpheus does the same.

I glance at Bryce, who's sound asleep. I try to shake him awake, but he doesn't budge. He's truly out to the world. Up ahead, I see the guys doing their best to open the gate, but every time they touch it or try to jump over it, they're flung backward. When they said barrier, what they really meant was an invisible force shield. Meanwhile, Mr. Westbrook is doing who knows what to Phoenix.

Rage takes over my body, making my stomach coil tight. Curling my fingers around the dagger's handle, I get out of the car. There's a humming right above my skin, a foreign sensation that I don't care to understand right now.

When the dagger pierced Rufio, it weakened him. Maybe if I strike the gate with it, I can dilute its force enough to allow Rufio and Morpheus to shatter it completely.

They're both are sent to the ground again by the time I near the gate. *Motherfucker. I'm done with this piece of shit hurting my guys.* Propelled by the fury coursing freely through my limbs, I run toward the gate, raising the dagger above my head.

"Daisy, don't get any closer!" Rufio screams, but I ignore him.

I let out a roar right before I strike. The dagger sinks into one of the rods in the wrought iron gate, sending white-hot pain up my arm. I sense the force of the field trying to push me back like it did Rufio and Morpheus, but I stand my ground. Clenching my jaw, I hold the dagger's handle with both hands and try to open the gate. It feels like I'm trying to move a mountain.

I think about Phoenix, how mangled he was when he came back from this place. I remember my parents and the night they were taken from me. All because of Idols like Mr. Westbrook.

A warm ball of fire seems to form in the middle of my chest. It spreads rapidly through my entire body, crackling like raw energy, making me feel invincible. The tension in the gate suddenly vanishes, and I'm able to pull it open after a hard yank.

I hear the guys behind me, but there's also a loud buzzing in my ears, and I can't make out their words. I don't stop to wait for them. Still propelled by this mysterious force in me, I take off. As I suspected, Mr. Westbrook has security guards on his property. Two come at me, but they're Fringes, not Idols. I slash at them with the dagger, cutting the neck of the first one when he gets close.

The second guard sends a gust of wind my way, but somehow it parts right down the middle, missing me completely. In a split second, I'm on him, burying the dagger deep in his gut. He makes a gurgling sound, looking at me with wide eyes. I pull the dagger free before he collapses.

I just killed two men and didn't even blink. It's almost like I'm having an out-of-body experience.

"Daisy, wait!" Rufio yells.

"Rufio, watch out," Morpheus warns.

I look over my shoulder as the guys engage with more security guards who have stormed the front of the house. Once again, I don't wait. The boys can handle those Fringes. I sprint up the stairs, prepared to kick the front door open, but surprisingly, I find it ajar.

Shit, this could be a trap. Slowing down, I correct the grip on the dagger. My hand is sweaty, and there's blood covering the handle, making it slippery.

The entry foyer is empty, but once I clear the narrow passageway, I see a flash of black from the corner of my eye. I turn, dagger ready to strike.

Vargas, Mr. Westbrook's butler, raises his hands in surrender. *Is he the one who opened the door for me?*

"Where is he?" I ask.

"The basement. That's where he usually takes his son." He points at the stairs going down.

"Do you know what he does to Phoenix?"

The man nods, bringing bile to my mouth.

"And you never thought to stop him?"

"I'm only a Fringe, miss."

Whatever. I don't have time for his poor excuses. I head for the basement on light feet, not knowing what other nasty surprises the wicked man has in store. When I reach the bottom of the stairs, I hear Phoenix's soft cries.

Throwing caution out the window, I push the only door in this lower level open and find Phoenix on the floor, naked and bleeding. His father is standing over him, still wearing his suit pants and white shirt. Only now the outfit doesn't look so pristine. It's speckled with Phoenix's blood.

Motherfucker. I'm going to kill him.

I charge, not caring that I'm about to collide with an Idol. His surprise wears off quickly, and with a flick of his wrist, he sends me flying against the mirrored wall to my left. At this speed, I'm going to shatter the glass completely. Only somehow, I slow down. Time seems to pass in slow motion, allowing me to twist my body and land on two feet instead of hitting the mirror. As soon as I touch the ground, the world resumes its normal speed.

"How the fuck did you do that?" His eyes widen, and then he glances at Phoenix. "You did that, you piece of shit?" He kicks Phoenix in his rib cage, and all he can do is curl into a ball on the floor.

With a roar, I run toward the man, ready to plunge the dagger into his heart. He turns just in time, grabbing me by the throat with one hand and my wrist with the other, forcing me to drop the dagger on the floor.

"You think you can invade my home and attack me, Norm scum? I'm going to hurt you so badly, you'll be begging for death before the night is over."

"Let... her... go," Phoenix grits out.

"Oh no. This is going to be fun. First, I'm going to break all her bones, and then I'm going to take you hard and let her watch."

He's squeezing my throat so tight that I'm beginning to see

dark spots in my vision. I can't pry his hand off my neck, so on a stupid move, I slam the heel of my free hand against his forehead. All the hit should have done is irritate the Idol even more. Instead he lets out a grunt and almost immediately lets me go. He staggers back, rubbing the place I hit him.

The fire churning in my core surges again. Disregarding my personal safety, I step into his space and grab his head with both hands. A tingling sensation concentrates in my palms at the same time that the asshole's legs fold and he drops to his knees.

He cries out as if he's in terrible pain. The veins in his forehead protrude as his eyes bulge. Only when my hands begin to hurt do I pull them away and step back. I feel sick to my stomach and light-headed.

Breathing hard, Mr. Westbrook glowers at me with murder in his eyes. He slowly rises to his feet, seething. "You little bitch. You'll pay for this."

He makes a violent movement with his arm, but nothing happens. "What the fuck?" His face twists savagely, becoming redder with the effort. He grunts. "What did you do to me? Why can't I use my powers?"

"Maybe because she took them away from you," Phoenix says from behind his father, back on his feet.

The man turns, his eyes almost popping out of his head. "How did you get up?"

Phoenix lifts his wrist, revealing nothing but unblemished skin. "Tattoo is gone, motherfucker."

Faster than a cobra, he plunges my dagger into his father's chest, twisting it for good measure. The hateful man staggers back, looking down as if he can't believe a common weapon could pierce his Idol skin. He finally drops to the ground, unmoving.

Phoenix's gaze meets mine. His face is bruised, his lower lip is busted, and there's a gash on his eyebrow that's bled, but the blood is dry now. His wide, naked chest expands and contracts rapidly as if he's been running a marathon. He slowly moves in my direction until he's right in front of me. Without breaking eye contact, he captures my face between his hands.

"You're not a Norm."

I blink fast while my mind is struggling to understand the meaning of his statement. "If I'm not a Norm, what am I?"

"I don't know, and I don't care." He kisses me then, and I taste the blood from his lip, but I don't stop. I need this connection with him after everything I've done, everything I've seen, even if it's making me cry.

49

DAISY

Rufio and Morpheus finally join us, breathing hard and sporting manic glints in their eyes. They glance at Phoenix's father, dead on the floor, then at us.

"What happened?" Rufio asks.

"I finally broke free from my shackles with Daisy's help," Phoenix replies, keeping his arms around me.

"You killed your father with the lighting-glass dagger." Morpheus's gaze is trained on the man.

"Yup. My only regret is that he went too quickly."

Rufio is staring at me with brows furrowed. "You could have been killed, Daisy. What the hell were you thinking?"

"I wasn't. All I cared about was saving Phoenix from that monster's clutches."

Glancing down, he runs a hand through his hair and exhales loudly. "Madness, complete madness." He lifts his gaze to meet mine. "Don't you ever do that again."

His order makes me see red, and maybe it's the adrenaline that's still coursing through my veins, but I step away from Phoenix's embrace, ready to show Rufio he can't boss me around.

"Holy fuck!" Morpheus blurts out.

"What?" we all ask at the same time.

"Daisy, can't you feel it?"

I frown. "Feel what?"

"The power in you."

Rufio squints, and then his jaw drops. "What the fuck?"

"Stop staring at me like I'm a freak!" I yell.

"You're not a freak. You're an Idol," Morpheus announces.

The air is sucked out of my lungs at the same time that my stomach bottoms out. "Impossible," I breathe out.

Phoenix holds my waist and turns me around. "I saw it with my own eyes, Daisy. You bent time, and you sucked my father's power right out of him."

My throat is tight, and my heart is slamming against my rib cage. "How can that be? Idols can only be born."

"I'm not... so sure," Bryce speaks from the door. He's clutching the doorframe as if he could collapse at any minute.

"Bryce, what are you doing here? You should be resting." I stride toward him but halt abruptly, afraid he won't accept my comfort now.

"Come here." He reaches for my hand and pulls me the rest of the way, engulfing me in a bear hug. Hiding his face in the crook of my neck, he inhales deeply before kissing a spot below my ear. "Don't be afraid, Daisy," he whispers. "We'll figure this out."

A throat clearing sounds behind us. Easing off the embrace, I look over Bryce's shoulders to see who the newcomer is. Vargas is standing there, accompanied by Xavier. His eyes are hard, troubled.

"Is Maximus dead?" he asks.

"Yes," Bryce replies.

"Then what are you waiting for? Move your asses! You can't be here when the authorities arrive."

"Who called the cops?" I glance at Vargas.

"It wasn't me, miss." He looks frightened.

"Vargas is not the enemy here. Now move. We don't have much time." Xavier motions toward the stairs.

Since Bryce is still recovering, I wrap his arm around my shoulder and steer him toward the exit. But before I reach the landing, I see Xavier stop Rufio.

"I need your assistance, kid."

"With what?"

"Getting rid of the body."

Understanding dawns on Rufio's face. He returns to the dungeon of horrors, disappearing from my sight.

"Go on, miss. You need to leave," Vargas insists.

Bryce and I don't speak until we're out of the house. In the courtyard below, the signs of battle linger. Several bodies are lying around, including the two Fringes I slayed. I skirt around them, closing my eyes so I don't catch even a glimpse of their lifeless faces.

Bryce hugs me tighter. "Don't feel bad about the fallen, Daisy. They worked for a horrible man. They weren't good."

"But did they know who Mr. Westbrook was?"

"No one can work for such a monster and not know."

When we finally reach the car, the others have already caught up. Phoenix has found a pair of sweatpants, but he's still shirtless and barefoot. He slides into the back seat with me and Bryce, sandwiching me in. Both boys reach for my hands, lacing their fingers with mine. I glance down, and seeing me connected to them like that makes a huge lump form in my throat. I have no idea what's going to happen now.

To distract me from my wretched heart, I ask, "How did Xa —I mean Mr. X find us?"

"Vargas," Rufio answers. "He called him as soon as we broke through the gates."

"So, do you think the butler was working for him this whole time?"

"I don't know, but we'll find out soon enough. He wants us to follow him."

"Follow him where?" Bryce asks.

"Don't know, but no matter where he's leading us, we're getting answers one way or another."

I HAVE no idea where we are when the car stops, but by the bumpier road we traveled on for the past ten minutes, I can make an educated guess that we veered off the main highway. I'm proven right when I exit the vehicle in front of a rustic cabin in the middle of a forest.

"Son of a bitch." Bryce tenses next to me.

"What is it?"

Xavier stops ahead to meet the man who just walked out of the house. They shake hands. There's no illumination on the porch, so I can't see him clearly until he steps down the short stairs and walks toward us. I suck in a sharp breath. Mr. Silverstone.

Before I can react, Bryce steps in front of me, arms raised and ready to fight. "What do you want with us?"

Bryce's reaction spurs the others, who also take an aggressive stance toward the man.

The blond Idol calmly raises an eyebrow and grins. "Take it easy, boys. I'm not here to harm you or Daisy."

I walk around the human shield the guys formed in front of me. "Why are we here?"

"To welcome you back to the fold, Daisy."

"What are you talking about?"

"I'm talking about your lineage."

"Magia. That's what this is about," Phoenix says.

"Who is Magia?" I ask.

"Magia was a powerful Idol who had her powers stripped

from her," Mr. Silverstone explains. We don't know if it was voluntarily or not. All that matters now is that you're her descendant, and somehow you recovered Magia's power. You're an Idol."

"But how is that even possible? Magia died millennia ago. The link to the demigods would be too thin," Rufio points out.

"We don't know that for a fact. Her powers were stripped, not diluted through the generations."

"How do you know all this?" Bryce asks.

Mr. Silverstone grins. "We know many things, boy. Morpheus is not the only Idol who has visions. The return of Magia's powers was foretold. Through centuries we've kept tabs on her descendants. We didn't know Daisy was the one destined to reestablish the link until she met the four of you."

All this information has turned me into a statue. My lungs are closing off; I can barely breathe. "How did I get Magia's powers back?" I croak.

"It was me, wasn't it?" Bryce chimes in. "When I saved Daisy, I somehow healed the broken link to Magia's powers. You kept me trapped long enough so Daisy would be unprotected. You wanted her to almost die."

"It was the only way. You didn't know about your healing powers. You needed to be triggered."

Bryce lets out a roar and sends a bolt of energy in Mr. Silverstone's direction. I don't even have time to yell. But the Knight isn't hit by Bryce's blast. He moved out of the way.

"I understand you're frustrated, but it all worked out in the end," he says from the other side of the clearing.

"Bryce, calm down." I touch his back, feeling the electric current surrounding his body. The power parts away from my hand, almost as if I'm canceling it out. I pull my hand back quickly.

"What kind of power did Magia have?" I ask Mr. Silverstone.

"The power to unmake Idols."

To be continued ...
HATEFUL HEROES available NOW!

BRYCE
GIFTED ACADEMY

ALSO BY MICHELLE HERCULES

Paranormal Romance:

Dark Prince (Blueblood Vampires #1)

Wild Thing (Blueblood Vampires #2)

Forgotten Heir (Blueblood Vampires #3)

Reckless Times (Gifted Academy #5)

Contemporary Romance:

Wonderwall (Love Me, I'm Famous #1)

Sugar, We're Going Down (Love Me, I'm Famous #2)

Wreck of the Day (Love Me, I'm Famous #3)

Devils Don't Fly (Love Me, I'm Famous #4)

Love Me Like You Do (Love Me, I'm Famous #5)

Catch You (Love Me, I'm Famous #6)

All The Right Moves

Heart Stopper (Rebels of Rushmore #1)

Heart Breaker (Rebels of Rushmore #2)

Heart Starter (Rebels of Rushmore #3)

Reverse Harem Romance:

Wicked Gods (Gifted Academy #1)

Ruthless Idols (Gifted Academy #2)

Hateful Heroes (Gifted Academy #3)

Broken Knights (Gifted Academy #4)

Lost Horizon (Oz in Space #1)

Magic Void (Oz in Space #2)

Red's Alphas (Wolves of Crimson Hollow #1)

Wolf's Calling (Wolves of Crimson Hollow #2)

Pack's Queen (Wolves of Crimson Hollow #3)

Mother of Wolves (Wolves of Crimson Hollow #4)

ABOUT THE AUTHOR

USA Today Bestselling Author Michelle Hercules always knew creative arts were her calling but not in a million years did she think she would become an author. With a background in fashion design she thought she would follow that path. But one day, out of the blue, she had an idea for a book. One page turned into ten pages, ten pages turned into a hundred, and before she knew, her first novel, The Prophecy of Arcadia, was born.

Michelle Hercules resides in Florida with her husband and daughter. She is currently working on the *Blueblood Vampires* series and the *Rebels of Rushmore* series.

Join Michelle Hercules' Reader Group:
https://www.facebook.com/groups/mhsoars

Follow Michelle Hercules on Instagram:
https://www.instagram.com/michelleherculesauthor/

Connect with Michelle Hercules:
www.michellehercules.com
books@mhsoars.com